Praise for Dan Walsh's Other Suspense Novels

The Discovery

"Dan Walsh's novel is rich with intrigue, history and romance...The Discovery is a sublime delight that shouldn't be missed."

— *USA Today*

"Yet again, Walsh has crafted a novel so engaging that you will lose all sense of time as he draws you in and makes the reader a part of the story."

— *RT Book Reviews Magazine.*

What Follows After

"Walsh excels once again with this psychological thriller...the author's narrative moves at a relentless pace, with tension building to an almost unbearable degree until the very end."

— *Library Journal*

"As is only to be expected from bestselling author Dan Walsh, *What Follows After* is a solid emotional thriller with a message...It has plenty that will appeal to both men and women."

— *Crosswalk.com*

For these and more of Dan Walsh's books, go to
http://danwalshbooks.com/books/

WHEN NIGHT COMES

WHEN NIGHT COMES

BY DAN WALSH

AUTHOR'S NOTE

If I'm a new author to you and you haven't yet read any of my other published novels (besides this one, there are a dozen others in print), let me start off by saying thanks for checking out *When Night Comes*. I hope you thoroughly enjoy it. If you do, at the end of the book I've included another note mentioning two recent novels that are the most similar to this one.

But in general, *When Night Comes* opens up something of a new door for my writing. The traditional rule in the publishing world is to stay locked into one genre, and only write books within that genre, because that's what your readers expect from you. For those of you who've read and enjoyed my other novels, you are familiar with my character–driven storylines, strong romantic threads, and a lot of page–turning suspense. You'll find all of that in *When Night Comes*.

So what's the difference?

Magazine and blog reviewers have often compared my books to the works of Nicholas Sparks. Because in addition to the things I've already mentioned, most of my novels include a strong spiritual theme and a powerful emotional punch. It's not uncommon for readers to get choked up while reading my books and many even cry (it's a good cry, though, not the sad kind).

That's probably not going to happen when you read *When Night Comes*. You'll be tempted to bite your nails a few times but not likely reach for the tissue box. I still enjoy writing my more "Nicholas Sparks type" books. In fact, I'm working on one right now.

But to be honest, when I read I'm not always in the mood for an intense, emotional ride. Sometimes, I just want to read a fun and entertaining novel of suspense. *When Night Comes,* represents that *other* kind of book I like to read…and to write.

A suspense novel.

I hope it's the first of many more to come. I'd love to be able to write both kinds of books in the days ahead. I won't be offended if you're the kind of reader who only likes one or the other, but I hope a lot of you are like me and enjoy reading both.

To make it easier to tell the difference, my suspense novels will have a totally different kind of cover than my other books. I decided to do it this way than to write under a different name.

If you want to write me and tell me your thoughts, feel free. I love to get reader emails and read all of them myself.

"*Combinations of wickedness would overwhelm the world... did not those who have long practiced betrayal grow faithless to each other.*"

— Samuel Johnson

1

DEAD BODIES HAVE a way of changing everything. Sergeant Joe Boyd drove his unmarked car down Chambers Road toward a possible homicide. He'd heard the officer on site reporting over the radio, his voice all jittery and pathetic. Sounded like he'd completely lost it, talking about throwing up and never seeing anything like it. Have a little dignity, Boyd thought. It was a Saturday morning. Figures it would be a Saturday, the one day in the week Boyd got to sleep in.

At this point in his career, he wasn't sure if he wanted to deal with a murder or not. Two months ago, he had been a homicide detective in the relentless, suffocating pace of Zone Five, arguably the toughest precinct in the Pittsburgh PD. He had worked there since coming out of the academy sixteen years ago and didn't relish the idea of leaving all that excitement to move down here to neighborly little Culpepper, Georgia.

But it was either that or his family. I'm out of here, Kate had said. It's them or me. Take your pick.

Kate had fallen in love with the town their first drive through. Boyd had to agree, Culpepper seemed like a better place to raise a family, a town the bad guys hadn't found yet. Since moving, he had been home for dinner more often than not. Started showing up at his son's Little League games; that was a first. At least three or four nights a week, his daughter could count on daddy reading her a bedtime story. He even made it to church most Sundays.

And now this.

Boyd pulled up to the scene, a two-story apartment building painted a cheap shade of blue. Must have been four patrol cars already there, the better part of the force. Boyd had learned in Culpepper a drunk driver rated at least two or three. "What you got, Hank?" Boyd asked, getting out of the car. Hank Jensen was the one patrolman Boyd thought had a chance of making it in the big leagues.

"Check it out, Joe. It's pretty strange." He met Boyd at the sidewalk and walked with him toward a black iron gate leading to the entrance of the apartment in question.

Another patrolman opened the gate and walked past without uttering a word, dread all over his face. "Hey," Boyd said. "Take care of that crowd over there. Keep everybody by the sidewalk."

"Okay, Sergeant."

The corner apartment door was wide open. Another officer rolled yellow tape between the pillars in the corridor, marking the scene. Boyd walked past a concrete stairway and stepped into the corridor.

"So, who died?" He walked through the door. A small two-room efficiency. Nothing unusual in the living or kitchen area. A little messy. No body. That's right, supposed to be in the bedroom.

"White male, twenty to twenty-five years of age," Hank said. "Probably a student at the University. Lots of them in this dump. Don't know his name yet. Haven't found any ID. Medical Examiner's on his way."

At least Hank tried to impress him. "Who found him?" Boyd looked at the busted door lock. Someone hurt his foot on that one.

"I think it was a friend."

"Where is he? Let's talk to him."

Hank hesitated. "We can't, Joe."

"What?"

"He's not here."

"He's gone? The friend's gone?" The look on Hank's face was Boyd's answer. He knew this scene looked too smooth, too organized for these guys.

"I didn't let him walk—"

"Then who did?"

A troubled–looking officer sat on the edge of the couch. He lifted his head and looked at Boyd. "He did," Hank said quietly. "That's John Dobbs. He's a rookie, Joe. He wasn't thinking."

So Dobbs was the guy he'd heard on the radio. Boyd had barely said two words to Dobbs before. A great way to get acquainted. He tried to calm down, remember his people skills. It was probably Dobbs' first homicide, he told himself. So what if he let a principal witness, maybe even the murderer go free. But it was okay. We can fix this. "You get his name, the name of the witness?" Boyd asked Dobbs, feigning politeness. "Maybe his address?"

"Well, no...not exactly," Dobbs said, rising to his feet.

He didn't get his name. *Did you lend him your squad car, maybe a little spending cash?*

"But I know he's a student at the university," Dobbs continued. "I'm sure I could pick him out if I looked at the school's computer. I'm sorry, Sergeant. I know I blew it here. I've just never seen anything like this before." Dobbs rubbed the sweat from his forehead.

He was tall and husky. Looked down at Boyd like a football player with his coach.

"It's all right," Boyd said. "Just tell me what happened."

"I got the call about an hour ago," Dobbs said. "When I got here there was this guy standing out by the sidewalk waving me down. He was pretty upset. He got sick, right as I pulled in. Said he was the guy that called us. That his friend was inside, dead, stiff and dead. I got outta my car, and we came in here. He was the one that kicked in the door, did it before I got here. I asked him what happened, then I walked into the bedroom and saw his friend. Then I got sick." Dobbs looked like he might throw up again just thinking about it.

Boyd listened, scribbled down a few notes. "What did this mystery friend say happened here? The exact words."

Dobbs seemed to shake off the wave of nausea. "He said they both attend Culpepper, history majors or something. He said he knocked and knocked, but there was no answer. Thought something might be wrong because they had talked a couple a nights ago about hiking somewhere this morning, and he was there to pick his friend up. He walked around the back and looked through the blinds to see if he was asleep or had his earplugs in. Then he sees him lying there. He banged on the window a couple of times, but the guy doesn't move. Then he knew something was wrong. He runs back around the front and starts kicking on the door and calling out his name. The door finally broke, and he went in. And there he was. Dead and his face—"

"Did you ask him if he touched anything? Did he touch the body? Move anything?"

"I didn't ask, but I'm sure he didn't. Soon as he knew his friend was dead, he said he ran out and got sick. Then he called us."

"When did you lose him?"

Dobbs looked down at the floor around his feet, as though the answer was down there somewhere. "I don't know, sir. He must have slipped out when some of the other guys showed up. I was explaining things to them, and we were setting things up for prints. I should have told him to stay put. But I really don't think he had anything to do with this."

"Sounds like he didn't," Boyd said, "but why would he take off like that?"

"I think I know why." Dobbs looked toward the bedroom door.

"Well, look Dobbs…I still wanna talk to this guy. Go over to the school. I don't know if they're open on Saturday. Try the registration building. See if someone'll let you take a look at their student files. Find out who this mystery friend is and let me know right away."

"Yes sir." Dobbs hurried out the door.

Guess it's a full time job being so ignorant. "Let's see what we got here," Boyd said to no one in particular. He felt a pressure building in his gut. The situation was playing ping–pong with his *Mini–Wheats*. He rearranged his waistband, tried to make some room. It didn't work. He walked past another officer on his knees, dusting the bedroom doorknob for fingerprints. Hank Jensen followed behind.

Boyd stood inside the doorway and took a slow pan of the room. By the way the others acted, he expected some Charles Manson scene of blood and gore, dismembered body parts, satanic slogans on the walls. Something. But there was no blood, no trashed room, no signs of violence or foul play. Just some cheap wall posters of jet planes and girls in bikinis. Some clothes hanging out of an open dresser drawer. A pair of high–top sneakers parked neatly beside the bathroom door. A pair of trousers in a pile beside the dresser. A dead body lying in a bed, looking very much like a sleeping college kid. "Anyone take any pictures of the scene?" he asked Hank.

"I did, before you got here."

"Good." Boyd looked at another officer kneeling by the bedroom door, dusting for prints.

"Get anything?"

"Yeah, plenty," the officer said without looking up. "My guess is…they're all gonna be our victim's."

"Why you say that?"

"That's just it, Joe," Hank piped in. "Look around. Except for the front door, there's no way in or out of this place. All the windows have been locked from the inside. I'm not sure we even *got* a homicide here."

Homicide or not, they definitely had a dead body in that bed. There was no mistaking that familiar smell. Boyd had never understood why people described it as sickening–sweet. Nothing sweet about it. He guessed by its intensity the boy probably died late last night, or in the early evening. He walked to the bed and looked down at the body, then at the kid's face.

Yeah, that's weird.

2

THE LOOK ON the decedent's face sent a chill through Boyd. Few things could. He'd seen a lot of dead people over the years, but he couldn't recall ever seeing anything quite like this.

The kid's face seemed more like a mask, like a still shot from a horror flick. Stark white in the center, olive green around the edges. His eyes flat—wide open in a horrific stare. Mouth frozen open in mid–scream. Bone dry. His hands clenched in fists around his sheet and blanket, tucked tightly beneath his chin. Bloody scratches highlighted his forehead and cheeks. Boyd noticed dried blood under his fingernails.

Looks like he attacked himself.

The boy's hair was dark and greasy and stuck out in several directions. Set against the odd color of his face, he looked more ghoulish than human. "You didn't find any ID?"

"No," Hank said. "Haven't searched the room myself. One of the guys did."

That gave Boyd no confidence. "How about the landlord? Where's he at?"

"We're trying to get hold of him now. The place's too small for a resident manager. We called the number we found on the internet. Unfortunately, we got voicemail."

"When's the M.E. supposed to get here?"

"I thought he'd be here by now."

Boyd walked into the front room and peered through the blinds. The M.E. did have a ways to drive, coming from the county seat. A Medivac van had arrived with two attendants killing time inside. Boyd went back into the bedroom, covered his mouth and nose with a handkerchief, and pulled at the bedcovers with his other hand.

"Joe, whatta you doing?" Hank said.

"I wanna see what killed this guy." He wrestled the covers from his fingers and peeled them back. No gunshots. No stab wounds. Just a skinny guy in a T–shirt. "Look, Hank."

Hank peeked over his shoulder. "I ain't surprised. I didn't think we had a murder here."

Boyd nodded. "Know what I think? I don't know how yet, but I think this guy died in his sleep. I want you to get to every guy that's been here—I mean you personally. Tell them not to say anything to the press about a murder. Tell them not to say anything at all. Just refer everyone to me. We don't need people thinking we got a murderer loose around town. We'll have hundreds of parents calling us and pulling their kids outta the college."

"I'll go right now."

"And Hank…"

"Yeah?"

"Don't worry about the guys in here. I'll tell them. You go after the guys out by the sidewalk and the ones who've left the scene."

"Right." Hank headed for the door.

"And Hank?" yelled Boyd.

Hank halted. "Yeah, Joe?"

"One more thing. I wanna put a lid on the scary look on this kid's face. If the M.E. confirms we got natural causes here, stories about the look on this kid's face alone could stir up all kinds of trouble we want no part of. We don't want word of this to get out to the public. Some people would have a field day with this. *'What scared this young man to death?'* You follow me?"

"Sure, Joe. That's the last thing this town needs, or this kid's family." Hank was off again.

Boyd covered the body up as best he could. The TV was still on, set to the blue screen. He hit the eject button and a DVD popped out. One of those slasher films by the look of it. How could anybody watch this crap? He looked again at the pair of jeans in a pile by the dresser. He bent down and patted the pockets, felt something hard and square beneath his fingers. "Don't tell me nobody looked in the kids jeans," Boyd shouted. "C'mon people."

Sure enough, it was a wallet, light brown leather. He tossed the pants back on the floor and opened it. Staring back at him was a student ID card on the left side, presumably the young man on the bed when he was having a better day. He looked down at the nightmarish face on the corpse and back again at the photo. It was a bit of a stretch. "Yeah, I see you in there," he finally said.

He read the name. "So, you are…Ralph Riesner, a senior at Culpepper University, military history major." He took a few steps forward and looked down at that horrific face.

"Must've been some dream you had, Mr. Riesner."

3

J ACK TURNER HOPED this little trip might be just the
thing.

He drove along the winding country roads just south of
Culpepper taking in the beautiful synergy of autumn colors, sipping a *Starbucks* latte, listening to *Michael Bublé* croon some big
band tunes. It was Sunday afternoon. After what he'd been through
the last few weeks with Gwen, his almost–fiancé, he needed this
diversion. And it would give him some time to make progress on
his new book. The best thing, though, was getting the chance to
return to his alma mater as the conquering king.

Well, maybe *king* was too strong a word.

His cell phone rang, startling him. He fumbled for it in the
passenger seat. "Hello?"

"Jack, that you?"

He recognized the voice instantly. "It's me, Professor." Professor
Thomas Thornton, Jack's former mentor and the man responsible
for this trip.

"I keep telling you, call me Thomas now."

"I can't see me doing that, Professor."

"Where are you?"

"If I remember it right…" Jack looked around, found some familiar landmarks, "…I'm about ten minutes south of you."

"Well, the reason I called is…just making sure you want to stay at that old place. I meant what I said, Jack. You can pick anywhere in town. I got that nice cabin out at Lake Sampson. Nice and quiet out there, great place to write. I was at that old apartment yesterday and—"

"It's what I want, Professor. Really, it'll be perfect." Jack had decided to stay at the same little place he'd rented the entire time he'd been a student at Culpepper—a little garage apartment at 433 Rambling Road. Seven years had passed since he'd last seen it.

"All right," said Thornton. "You're still planning your first lecture on those Pearl Harbor conspiracy theories, right? We're studying Pearl Harbor at the moment."

"I haven't forgotten. And you remember I can't get into the series I'm writing about now. My publisher's got them off limits until after the book hits the shelves. I can't even field any questions about it."

"I know. A colleague heard part of the series when you taught at Gettysburg. Some fascinating angles you're working there."

Jack's new book explored the question: *What if the political and military leaders during World War Two had to contend with today's hi-tech 24/7 news media?* "It's really pretty silly, all this secrecy. You'd think we were guarding a military secret."

"Guess I'll have to wait for the book like everyone else."

"Well, nothing in the contract says I can't talk with an old friend off the record."

Thornton laughed. "You've done well for yourself. But clearly you've changed."

Jack wondered what Thornton meant. "I have?"

"Your looks. I hardly recognized you from your bio picture."

"Really?"

"I guess it's your hair, Jack. You remind me of that actor, what's his name? He's in all kinds of movies these days. I can't think of any of his newer ones, but he was the lead actor on *Pirates of the Caribbean.*"

"Johnny Depp?"

"That's him."

Jack laughed. "Guess I am wearing my hair longer. I got real busy last year, missed a few haircuts. The girl I was seeing thought I should go with a longer style." So far, it hadn't stopped anyone in the academic world from hiring him to speak. "Is it a problem?"

"No, just a surprise. In my day, short hair and a trimmed beard was the mark of distinction for an academic. Maybe a refined mustache. Folks figured you got even smarter when it started to turn gray. By the way, I left you a little present at the apartment, should find it right on the coffee table."

"What is it?"

"Found it a few weeks ago. A Life magazine issue from 1949, big article in there about Pearl Harbor. Not a copy, mind you, an original. I know you like to collect such things. And you'll find all the books you asked for from the library, in a box on the sofa."

"Thanks, I'm going need those for my research."

"Made any plans for dinner tomorrow night?"

"Not yet."

"Now you have. Come over to my place. I've got it all arranged. Just be the two of us, nothing elaborate. We can get caught up. You can tell me about all your exploits."

"I'd like that, but there's not much to tell."

"Remember how to get here?"

"Sure do."

"Seven all right?"

"Fine."

"Will you be ready for your first lecture tomorrow morning? If you need more time—"

"I'll be ready, Professor. It's at ten, right?"

"Yes."

"Same classroom?"

"Nothing's changed, Jack."

"See you then." Jack laid the cell phone down in the seat. He'd always considered Thornton a brilliant educator, very underrated in this business. He recognized they were teaching a video generation now and incorporated documentaries and docu–dramas in his lectures every chance he could. He was also a master at Q&A.

Jack had begun attending Culpepper twelve years ago, thanks to the GI Bill and some miscellaneous grants. Even that didn't close the gap, so Jack had worked as Thornton's research assistant. Eventually he'd received his BA, then a Master's in Military History.

It was pretty satisfying driving back there now as a guest lecturer, at the invitation of—actually the pleading of—the same professor he'd worked for all those years. When Thornton had first called, Jack said no. He didn't need the money. He needed peace and quiet, a place to write his book. Thornton upped the offer to include room and board anywhere in town. Jack could dictate his own hours and have no administrative duties.

Jack changed his mind. In some ways, he owed Thornton.

Shortly after Jack graduated, Thornton had submitted one of his essays to an editor friend at *Military History Quarterly*. It was quickly accepted and published. Soon more articles were being accepted by other military publications. Editors and readers said

Jack's writing made history leap off the pages. He began getting invitations to lecture at various colleges and universities. It turned out Jack wasn't just a good writer, he could speak. Things were going so well, his agent said recently she felt certain after Jack's next book came out, she could get him an expert–contributor spot on *Fox News*.

A sharp curve in the road brought Jack's mind back to the present. Frank's Service Station was just up ahead. Only a few minutes from the apartment now. Driving across a narrow bridge spanning the Chambers River, he glanced at the hills dropping sharply on either side. Oak, maple, and sycamore trees fanned out across the scene, arrayed in brilliant fall colors.

Yeah, this is what he needed.

As he entered the city limits, it was as if the car knew the way by itself. The town square was a scene frozen in time, altered through the years only by the changing styles of the cars and clothes. The town hall stood proudly on the north end, with its majestic pillars and granite steps. Two–story shops and businesses, bordered the square, all of awnings and window displays. A grassy, tree–lined park framed the center, complete with gazebo and black ornamental benches.

A few blocks later, Jack turned onto Rambling Road. He didn't need to read the mailboxes or street numbers. There it was on the right. The yellow, clapboard house with the white shutters. Professor Thornton had mentioned it was still owned by the Martins, his old landlords. They had to be, what, in their eighties now?

He pulled into the loose–gravel driveway. Thornton was right. The apartment wasn't much to look at; a little wooden cottage sitting atop a concrete garage. Like the main house, badly in need of a paint job and new roof. Grabbing his laptop and suitcase from the backseat, he moved quietly across the stones to avoid alerting the Martins to his arrival.

He walked up the wooden stairway on the right side, attached to a small landing, and carefully opened the screened door. Several potted plants in various stages of demise moped about the perimeter. The key was under the mat, as arranged. He unlocked the deadbolt and stepped inside. Odd, he thought, that such a pathetic little place should feel like home, but it did. He went back to the car for the rest of his things.

His immediate plans were simple: heater on, Benny Goodman playing quietly in the background, clothes unpacked, hot shower, a long nap.

*

The man wore a gray hooded sweatshirt and baseball cap, dark sunglasses to hide the crows' feet around his eyes, blue jeans, and a pair of *Converse* high tops. To give the look more authority, he carried a short stack of textbooks under his arm stolen from a table in the Media Center. Nigel Avery, the name he was going by these days, had the long, lean body of a man half his age. By all accounts, he blended well with the student population.

Truth was, Avery and books had never gotten along. What he excelled at was surveillance. That and making people die in staged accidents or petty crimes.

At the moment, his orders were simple: tail a certain professor named Thornton and build a file on his schedule, habits, and close relationships. But he had a feeling his other skills might be called upon very soon.

He'd already concluded Thornton had little in the way of a social life. No romantic connections. He was highly regarded by students on campus. Kind. Considerate. The smartest professor at the school some had said.

Apparently not smart enough, Avery thought, walking now about fifty yards behind the professor toward the Murray Building.

Else I wouldn't be here numbering your days.

4

"I'VE GOTTA REEL it in guys," Jack announced. "Look at the clock." The clamoring in the classroom died down. "You've been a great bunch. I can tell I'm gonna enjoy my time here. Let's wrap up. As I said, the evidence is pretty clear... the public wasn't told the whole truth about Pearl Harbor. Even without all the evidence that's surfaced in the last seventy years, any thinking person would have to conclude a lot more went on here than we see in the official record."

Jack paused a moment to let that sink in. Every eye was glued on him, including one attractive young lady standing in the back. Jack was sure she'd been looking at him a certain way the better part of the last hour. He'd have to find out her name. She'd said it once during the Q&A, Rachel something. He wasn't sure, but she looked older than the average senior.

What are you doing, he scolded himself. That's not why you're here.

He finished his review and stood off to the side, allowing Thornton to take the podium. The class applauded. This wasn't new for Jack. Experiencing it at his old school was, in the very hall he'd spent so much time as a student.

"Thank you, Mr. Turner," Thornton said. "Class, Mr. Turner will be with us off and on over the next two months, but I must add...he's primarily here to write his new book, so please respect that and don't put on him any undue social expectations."

Jack put his iPad in his brief bag as the class made their way toward the doors. "Remarkable," Thornton whispered. "You had them in the palm of your hands."

"You accomplished that every day I was in your class, Professor. I'm just the flavor of the month."

"That's kind," Thornton said. "But you're far more than a novelty, Jack. I don't think my mind was ever that sharp, nor the line between my mind and mouth ever that straight." Thornton walked toward the inner door leading to his office.

Jack looked up. That attractive young lady was staring at him. When she saw Jack noticing her, she didn't look away. Instead, she flashed a photogenic smile. He couldn't help but respond. She got up and walked toward the door, looking back once before exiting into the hall. Something in that last look was vaguely familiar.

Thornton apparently caught this. He walked back over and whispered, "That's General Cook's daughter, Jack. Proceed with caution."

"General William Cook?" Jack asked.

Thornton nodded. "You know him?"

"Yeah. Not personally. I was stationed at his base in Ramstein, Germany for a year. My last six months there I served as his driver off and on."

"Rachel's not a student," Thornton said. "She graduated a few years ago. Works as a teaching assistant in the political science department. She decided to take my class for some reason. Told me why once, but I can't remember. Something to do with her dad."

"I'm not in the market right now anyway, not after what I've just been through." Jack snapped the latch on his bag.

"You mentioned something about that. Broke off an engagement recently? What was her name?"

"Gwen. But we never actually got engaged." Jack walked toward the main hallway.

"Are we still on for tonight?" Thornton called out.

"Definitely," Jack said. "See you at seven."

*

Jack drove along the familiar route from the University to Rambling Road, oblivious to his surroundings. Gwen was the last thing he wanted to think about but his thoughts still drifted there, to their last date three weeks ago. How could he have been so wrong about her? How could he have missed the signs? Except for his traveling, they had been inseparable the last year. They'd never fought, talked everything through, respected each other, laughed all the time. He never saw it coming.

During that final conversation, they were sitting at a quaint corner table at the *Macaroni Grille*, her favorite restaurant. Candles lit, a bottle of house wine freshly uncorked. The restaurant's best tenor had just begun to sing *Con Te Partiro'*, something Jack had also arranged. The kid was no *Andrea Bocelli*, but he did a passable job. Jack kept looking back and forth at Gwen's eyes, trying to measure her reaction. If anything, she seemed distracted, on edge. He leaned over. "Something wrong?"

"Let the man finish," she scolded gently, motioning toward the waiter.

Jack reached into his pocket, feeling the velvet box containing the three–quarter–carat diamond ring. He planned to give it to her just as the waiter finished his song. He didn't remember what he'd attributed her peculiar mood to, but he was certain everything would be fine the moment he got down on one knee and Gwen feasted her eyes on that ring. Finally, the song ended. Everyone nearby clapped. Jack nodded his thanks to the waiter. Twenty dollars well spent. He turned to face Gwen, that wrong look on her face again. She wasn't even smiling. "Gwen, what's wrong?"

"We need to talk, Jack."

"I'm listening."

"I should have told you this two months ago."

"Told me what?"

She looked around the restaurant, then back at him. He remembered now, she never fixed on his eyes. "I should just say it. I've practiced it in my head so many times. There isn't any good way to—"

"What is it, Gwen?"

"It's over between us. I don't love you anymore. I've found someone else. There, I said it."

Jack was stunned. "I don't understand."

"It's not you. It's me. Don't blame yourself."

"I don't blame myself." It's all he could think of to say.

"I could see you were getting way too serious about me."

"Serious? You've said you loved me, at least a dozen times."

"But have I said it lately?"

"What?"

"In the last couple of months I've been pulling away, haven't you noticed?"

Jack shook his head.

"We're just too different, Jack. I know the way you're wired… you were thinking marriage. I don't want to get married now."

"I can wait, Gwen. We don't have to be in a hurry."

"But you'd want us to be married, and I don't. That's the problem. And I'd feel pressure from you the whole time. Look, it doesn't matter. I've already found someone else. Someone who's living in the present."

"What's that supposed to mean?"

"Nothing. I shouldn't have said that."

"But you did. What's it mean?"

"You're a hopeless romantic, Jack. I'll admit, at first, I liked it. A lot. But now it's like watching an old movie with bad dialog."

"What?"

"All this history stuff. You can't live in the past, Jack. Well, maybe you can, but I can't."

"I don't live in the past."

"Yes, you do. You don't even see it. All the roses and mushy cards. The schmaltzy music you always listen to. The black and white pictures on your walls of all those dead generals. Jack, who has pictures of dead generals on the walls of their living room?"

"Gwen, I teach military history." But the disgust in her voice, coupled with the betrayal, had finally hit its mark. "All right, you've made your point." The waiter walked up all smiles, the platter of delicious food in his hands. Jack stood up and tossed a hundred dollar bill on the table. "That should be enough for the meal, your tip, and a cab for the young lady."

"Jack," she called out as he walked away. He never looked back.

She had called a few times over the next week, but Jack didn't return them. The calls wouldn't be apologies or requests to get back together. They'd have been about alleviating her guilt. *I'm not such a bad person. Let's keep this positive, Jack. Can't we still be friends?*

Someone like Gwen needed to feel as much guilt as her shallow little system could absorb.

"You don't know jack about women," he muttered aloud, as he turned into the gravel driveway on Rambling Road, then laughed at the unintended play on words. As he walked up the wooden steps, he reflected on his first session in Thornton's class this morning. Not so much about the class's reaction to his lecture but about that attractive brunette who kept smiling at him the whole while. What was her name again? That's right, Rachel. Rachel Cook, the General's daughter. Proceed with caution. The screen door slapped shut behind him, making him suddenly aware of what he was doing.

Was this some kind of curse or what?

*

Sitting on a campus bench, just outside the Murray building, Nigel Avery reached for his phone from a backpack. He looked up at the sun. It had been moving in and out of the clouds all morning, changing the temperature ten degrees either way. A cute blonde walked by and smiled. He lowered his sunglasses to get a better look. As expected, she glanced over her shoulder a few feet past him. He saluted with one finger. She smiled and quickly turned away. He dialed a number in Falls Church, Virginia, a suburb of Washington, DC. The man who'd hired him picked up the other end. "Jameison?"

"It's me. You got something worthwhile? I've got patients waiting, sort of in a hurry."

"You sure about this guy, Doc? I mean, really, what am I doing here? This professor's got no life. I'm here almost a week and, except for him tutoring one or two students in his condo, I got nothing to report."

"Are you listening yet or just watching?" Jameison asked.

"Watching. I'll have the bugs in place the next day or so. Then I get to sit in a dark van all day."

"Look, I wouldn't be spending all this money if I didn't think it was necessary. I need to know what this professor is up to. I've got a lot riding on this. Get those listening devices working. See who he's spending time with on the phone. If he has any visitors, spends any more time with any of his students. If nothing turns up by the end of the week, call me back. Maybe I'll reconsider."

"All right," Avery said. "But you don't want to be wasting my time, Doc."

A pause. "Just do as I ask," Jameison said. "You won't regret it."

5

SGT. JOE BOYD swigged his last gulp of soda. He had just inhaled a Big Mac and some fries. He was on his way to Dunedin, the county seat. He had told the Medical Examiner he would be there at 1PM sharp, and he intended to be on time.

When the M.E. finally arrived at the scene on Saturday, he'd agreed with Boyd that this probably wasn't going to be a homicide. Still, an autopsy was required, so he had Riesner's body sent to his lab. Not a big hassle for Boyd. Just an extra forty–minute drive along some pretty country roads.

In these idle moments, Boyd thought about the case. It had been difficult keeping a lid on Riesner's death, especially with the scary face thing. With Hank's help, they'd finally gotten the rest of the guys in the squad to understand the need to keep their mouths shut. So far, Boyd had been unable to locate Riesner's parents who lived in Charlotte. The next door neighbors said they had gone to Florida for a short vacation but he didn't have a number to reach them. A terrible thing, Boyd told the guys. How would they like to hear about their own kid dying like that through the grapevine or on the news? And think of the havoc such publicity would raise at the school?

Boyd had used the same arguments with Riesner's friend, the student who'd found him at the apartment. Dobbs had finally located him late Saturday afternoon. It took some doing, the kid being so shook up, but Boyd finally made him see the importance of keeping quiet. It would only be for a few more days until they could locate the parents. The kid had been so pathetic. It was all Boyd could do to keep from slapping him.

Boyd arrived at the County Administration building in Dunedin. Once inside, he found a directory board indicating the pathology lab was on the first floor. He wandered the slick marble floors reading door numbers until he found it. Once inside the reception room, he was greeted by an invisible dome of flowery perfume. He looked for and found a kindly–faced older woman with close–curled silver hair.

"Can I help you?" she said warmly.

"Hi. I'm Sergeant Joe Boyd, here to see Dr. Hargrove."

"I'll just tell him you're here, Sergeant." She smiled. "Wait right there. I'll be right back. Care for a donut, some coffee?"

"No, thanks." He eyed the donuts. She disappeared behind a solid wooden door. No one else in the waiting room. Not like an M.E. to have a steady stream of patients. He scanned an end table for some reading material. Nothing but health magazines. He grabbed a donut.

The woman returned as he finished the last bite. "Go right in, Sergeant. There's a doorway to a little room down the hall on your right. Dr. Hargrove will meet you there."

"Thank you."

He found the room and entered. Almost instantly, a man in

green scrubs walked through a door, pulling a protective mask off his face. "You got anything for me, Doc? I'm Sergeant Joe Boyd. We talked on Saturday. I'm here about the kid with the scary face." Boyd offered his hand.

Doctor Hargrove snapped off a soiled latex glove, flung it into a hazmat container and shook Boyd's hand. It was then Boyd noticed they were meeting in a room adjacent to the autopsy room, separated by glass partitions. It wasn't easy, but Boyd tried to keep firm eye contact with Hargrove as they spoke. If his eyes wandered two inches to the right of Hargrove's face, he could see the good doctor's handiwork on young Riesner, who now lay rigid on his back, half–dissected on a steel table partially covered by a towel. What appeared to be a vital organ hung suspended from a scale.

Autopsies were something Boyd had never grown used to. It made Boyd feel strange to shake hands with someone who knew what he looked like on the inside. He wondered if men like Hargrove casually dissected people with their eyes.

"The scary face?" Hargrove said, "You're referring to my cadaver, Mr. Riesner. I've got a few more tests to run on him."

Cadaver, Boyd thought. He'd been rehearsing the list of sympathetic words he'd use to explain things to Riesner's parents, when he finally found them. He hoped cadaver didn't slip out accidentally. "Do you know what we're looking at here, Doctor? Did the cadaver—I mean, Riesner—die from natural causes? Something kill him like gas or poison, cause I didn't see any marks? Except maybe those claw marks on his face, but I figured he did that to himself."

"There's no doubt about the cause of death. His heart went into full cardiac arrest. I can't tell you why, just yet. His medical records may shed some light. Right now, I'm exploring for congenital heart defects. I think I've spotted one, a ventricular septal defect. That could certainly be the cause."

Hargrove lost Boyd on that one. He seemed to notice and added, "You remember that college basketball player who died a few years ago when his heart just snapped after snorting cocaine?"

Boyd nodded, "You think this kid died from snorting cocaine?"

"No. I'm talking about the heart defect. It was congenital… that means he had it since birth."

Boyd knew what congenital meant.

"A ventricular septal defect killed that basketball player. It was hiding there, dormant, not affecting his life until that critical moment. I think our lad here had something similar. I'll know in a little while. If it's true, I can say he died very quickly, if that's any consolation to the family."

Boyd sighed. "I'm sure that'll help some. But what made his heart snap?"

"That I can't tell you. My preliminary tests don't show any presence of illegal substances or alcohol. Nothing that would create sufficient shock to trigger this kind of defect."

"Do you think it's possible this heart attack could have made his face all twisted up like it was?"

Hargrove thought a moment. "It's quite possible. If the cardiac arrest happened in his sleep—and I believe this did—it would have produced a tremendous surge of pain. Although, I've never seen anything quite so dramatic before. Except in the movies."

A picture of Riesner's face flashed into Boyd's mind. "Could a nightmare have triggered this…septal defect?" Boyd hoped he got the word right.

"I was thinking that very thing. But it would have to be the mother of all nightmares."

"How about those marks on his face," Boyd added.

"I agree, self–inflicted. Very strange. It's what's leading me toward the nightmare theory. It's almost as if he was trying to get something off his face."

"Know when he died, approximately?"

"I'm thinking death occurred sometime late Friday night, or very early Saturday morning. Sometime between 11:00pm and 2:00am. Will you need an exact time for your investigation?"

"Not for a heart attack, if that's all it is." Boyd rubbed his chin a moment. "Could I ask you a favor, Doc?"

"What is it, Sergeant?"

"I know this may sound strange, but since Riesner died of natural causes, could you leave the way his face looked out of your report, or at least be real vague about it?"

"Do you mind telling me why?"

"Well, the guys who answered this call got real spooked by the look on the kid's face." Boyd pointed toward Riesner's body, then instantly recoiled at the sight. "I'd like to have something real rational–sounding to take back. Can I just say it was a look of pain brought on by the heart attack?"

"I suppose you can tell them that. But what does that have to do with my report?"

"I was just hoping since there's no foul play involved, you might overlook the expression on his face."

"I still don't understand, why should it matter what I say about his face? If this isn't a homicide, who's going to read my report anyway?"

"Well, there's something else. You know this story's gonna be in the local news, him being a student at the school. It's just, I'd like to keep this in the *local* news, if you know what I mean. There are people in the media, especially the cable news folks, who'd like to turn something like this into a circus if they got hold of it. You know, people start talking about what terrible thing he must have seen or what scared this young man to death? They'll dig up your report, pick out—"

"I see."

"That kind of stuff wouldn't be good for the town, the college, or this kid's folks. See what I mean? If this was a homicide I'd say throw down the gloves and let's go for it. But since it's not, I'd hate to see this be anything more than a tragic loss for one family."

"I guess I don't have a problem with that. The look on his face carries no real medical significance, anyway."

"Thank you, Dr. Hargrove. Can you email me your report when it's complete?"

"You'll have it late this afternoon, tomorrow morning at the latest."

"Great. And thanks for getting with me here, Doc. You just made my week a whole lot easier."

When Boyd got out to the parking lot, he called Hank Jensen to update him on the good news. He asked Hank to start circulating the word around the shop about the kid's death being a heart attack.

What a break.

On the drive back to Culpepper, he thought about his reaction to the news. He couldn't believe how quickly he was turning into a small town cop. A few months ago he'd have been hounding a guy like Hargrove, looking for dirt, even if there was none. Now he was more excited about his son's basketball practice tonight. They were all going out for pizza afterwards. A murder investigation was the last thing he wanted to strap on right now.

6

THE FAMILIAR STONE wall flashed in Jack's headlights. He braked as he rounded the curve. The wall, covered in ivy, encircled The Whispering Hills, the condominium where Thornton lived. He'd been to Thornton's many times before, years ago, but only to give Thornton the occasional lift home. It was different being welcomed through the security gate and directed toward visitor parking.

Getting out of the car, Jack stood a moment to take it in. Whispering Hills was an attractive complex of garden–style buildings—some two, some three stories tall. Lots of trees. He walked to the glass security booth in front of Thornton's building, checked the board and dialed Thornton's number. Thornton buzzed him through. A few minutes later he was ringing the doorbell.

"Come in, Jack. Come in." Thornton was smiling widely. He turned and walked down a dimly–lit hallway. "You can put your coat in the closet there beside the door," he said over his shoulder. "You like Chinese, I hope?"

Was it Jack's imagination or did Thornton seem drunk? He never drank, as Jack recalled, but he walked down the hallway just now like a man navigating the deck of a ship. Seeing him in the dining room light, it dawned on Jack this was the first time he'd ever been with Thornton informally. He'd never been physically fit, ranging somewhere between out-of-shape and ready for a bypass. Every day in class he wore the same wrinkled brown tweed suit. Still did. It appeared going casual at home meant losing the coat, tie, and shoes.

"We've got four entrées to pick from," Thornton said as he walked into the dining room. "Stuff is so cheap, didn't want to take a chance I'd pick something you didn't like."

It was an odd table setting. Fancy white china, linen napkins, lit candles, then an array of small white cardboard boxes with red stripes spread out around a floral centerpiece. Jack looked into the living area. Nicely decorated, though a bit messy. A fieldstone fireplace centered the main wall. The back wall was covered by drapes and vertical blinds.

"Sweet and sour pork, General Tso's chicken, pepper steak and broccoli, stir-fry shrimp and vegetables," he called out. "Have a seat. Take your pick. I like them all the same."

Jack obeyed and began to pour the shrimp and vegetables over a mound of white rice. Moments later, Thornton came in and set a frosted glass full of wine in front of him and a chilled bottle of white zinfandel. Jack noticed a half-empty bottle of the same wine across the table by Thornton's seat. "A whole bottle?" Jack asked.

"A gift," he said as he took his seat. "Just drink what you want, take the rest home."

For the next hour as they ate, the conversation graduated from small talk to catching up. He learned Thornton was still unmarried. Too preoccupied with his work to get entangled in such relationships. It sounded like an excuse. He'd come under some pressure at the school to get published again. By rights, he was next in line to become Dean of History, but the regents wanted him to be more visible. Attend more alumni events, attend more fundraisers. Thornton sounded like he wasn't up for all the politics. He became increasingly edgy as he spoke.

"Why don't you just stay where you are?" Jack said. "Who cares about becoming Dean? If you're happy teaching…you do it well. Best teacher I ever had."

Thornton sighed. "Nice of you to say, Jack. But I'm not sure what I'm going to do. Becoming Dean was a goal I set for myself when I was your age. But the job was different then. Education was different. I've found myself thinking of other options." He was staring off toward the unlit fireplace. He refocused on Jack and said, "So, now that you've finished eating, let's hear about you."

Jack spent the next few minutes trying to be as vague as possible. By comparison, since they'd last met his life had been full of superlative experiences and ever–widening opportunities.

"I'll bet you even have an agent and a publicist, don't you?" Thornton asked.

"What?"

"For your books, your lectures."

"Actually, I do." Jack felt like he was apologizing. "It was just getting too much for me to manage."

"I imagine it would."

Jack wanted to think of some way to change the subject. He was aware of the gossip circulating in the academic world about guys like him. He hadn't even earned his Ph.D. yet or served on the faculty of a reputable school. By most accounts, he was only half–way through his educational journey. But here he was being treated as one of the new fair–haired boys, making three times the money and wielding ten times the influence as the hundreds of faithful history professors working in the trenches. Still, if they did resent him, they didn't hesitate to call on him to speak at their schools.

Did Thornton feel this way, too?

"Don't get me wrong, Jack. I'm glad someone from our school is getting his share of what's out there."

The thing was, he didn't sound glad. "Have you ever thought about the lecture circuit, Professor? You're a remarkable communicator. I could put in a word with my agent, test the waters a little, see if—"

"No, please don't do that. Not my cup of tea. I've got, as they say, a face made for radio. And I couldn't say anything meaningful in a sound bite. You've got the looks. You're sharp, witty, charming." Thornton sighed again.

And these didn't sound like compliments. The whole conversation was heading in a wrong direction. Jack didn't feel up to the role of playing Thornton's confidant. "Well, I really better be going. If I'm going to keep up the lecture schedule we discussed, I've got to do my writing at night." He stood before Thornton could talk him out of it.

"I understand. Don't forget your bottle."

Jack picked it up then walked to the hall closet to get his coat.

Thornton came up behind him. "It was great to see you again, Jack. I couldn't have been happier with the way things went this morning. What did you think?"

Jack opened the front door. "It was nice, but it was strange teaching in the same lecture hall I spent so much time in as a student."

"You'll get used to it," Thornton said as Jack crossed the threshold. "Well, don't work too late. A young man needs his sleep."

"Right," Jack said. "And thanks again for dinner." As he walked to his car, he wondered if it might be a mistake developing this kind of relationship with Thornton. Maybe he should keep things like they were, distant and formal.

*

Nigel Avery watched a man in his early thirties make his way down the stairs and out to his car. He'd gotten his name from one of Thornton's students that afternoon, some kind of guest lecturer the girl had said, Jack Turner. He used to attend Culpepper years ago. Probably nothing, Avery thought, but this was only the third person Thornton had been seen with informally since he'd started his surveillance. As it drove by, Avery took down the make and model of Turner's sporty new BMW.

Tomorrow, he decided, he'd get inside Thornton's place and set up the bugs.

7

JACK RETURNED TO the comfort of his garage apartment. The temperature outside had dropped dramatically. Inside, an aging radiator sat to the side like a faithful dog, closing the gap on the chill. He yawned as he turned on the kitchen light and saw the time. Couldn't believe it was ten o'clock already. Way too early to be this sleepy. Maybe it was the long day. Or maybe it was just the release of tension now that he was free of Thornton's company.

It had been a strange evening.

He'd never thought of Thornton as anything but a success before. He still felt that way. Thornton had probably fallen into some reflective mood brought on by the wine. That was probably all it was. Jack turned the kitchen light out and walked into the living room.

He had decided against writing tonight when the yawns began in the car ride home. Instead, he sat on the couch and picked up the 1949 issue of Life magazine Thornton had given him. He turned to the cover article on Pearl Harbor. It had that old–timey look and feel to it, an ad for a 1950 Studebaker even appearing on the opposite page, going for all of eight hundred bucks.

Imagine.

After a couple more yawns, Jack got up and turned the light out in the living room. He carried the magazine and a bottle of water back to the nightstand. He propped up some pillows, flopped down on the bed and began to read. All the while, his body beckoned for sleep. He managed to read the Pearl Harbor article through twice but finally gave in. He fell asleep without ever getting out of his clothes.

*

Jack awoke to the strange sensation of someone shaking his toes. The problem was…Jack had the apartment to himself. As he turned on his back, he felt a warm breeze blow over him from a window overhead. But it was the fall in Georgia. There were no more warm breezes, hadn't been any for over a month. And the window in his apartment was on the right side of the room, not overhead.

"C'mon Turner, you better get outta the sack. It's six–forty–five. You and me got AA duty at 0800 hours. I don't know 'bout you, but I intend to eat before then."

Someone was in his room. A friendly voice, with a noticeable New York accent. Slowly, Jack reached his hands around a stiff narrow mattress and felt the cold steel of a military–style bunk. He lay motionless then opened his eyes slightly, almost against his will.

"Okay, Turner. Suit yourself. I ain't comin' back for you no more. You ain't out there at 0800, the Sarge will have *you* for breakfast, I'm tellin' ya."

Standing at the foot of his bed was a short, muscular Italian–looking guy in a T–shirt and khaki–colored pants. A plain white towel was draped around his shoulders. Spots of shaving cream punctuated his face and neck.

Jack noticed the size of the room, way too big for his bedroom. Bunks lined three walls, all occupied, and a row of steel lockers stretched along the fourth. Cold fear gripped him. He didn't seem to be in danger; this Italian GI seemed friendly enough. But everything was wrong. Who was this guy? *What is this place?*

Convinced he had to be dreaming, Jack rolled back on his side, slammed his eyes shut, and covered himself with the sheet. He searched the darkened corridors of his mind for a better dream. He heard the Italian GI's footsteps walk away from his bunk.

"Suit yourself, Turner," said the fading voice.

Jack lay there for several anguishing minutes. He couldn't fall back to sleep; his body was done. Besides, he was already asleep, wasn't he? Slowly, he rolled over in his bunk and reopened his eyes. It was all there again: the bunks, the lockers, the warm breeze. I've gotta be asleep, he thought. I can't be in some army barracks. This has got to be a dream.

Why can't I wake up?

But what if he wasn't dreaming? What if he really was in this strange place? Jack rarely dreamed and, when he did, he'd forget them completely before stepping into the shower. The few dreams he could recall were only snippets and images that made no sense. Blurred things, like bad music videos. Certainly nothing this real. Everything he saw bore the undeniable imprint of reality.

A shower. Maybe if he took a shower he'd wake up. He sat up, instinctively scratching his head. Where his hair should have been he felt a stubby, prickly crew cut.

He tried to assess the situation logically. Last night was what… Monday? He had read that WW2 article before bed. Before that, he had dinner with Professor Thornton. Earlier that day he had given his first lecture in Thornton's class. He remembered. "That's my life. This is *not* my life."

He got up from the bunk and walked slowly toward a doorway at the far end of the room, searching for a shower. The faint sound of trickling water suggested a bathroom. He walked past a square pillar in the center aisle of the room and stopped to notice a dozen rifles neatly stacked around a wooden rack. There were three such pillars in the room about fifteen feet apart.

He looked back at his bunk, placed against the only wall facing outdoors. He could see the fronds of palm trees gently yielding to the wind outside. He ran to look. There were no palm trees in Culpepper. There was a road outside, partially lined with old cars. Across the street, a baseball field. He turned and examined the roomful of sleeping GI's. At the foot of each bunk, a wooden footlocker rested on a short stand. Jack's footlocker had his name stenciled across the top.

"This is crazy," he said aloud. A set of dog tags brushed against his chest. He grabbed at it. It identified him as Pfc. Jack Turner, the property of the US Army, with a serial number he did not recognize. U.S. Army? Lord…where am I? As he neared the doorway to the bathroom, he peeked inside.

"Hey, glad you finally decided to rejoin the land of the living. But as you can see I'm done." It was the Italian GI buttoning the last of his shirt buttons. "You want I should save you a spot?"

"Excuse me?"

"A spot…a place at the mess hall. You gonna chow down or what?"

Jack stared at him dumbly. "Listen, this may sound crazy to you, but I'm not supposed to be here."

"You're talking to the wrong guy about that. I'm just a Pfc. like you. They don't ask me to make duty rosters yet."

"No, I mean in these barracks. I'm not supposed to be here in these barracks. I don't belong here."

"What, somebody smack you good last night? Whatta you mean you're not supposed to be here?"

"I don't know. Nothing's making any sense right now."

"You musta tied on a big one last night, Jack. But you better snap out of it. Here's the skinny…you gotta get dressed, get some grub, get your gear, and be down at our duty station in less than an hour. I'll get the guns checked out. But you better get it together. Pronto." He was poking his index finger gently into Jack's chest.

Here's the *skinny*? Who talks like that?

The GI threw his towel into a laundry bin and walked past Jack. He headed down the center aisle toward a doorway in the far corner of the room. "You better get a move on it, Jack," he whispered loudly.

Somebody moaned "shut up" as the GI disappeared through the doorway.

8

J ACK WALKED BACK to the bathroom. A naked light bulb glared down at him from the ceiling. The toilets and urinals must be in the next room; he could tell by the smell. On a shelf to his left were a stack of plain white towels, the kind you get in a cheap motel. Jack grabbed one and walked toward a shower nozzle. He hung his towel and khaki–colored underwear on a wooden dowel and placed his watch on a shelf set about head–high.

He reached for the shower knob, careful to pick the one with an "H," and stood off to the right. Ice cold water blasted out. Chills from the wet spray zapped his neck and arms. At his feet, a puddle of icy water quickly gathered on the cement floor in search of the drain. He danced out of its way.

In a few moments, it finally warmed up. As the shower drenched his head and face, he ducked and closed his eyes. A thick stream poured off his chin like a faucet. When he opened his eyes, he expected to be standing in his antique porcelain tub with its four little legs in his garage apartment at 433 Rambling Road. It would be Tuesday morning. He would get on with the rest of his day, get some work done on his new book. This whole bizarre dream would start slipping from his grasp so fast he wouldn't recall a fraction of it by breakfast, even if he wanted to.

With his eyes still shut, he reached down for the hot and cold water knobs in his tub, fully expecting them to be there. Instead, he felt a rough cement wall. Not a good sign. His fingers spidered up the wall until they felt the same military knobs as before. He turned them off and stood there stiffly, fighting a wave of nausea. He opened his eyes, squinting at first, and panned the room.

Nothing had changed.

He slapped his palm against the wall. His last hopes for a rational conclusion to this nightmare were gone. Reaching for the towel, he dried himself off and faced the unwelcome reality that he would have to play this thing out, whatever it was. Maybe some sense would come of it later.

After his shower, Jack found a set of fatigues in one of the metal lockers along the wall. Not surprisingly, the locker had his name on it. Everything in the locker fit, even the boots. He studied its contents carefully. It yielded no clues.

He found the mess hall in the interior of the building by following a couple of hungry-looking GI's. Ten minutes later, he was looking at breakfast: some greenish scrambled eggs, two shiny sausage patties, and a clump of oatmeal. He had no appetite.

He quickly located the Italian GI again among thirty or forty others. Within a few minutes, he'd learned his name was Salvatore Bertelli, Sal for short. Sal was from the Bronx, and Sal had the hardest time believing Jack didn't know his name or anything about him. "What you got magnesia, or somethin?" he asked.

Jack looked across the noisy table at Sal. "Let's just say I've got amnesia," he whispered. "Let's just say I did get hit over the head in a bar last night. Right now, I need your help. I don't know where I am. I don't know what I'm doing here. I don't even know what I'm supposed to do with you on duty. Could I just follow you around for a while? I'm sure I'll snap outta this. But for now—"

"Geez, Jack. You're serious."

Jack stared directly into Sal's eyes. "Completely."

"Maybe after duty, you better go see the Doc down at Tripler. Let him give you a look."

Tripler, Jack thought, where have I heard that name before? "I'll do that," Jack said. "But for now…can you help me out?"

"Right now you and me, we gotta go. You gonna eat that?"

"I'm not hungry."

"Well, c'mon. We got exactly twenty–five minutes till we make the Sarge's hate list. I don't want to spend the weekend digging holes and filling 'em back up again. Let's get our gear." He pushed himself away from the table and headed for the door.

Sal hurried through the halls back to the barracks with Jack in pursuit. A few more GIs had crawled out of bed, slowly making their way to the showers. Jack gave Sal his full attention, imitating everything he did.

Sal opened his footlocker and pulled out a waist belt holding a bayonet and canteen. He went into the bathroom, rinsed out the canteen, and refilled it. Then he went back to the locker, pulled out a pie–pan steel helmet and put it on. Jack had the same gear in his footlocker. Sal then thumbed through the rifles in the center gun rack, grabbing one in particular. He exited out a side door next to the row of lockers. "Let's do it, Jack."

Jack grabbed a rifle—any rifle—and followed Sal out the door, wrestling with the waist belt as he went. In his four years in the Air Force, Jack had pulled duty a number of times but had never seen rifles like these. He wasn't a *Guns–and–Ammo* kind of guy, but they looked like antiques.

Barely a few steps from the barracks into the fresh morning air and he stopped dead in his tracks. Directly ahead, about seventy–five yards away, were two rows of large airplane hangars. What he saw caused his heart to skip a beat. Between the two closest hangars were several B–17 Flying Fortresses, World War II bombers, parked wingtip to wingtip. There could be no mistake. In his whole life, he'd only seen one at an air show, well–worn with age. These beauties glistened like new in the early morning sun.

He turned for a moment to look at the barracks building and the handsome row of palm trees, all about fifteen feet high, evenly spaced around the border of the property. It was an odd–shaped, three–storied building. Jack had seen it somewhere before, maybe in a picture or a movie, but he couldn't place it. Then he noticed the backside of a wooden sign along a walkway facing the hangars. He ran over and read the words on front:

Halemakai Barracks
Hickam Field – US Army Air Force
Honolulu, Hawaii

"Halemakai Barracks? Hickam Field?"

That's where he'd seen this scene before. It was too incredible to comprehend. Somehow, he was in Hawaii. Hickam Field was one of the air bases at Pearl Harbor. His eyes focused on the third line: "US Army Air Force."

US Army? The Air Force hadn't been part of the Army since… since World War II. He looked back at the B–17's. Back at the sign. He looked all around in disbelief then began to sweat.

He noticed the age of the cars parked along the roadside: vintage Buicks, Chevys, Fords, Packards, and Studebakers—all in mint condition. There was even an old trolley–style bus. But it wasn't old; it was like new. Not a modern vehicle in sight. He looked back at the airfield. No jets, no turbo–props, no helicopters. Just the B–17's and some other old planes he couldn't identify.

He looked and found Sal about one hundred yards away, walking along the hangars toward the end of the runway. "Wait! Sal, wait up." Jack sprinted, his rifle banging him in the butt with each stride. "Sal, what's today's date?"

"What?"

"Today's date…what's today's date?"

"Today's Sunday. You don't even remember that?" Sal kept walking, didn't even look up.

"No. I said the *date*. Not the day, the *date*."

"I don't know. It's the sixth or seventh. I don't know. What's it matter? I'm here fourteen more months, that's all I know." He kept walking, the anti–aircraft battery now in sight.

"Is it December?"

Sal stopped for a moment and stared at Jack. "You serious? You *are* serious. Course it's December. No snow's on the ground, but I'm not having any trouble remembering what month I'm in. What's a matter with you, Jack?"

"Is it…1941?"

"You don't even know what year you're in? Maybe you should see the Doc now." Sal turned and began to walk again, shaking his head in disgust.

Jack looked at his watch. It was 7:35am. He couldn't believe it. But it all added up. Somehow, some way, he was standing at Hickam field in Pearl Harbor on the morning of that fateful day.

That great day of infamy.

9

I

T FELT LIKE something out of the *Twilight Zone*.

Jack ran and caught up with Sal, all the while scanning the scene, looking for something to parlay his fears. The B–17's were in plain view, and they were brand new. Showroom condition. A sailor sputtered past on an antique motorcycle, also brand new.

"Sal," he said, gently grabbing his arm.

"What!" Sal pulled away. "Jack, you gotta come outta this. They're gonna put you away you keep talking like this."

"Sal, you've gotta believe me. Something terrible is going to happen here about twenty minutes from now."

"Whatta you talking about? Now you know the future. Five seconds ago you didn't even know what year you were in." Sal resumed his hectic pace toward the battery, now about twenty yards ahead.

Jack realized how foolish he must sound. The words sounded foolish leaving his mouth. How could he be in Pearl Harbor in 1941? This didn't seem like a dream. Did he travel back in time somehow? Maybe his body was lying helpless in a coma somewhere, locked into some weird mental illusion.

None of these theories satisfactorily explained why everything was so real. He was experiencing something as real as his old life used to be, as real as life is to anyone who lives it. He had to consider the possibility all this *was* real, at least for the time being. He decided to take full advantage of his knowledge of the Pearl Harbor attack to survive the next hour.

Sal finally reached the anti–aircraft battery, with Jack close behind, and relieved the two weary airmen standing there.

"You're early," one of them said.

"That's okay," Sal answered. You guys go get some chow or some sleep. We'll take it from here." He lifted a boot on a fifty–caliber ammo box, grabbed hold of the handles on the machine gun, and swiveled it around pretending to shoot down a plane.

The two airmen walked by Jack and nodded politely. He stepped into the circle of sandbags and looked at his watch again. 7:45am. Ten minutes. Only ten minutes. He looked up. What direction did the planes come from? He couldn't remember. From the north? Yes, the north. Looking at the sky now, it was hard to imagine several hundred Japanese planes were already in the air, headed this way.

When Jack was sure the two airmen were too far to hear, he said, "I'm going to tell you something, Sal. You're gonna have a hard time believing it. But you've *got* to believe it. Your life may depend on it."

Sal cast a "yeah, right" look in Jack's direction. He continued through his paces checking out the gun.

"In ten minutes, six carriers worth of Japanese fighters and bombers are going to attack Pearl Harbor and all the air bases, too. Hickam is going to get hit—bad. We gotta get out of here, start warning people, sound some kind of alarm."

"What? Jack…" Sal had a frustrated, angry look on his face

now. "You don't know how stupid you sound. We ain't goin' nowhere. And no Japs are coming here."

"It's not stupid, Sal. If this is December 7th, and it's 1941, it's going to happen."

"No, I'll tell you what. We're gonna sit here, do our four hours like we always do, stare at the birds and the trees, watch planes take off and land. Some other couple of suckers, whose Sunday got ruined too, are gonna take our place. And then I'm heading down to Waikiki for a swim, show these Hawaiian dames what a real man looks like."

"No, Sal. The Japanese *are* coming. Right here. They're going to sink most of our battleships. Hundreds are gonna die. I'm not joking, and I'm not crazy. We've got less than ten minutes."

"Don't you think the brass would know it if the Japs were coming?" Sal's eyes widened; his nostrils flared. "You think they'd let everybody sleep in like this? You think the General would order us to line all them planes up like that if there was a even a *chance* we'd get attacked? You gotta be—"

"General Short blew it!" Jack shouted loudly, cutting Sal off. "He didn't see it coming. He had his head in the sand. Everybody did. He's getting ready to play golf right now!"

"Better watch what you say, Jack." Sal leaned forward. He seemed only seconds from punching Jack out.

Jack turned and looked behind him. Their anti–aircraft battery was directly in line with the bombers positioned on the apron beside the runway. He realized the very spot they were standing would be bombed or strafed very soon. "You see all those beautiful planes over there?"

"Course I see 'em."

"According to history, eighteen of those bombers are going to be destroyed before you digest your breakfast. Over a hundred guys on this base are going to be killed and more than two hundred others wounded!"

"Jack, no Japanese are going to attack this base. You don't know what you're talking about. You're just sick in the head. We ain't even at war with the Japs."

"It was a surprise attack. They came—"

"Whatta you mean *was*? Listen to you."

"I mean *is*...it *is* going to be a surprise attack. They're coming out of the north. Their plan was to try and cripple our Pacific Fleet to buy them time to consolidate their gains and strengthen their defenses." Jack was reciting history straight out of the textbooks. He looked at his watch. "Now we've got...about five minutes, maybe less. We've got to warn the others, Sal. We can't just sit here and do nothing."

"You go warn 'em. Go ahead. Maybe they'll even thank you. 'Thank you Private Turner for waking me up early on Sunday so you can tell me the Japs are coming. I was gonna sleep in and miss it.' See what that gets ya. As for me...I'm gonna just sit here and unwind and enjoy the view." Sal leaned back against one of the sandbag walls, his hands behind his head, sunning his face.

Jack turned to face the planes and hangars, then looked at the barracks building set against the bright blue sky. Such a quiet and placid scene. So entirely normal. A few men milled about in the nearest hangar drinking coffee, laughing, probably exchanging stories from the night before. Just outside, a group of about twenty mechanics were already busy working on several bombers, preparing them for routine training flights. No big surprise. That's what people do in peacetime—routine training. Officers, noncoms, and enlisted men walked about, saluting each other, going in and out of buildings. Every one of these guys were probably thanking God for the chance to spend his tour in this tropical paradise. What was he supposed to do? Run around like Chicken Little telling everyone the sky is falling?

Images began invading his thoughts, historic photographs of Hickam Field before, during, and after the attack. He looked back at the barracks building. No wonder it had looked so familiar. But it was odd seeing everything in color. All the photographs and documentaries he'd seen of Pearl Harbor were in black and white.

"What was that?" Jack asked, jolted from his thoughts.

"What was what?"

"Those booms. They came from over there." Jack pointed in a northerly direction. "Which way is Battleship Row and Ford Island?"

"You know which way."

"Which way?"

"Right where you pointed."

"You hear that?" asked Jack. More low, rumbling booms and then another sound. A deep droning, buzzing sound. Radial engine planes flying at low altitude. Jack recognized them from the dozens of air shows he'd seen. He strained his eyes in their general direction but couldn't see a thing. He looked at his watch. "7:55am. It's happening now. It's really happening." Jack was squinting, searching the sky for planes.

"That ain't Japs, Jack. Them Navy boys are always flying practice runs in the morning. They're gonna catch some flak for doin' it on a Sunday, but—" Suddenly Sal stopped talking and rose slowly to his feet. A pale, sick expression replaced his bragging smirk. He stared in the direction Jack had pointed a moment ago. Jack turned again to look for himself. Toward the north, in the direction of

Ford's Island, thick billowing clouds of smoke began to rise above the buildings.

Instantly, the loud humming of planes grew louder, much louder. "There. There they are!" Jack shouted, pointing now to the opposite end of the runway. A thin line of white planes was diving straight for them. They stood like two men watching a movie. More booms could be heard in the distance. The planes came closer. Jack saw clearly the fixed landing gear beneath their wings.

"Vals!" he shouted. "Dive bombers. Sal, get down." Jack immediately dropped to the ground, curled up into a ball, and wedged himself tightly against the sandbags. He reached over and grabbed Sal's ankle and shouted his warning again. Sal stood there motionless.

"Sal," he shouted again. "Get down!"

Next came the deafening sound, several loud explosions in quick succession. He felt the impact of the bombs against the sandbag wall. It shook the ground beneath him. He knew from history, now from instinct, that several of the hangars he'd walked past twenty minutes ago were flaming ruins. He tucked tighter against the sandbags. The planes roared overhead as the sound of bullets tore into the pavement, then into the sandbags in a terrifying rhythm.

Sal's ankle was suddenly yanked from Jack's grasp. He heard Sal's body hit hard against the opposite sandbag wall. Sal uttered an emotionless, "Uh."

"Sal?" Jack reached over with his hand, his head still down, the rest of his body still locked tight in a fetal position. He felt Sal's leg and shook it. "Sal?"

Sal didn't answer.

For a moment, the sound of planes had faded. Now Jack heard

the cries of men screaming in agony and swearing in anger. More explosions in the direction of Battleship Row. Jack unfurled for a moment and looked at Sal.

Sal was half–sitting, half–lying with his back against the sand-bag wall. His head hung unnaturally off to the side, his face still set in that unbelieving stare. Three bullet holes in equal distances spread across his abdomen.

Sal was gone.

10

JACK JUMPED OVER the sandbag wall to flee the maddening scene. He had seen death before but always in natural, civilized doses. Wakes, memorial services, funerals. He'd never seen anyone die like that. He ran toward the barracks. The planes returned. New planes. This time from the opposite direction, behind him.

Before he had a chance to turn around, he heard a bomb whistling through the air. He glanced to his right in time to see that group of twenty mechanics disintegrate in a blinding flash, along with the planes they'd been tending. It was so close he could feel the heat from the explosion. The impact wave knocked him off balance. He buried his head in the grass, covered his helmet with his hands. Several more earsplitting explosions thundered down the flight line. Jack knew the B–17's were their target. They, too, were now gone.

God, he prayed, *please don't let me die here. Please let me get back to where I belong.*

Pieces of planes, buildings, and people started to rain down from the sky in a sickening cascade. Again, the Japanese planes faded into the distance. Jack looked up toward the barracks.

Through the thickening smoke, he could see the outline of a building. He had to make a run for it.

He took off toward Halemakai Barracks, limping slightly, jumping over chunks of buildings and human debris. He tried not to focus on the gruesome sights as he choked on the smoke and oil fumes that filled the air. He saw bleeding and wounded men, some crawling, others running in different directions. He remembered another black and white photo, a picture of a building on fire. Looking up, he saw a perfect match in color. It was Halemakai. The barracks, they get hit. So does the Mess Hall. Over thirty guys die.

Jack made his way there to warn them all to get out. Through the smoke, he saw it was still intact. As he ran, he tried to remember whether Halemakai got hit in the first or second wave of attacks. How much time did he have?

Moving toward the barracks as fast as his legs would go, he ignored the pain in his knee. He dashed across the street away from the intense heat from two hangars, now burning out of control. He looked for the doorway he'd come out of before. He couldn't afford to get lost on his way to the mess hall. He may only have seconds to spare once inside.

Another louder explosion stopped him in his tracks. It came up ahead in the direction of Battleship Row. Immediately followed by another explosion greater than the first. It sounded like the earth splitting in two. The ground rumbled like an earthquake. He felt the vibrations through the soles of his boots. A large, black mushroom cloud started to billow and rise off in the distance over the harbor.

The Arizona! The greatest single tragedy of the entire attack. A bomb from one of the Val dive bombers had just broken through several decks and ignited the powder magazine. That was the second explosion Jack had heard.

Eleven hundred men had just died.

A moment later, the dreaded sound of radial engines returned, zooming down over his left shoulder. He looked up in time to see three more dive bombers in a tight V–formation swooping directly toward Halemakai Barracks. Jack watched the birds of prey descend as he ran.

The whole scene moved in slow motion. He ran faster, as if he might outrun them, but they sailed right past. Machine guns blasted from their wings overhead. Bullets danced in straight lines, kicking up dirt and grass several feet into the air about fifty yards ahead. They found their target. Four airmen also running toward Halemakai. The bullets raked right over them. Three of them twisted and writhed in horrific spasms as they fell to the ground. The fourth stood perfectly still as the bullets raced past. He looked down with a stunned expression at his three dead friends. Together, Jack and this airman watched the planes finish what they came to do.

The planes flew directly over Halemakai's roof and back up into the sky. The center of the barracks erupted like a volcano of lumber and cement. Flames shot two hundred feet in the air. Both men hit the ground. As he lay there clutching his helmet, pictures of the mess hall began to form in Jack's mind. He wondered if any of the men he had casually nodded to were among those whose lives had just been snuffed out. How many of the men sleeping in the bunks finally made it over to the mess hall, just in time to meet their doom? Why couldn't he have figured all this out sooner? Even if he had, who would have listened? Would anyone have taken him more seriously than Sal?

Sal. Jack could see him lying there against the sandbag wall. The bullets puncturing his abdomen.

As he laid there, other images of the last few hours began to swirl around his mind in a nightmarish carousel. He tried to block them out, closing his eyes as tightly as he could. He covered his ears, trying to cut off the sounds of men dying, of piercing explosions and flames devouring ships and buildings.

He felt drained and exhausted. He seemed to be fading. It felt like he was losing consciousness.

Or...was he merely falling back to sleep?

*

When Jack awoke, the first thing he noticed was the absence of the acrid, choking smoke. Next, the silence. It was over. He had survived the attack on Pearl Harbor. He listened for the battle sounds, his eyes still closed. Gradually, he became aware of a strange softness beneath him. A second squeeze confirmed—a pillow.

He bounced up on his hands and knees and looked down. "I'm in bed!" he shouted. He rolled on his back, gazing at the ceiling with an exhilarated smile. There was the familiar water stain in the corner, the dusty floral globe covering the ceiling light. It was just a dream. He looked around the room. Yes. He was back at 433 Rambling Road. No warm breezes. No palm trees. No epic battles.

He jumped up and raced through the doorway to his bathroom, skidding the last few feet over the wooden floorboards in his socks. He smiled at his antique porcelain tub with its stubby little legs, as if greeting a long lost friend. He marched in, pushed the shower curtain back, and turned the water on. As he straightened up, he looked at his face through the crack in the medicine cabinet mirror. He looked terrible, but he was alive. And he was back home. And it was just a dream, a scary stupid dream.

The steam from the shower quickly fogged the mirror. He undressed, letting his sweaty clothes drop to the floor, and stepped into the soothing wet heat. He grinned as he watched the tornado of water form in the drain. This was the shower he had wanted to take back in the barracks. The one that washes bad dreams away. He got out and dried off. Stepping into the hallway, he took a whiff of the freshly–brewed coffee coming from the kitchen, compliments of his automatic timer.

Then it happened.

A vivid, piercing picture of Sal's bullet–ridden body blasted into his mind. He could see his face, that cold dead stare, the weird slant of his head. Then an image of those twenty mechanics being blown to pieces by that whistling bomb, debris falling down all around him. Then the sight of the four men running toward the barracks, three of them cut down by strafing bombers. He could almost hear the planes coming from behind, as though flying right through the bathroom into the kitchen. He winced and ducked down.

He ran back to the bathroom, turned on the cold water, and flushed his face and eyes. Grabbing hold of the sides of the sink, he slammed his eyes shut. The flashback was so powerful he feared it might somehow pull him back to Pearl, back to the aftermath of the battle. He looked at his petrified face in the mirror. In a loud, trembling voice he declared: "You are awake. That was a dream. It never happened!"

He was sure he was battling for his sanity.

11

LATER THAT MORNING, a few minutes after eleven, the warming sun began to pour through the blinds in Jack's apartment. A pleasant song played through his iPod speakers. Jack sat at his desk, staring past his laptop at the dust molecules dancing in the sunbeams.

He had just come in from the gravel driveway downstairs, shuffling like a zombie, still hungover from The Dream. He had walked down to the sidewalk to get the morning paper. He needed something, anything to keep his mind off The Dream. In the last few hours, the intensity had subsided, but when the images came they were still vivid. Keeping them at bay over the last few hours had given him a headache.

His concentration was broken by a car skidding to a halt in the driveway. He peeked out from the curtains but didn't recognize it. He did recognize the beautiful young woman who got out. It was Rachel Cook, the General's daughter. What was she doing here? She lifted her collar against the wind and pulled her gloves from her coat pockets.

Jack peeked out a crack in the curtain. As she made her way up the stairs he saw her cradling a large platter covered in plastic wrap. The screened door squeaked loudly. Before she knocked on the kitchen door, he opened it. Up close, her face was stunning, like a model's. High cheek bones, deep brown eyes, a natural blush provided by the cold. He snapped out of his stare. "Hi…it's Rachel, right?"

"You remembered my name."

"Well, you were only one of three girls in the lecture hall yesterday. I asked Professor Thornton about you." Jack backed up. "It's miserable out there. Better leave your coat on a few minutes. The heat in this place isn't too good."

"I really can't stay."

Jack looked down at the platter. Looked like the makings for hoagies. "So, what brings you here?" Only a handful of people knew where he was staying, so she must have asked around.

"I'm sorry, this was probably a stupid idea. You're busy, got your lectures to prepare for, your book to write."

"No, I'm glad you stopped by. I am supposed to be writing my book, but the lectures really aren't any work for me, they're all reruns."

She laughed. "Officially, I'm here just offering some Culpepper hospitality."

"And…unofficially?" Jack took the platter and set it on the counter.

"You don't remember me, do you? This isn't the first time we've met."

"No?" It had been twelve years since Jack served her father in Ramstein, Germany. He looked closely at her eyes, her smile, her hair. But she would have been so much younger. No, it couldn't be.

"You don't remember. I'm glad. I was fourteen, almost the same height as I am now, but I was a toothpick with braces. My dad wouldn't let me wear makeup. He'd only buy me the plainest clothes, and every day back then was a bad hair day. But you were always very nice to me."

Vague flashes of a homely teenage girl greeting him at the General's door or peeking out behind the living room curtain began to percolate. He looked back at her now. The transformation was astounding. "You know, I am starting to remember."

"Liar," she said smiling.

"No, I do…but, you've got to know how much you've changed."

She started tossing the salad. "I couldn't believe it when Professor Thornton announced you were coming back to Culpepper. I didn't think I'd ever see you again."

She instantly seemed to regret that last remark. The picture was becoming clear. A teenage crush. He had never suspected. "Small world."

"What I mean," she said, "who could have imagined out of six billion people going six billion different ways our lives would suddenly intersect again?"

She still seemed uneasy saying that. Jack wished he could think of a way to ease her embarrassment, but he rather enjoyed it. And coming over here unannounced wasn't very subtle. But then he began to rethink the moment. He was supposed to be still getting over Gwen. This trip was supposed to be a break in the action, let him readjust his focus. Some downtime to write his book.

"Are you all right?"

He smiled and looked away. "Just had a really rough night of sleep," he said. "Bed's too soft, I guess."

"Nice little place," she said.

"I roomed here when I attended the school."

"Really."

"Professor Thornton offered me any place in town, but I wanted to be here. Would you like a tour of the west wing or the east wing first?"

"Which is more impressive?"

"The east by far. The bathroom is in the east wing, hot and cold running water. But we'll start in the west wing, let the suspense build."

Jack led her into his miniature living room. He watched her as she observed the sparse collection of upholstered antiques. Several thin throw rugs dotted the wooden floor. Doilies covered the dried glass rings on the dark wooden end tables. It looked like the apartment of an old woman, except for the black–and–white World War II magazines spread out on the coffee table. "The apartment came furnished."

Rachel nodded. A doorway led into the single bedroom containing a small desk, a matching double–bed and dresser. "I like the song playing on your iPod," she said.

"You do?" That surprised him. Gwen hated his big band music. "Downloaded it on iTunes just before I left."

"And I like your little place, Mr. Turner."

"*Mister*?" he said. "I can't be that much older than you, am I?"

"I'm sorry. I only meant—"

"Please call me Jack."

She walked through another doorway leading back to the kitchen; the bathroom was on her left. She stopped for a moment. "I love those old tubs with the cute little feet."

"You sure you can't stay?"

"Professor Thornton said we needed to give you some space."

She walked back into the kitchen. "You'll find everything you need here for a nice lunch."

"I'd like you to stay," he said. "If you can. Looks like plenty of food for two." What was he saying? She had just given him an out.

She hesitated a moment. "I really should go."

"You can go right after we eat, how's that?"

"All right," she said. "Here, you have a seat and I'll finish putting this together. Won't take me five minutes."

"Are you warm enough? I can take your coat. You drink coffee? Just made a fresh pot."

"I had some on the way here. Have any tea?"

"Some iced tea. I could put it in the microwave, try and reverse the damage."

"I can drink it cold. By the way, I really enjoyed your Pearl Harbor lecture. Can't wait to hear the next one."

Jack walked over to the fridge, poured her a glass. "I'm just going to use the restroom for a minute."

"Should be all ready when you get back."

Jack closed the bathroom door and took a deep breath. *Pearl Harbor.* Why did she have to mention Pearl Harbor? Without warning a flashback of the men running across the field toward Halemakai Barracks rushed to his mind. Once again, Jack watched the bullets mow them down. Once again, saw them twisting and turning as they fell. Once again, the screams. He shook his head and opened his eyes, then stared at himself again in the mirror. "You were never at Pearl Harbor," he whispered aloud. "It was just a dream." He flushed cold water on his face.

Why was the spell of this dream so hard to break? The memories were nothing like dream memories. More like he'd really been there. Like the day after must have felt for the guys who survived the attack. He had to get back in control. His headache began to pound again. After a few deep inhales and exhales, he straightened up and came back out. The hoagies were made, the table set.

"I didn't know what you like on yours, so I made the standard Italian. You like mustard or mayo?"

"Both," Jack said. "Rachel, it's really nice of you to come over."

"Well, I'm a nice person. Lettuce and onions?"

Jack feigned a smile. She really was nice. And so beautiful.

"Are you alright? You don't look so good."

"I had a bad headache before you came. It went away for a few minutes, but now it's back."

"Have anything for it?"

"Not really."

She reached into her purse. "Let me give you some ibuprofen." She fished them out and handed them to him. "I really should go then, and let you get some rest."

He paused a moment. "I feel bad. You coming over here like this, making me lunch."

"Don't. It's not your fault you got a headache. I wasn't going to stay anyway."

"At least stay and eat. I can rest after you go."

"No, we can catch up some other time."

"At least take your sub with you."

She smiled. "No, I'll just wrap it up, and you can have it tomorrow. I didn't put anything on it yet to make it soggy."

Within a few minutes, she had the second sub in the refrigerator, her coat and gloves on. She smiled as she walked out the door. Jack walked onto the landing as she made her way down the steps. He was almost tempted to follow her and keep the conversation going but reminded himself he hadn't come back to Culpepper to get sucked into another relationship.

He watched her get into her car. "Thanks Rachel," he shouted. "Sorry about this." She looked up and smiled, but he thought he detected a slight look of regret in her eyes.

Maybe it was just wishful thinking.

"See you in class on Wednesday," he yelled as she backed out of the driveway.

12

ONE HOUR LATER, a man in a gray jogging suit stepped out of a rented car parked along the roadside, a block from the Whispering Hills condominium complex. He wasn't there to jog, nor did he need to. Nigel Avery already knew Professor Thornton wouldn't be home. Lifting the cottony hood of his sweatshirt over his jet–black hair, he tied the drawstring in a loose knot beneath his chin. He wore a pair of inexpensive sneakers, purchased at a nearby Wal–Mart because their tread patterns matched the sneakers of several hundred other cheapskates around town. He wore black leather gloves to ward off the cold. And fingerprints. He reached through the driver–side window, picked up a pair of sunglasses, and put them on. Ostensibly, to shield his eyes from the glaring afternoon sun.

Feigning a few stretching exercises to make sure he was alone, he jogged down the sidewalk. Just before reaching the stone wall that bordered the property, he darted into the woods. The dense shrubbery closed behind him like saloon doors.

Once in the woods, he stopped running. Even walking, he soon came to where the stone wall cut through the forest. The wall was icy cold, about eight feet tall, covered with dark ivy. He was over it in seconds, standing safely inside the perimeter of the complex. It was a brief detour but necessary. It served to spare the life of the aging security guard monitoring the front gate, who undoubtedly would not have allowed him to pass through in his car.

The hair, the padded suit, the sunglasses, and of course the southern accent, were simple components of his disguise. All designed to give Avery an altogether forgettable appearance. For two decades Avery had been a contract employee for the CIA. Then two years more with the NSA. But neither agency could lay claim to his loyalty now. Avery was for Avery. Money mattered some. The thrill mattered more. The more complex the job, the better.

So far, this job was falling woefully short of expectations.

He stood a moment in a grassy strip between the stone wall and parking lot, then jogged along the asphalt, crossed between two cars, then along the sidewalk, panting profusely to keep in character. He nodded to a nearby maintenance man in soiled green coveralls, lazily filling up a trash bag with wet leaves. Thornton's building was just ahead. Getting through the locked glass security booth would prove only a minor inconvenience. It amazed him that people in condos and apartments derived any sense of security from these things.

A young boy walked toward him carrying a small backpack over one shoulder. The boy turned into the booth in front of Thornton's building. Avery jogged right behind him, taking out a set of keys for appearances, after the young man produced his own. The boy opened the lock to the second door with his keys, while Avery stood closely behind, studying the digital menu next to the security phone, confirming Thornton's apartment number.

"You coming?" the boy asked.

"Yeah, thanks," Avery said, putting his keys back in his sweats.

The boy nodded and smiled shyly, then walked away.

Avery quickly turned and continued jogging in the opposite direction. He ducked inside the first hallway. He leaned up against the wall, pretending to catch his breath. A quick look verified he was alone again. He walked straight to Thornton's front door.

Thornton had only locked the front door using the doorknob, ignoring the deadbolt. A man who's never been robbed, he thought. A few surgical tweaks with a credit card and he was neatly inside. He stood in the darkened hallway a couple of seconds allowing his eyes to adjust. He took a few cautious steps forward until he came to the kitchen doorway on his right.

Several dishes were stacked in the sink. On the stove were four opened boxes of Chinese food, two with spoons sticking out the top. A newspaper sprawled across the dinette table beside a bowl of flakes which had coagulated into an indiscernible mush.

Moving to the living area, it was no better. Clothes were lying about, glasses and silverware left out on the dining table, stacks of files on the coffee table. He noticed the wall of bookshelves on either side of the fireplace. Then the miniature TV Thornton had propped on a wooden stand. No DVD. No surround–sound. Thornton was definitely not into movies or sports.

He glanced through the sliding glass doors to see if any neighbors lurked outside. The coast was clear. He moved catlike along the edge of the fireplace and then around the wall facing the outside. He closed the vertical blinds, making the living room as dark as the hallway, but still enough light to accomplish his task. He could wire this place in his sleep.

He walked from room to room taking inventory and was just about to pop the phone next to the bed in half when his ears picked up the faint sound of jingling keys.

He froze. There it was again.

Now the keys were in the door.

The door opened.

Thornton was supposed to be gone until late afternoon. He hadn't altered his schedule once the entire time Avery had watched him. Without a sound, Avery set the phone back on the stand, grabbed a pillow, tiptoed around the bed, and retreated into the darkness of a walk–in closet. He backed into a rack of dress shirts then reached for the holster strapped to his leg. He pulled out a small–caliber handgun that he'd bought for sixty dollars in Atlanta. Its former owner was some kid no older than fifteen. Avery was certain ballistics would match any bullets taken from this gun to a host of drug–related crimes or drive–by shootings.

He hadn't planned on killing anyone today, but it wasn't an emotional decision. Dying is part of life. Just happens to be the last part. Avery was an ambassador of fate, hand–picked by the Grim Reaper to usher selected souls into the eternal abode. He'd sent so many there over the years, more than he could count. Perhaps today was Thornton's day.

He waited a few moments in the closet, gaining control over his emotions and reflexes. As the door slammed shut, he heard a woman's voice singing in the hallway.

"Ama–zee–ing grace, how sweet da sound." After a few more bars, she began to hum. She took a few steps into the kitchen and said, "Oh Professor, choo are such a slobe. And why ees it so dark in here?" He heard her roll back the vertical blinds. "Dats better."

Obviously, it was Thornton's maid. How could he have missed this?

He continued to listen, trying to conjure an image for each move she made. If she came near, the last thing she'd hear on earth would be a muffled popping sound through a bed pillow. But what if she ignored the closet? How long would it take her to clean up this pigsty? Was her life worth waiting in this stuffy closet for an hour? Two?

Avery was not a patient man.

After she had spent almost thirty minutes on the kitchen alone, Avery was about ready to walk out in broad daylight and blow Ms. Hispanic away. He was burning up in this stupid disguise. It wouldn't be the first time someone walked into a burglary and paid for it with their lives. That's how this could go down. He'd given so many local homicide detectives routine burglary–turned–sour investigations to conduct. It was not a sophisticated MO, but none had ever come back to haunt him.

He smiled as he thought about the way hit men were depicted in movies. All kinds of hi–tech, complicated methods. But there was no need to kill fancy, not with so much killing going on now over drugs and ex–girlfriends. Innocent people always got caught in the crossfire. The thing now was too make your hits look like any-thing but a pro did it. You had to think like a young punk who just got disrespected, maybe somebody looking for a little extra cash. Leave a trail that points the cops back to the hood. Quickest way to get them to move the case to the unsolvable bin. Or else they'd wind up arresting somebody who had it coming anyway.

If it came to it, Avery would simply off the cleaning lady, grab a few valuables, drive one town over, put everything in a trash bag, and throw the bag in a dumpster. What was that—a thirty to forty minute delay?

The cleaning lady walked from the kitchen into the living area. "Guess I'll get started on da laundry," she said, groaning. Avery imagined her bending down to pick up a pair of dirty socks from the carpet then walking around the living room snatching one item after another from wherever Thornton had shed them.

Avery glanced down at an overflowing hamper against the back wall of the closet. She'd be coming here soon. It was perfect. Perfect angle. Perfect location. The insulated walls of the closet would even help muffle the gunshot. She'd never even see her assailant, or mercifully, feel a tinge of fright. She would simply bend over to pick up the hamper and slip through the boundaries of this life to the next.

A few moments later, he heard the soft depressions on the living room carpet heading for the master bedroom. He heard her soft humming as she crossed the threshold. The same tune as before—*Amazing Grace.*

"Look at dees, dark in here, too."

He heard the sound of the drapes swing open, as light from the window invaded the closet through the louvered doors. His presence was still shrouded in shadows. Through the slats, he saw a stocky feminine shape toss a collection of dirty clothes on the floor next to the unmade bed. Casually she began to sort them. She had no idea these monotonous, meaningless tasks were buying her precious moments of life. He heard bed sheets being rustled from the bed, the corners of the fitted sheet snapping in the air as it pried loose. He lifted the barrel of his nine–millimeter semi–automatic pistol slightly upwards and shoved it into the pillow.

"Da hamper! I almost forgot."

Here she comes. She grabbed the doorknob and pulled the closet door open. He moistened his lips, took a deep silent breath. He felt her presence inches away. A cell phone rang, sounded like from the living room. She stopped. It rang again. She pulled back. "I'm coming. I'm coming. Hold choor horses!"

He exhaled slowly but kept every other muscle in focus. As soon as she was off the phone, she'd be back.

"Hello?" A brief pause. "Juan? What's wrong? Roberto? What's wrong with Roberto? Can't you peek heem up? I'm working. I can't leev now. What? An interview? With who? Oh, Juan, thass wonderful! Well, for dat I will be happy to get heem. Let me see, I can be there in fifteen minutes. Perhaps, if I bring him back here I can still feenish on time. I know he will hate it, but I have no time to drop him home first. Jest go and get that jobe, you let me worry 'bout Roberto. Yes, bye."

She hung up. "Oh, Jesus, plees let Juan get dees jobe."

He heard the sound of car keys jingling and hurried footsteps heading down the hall to the front door. The door opened abruptly and closed. Then silence. He lowered his gun and came out of the closet. He tossed the pillow on the bed, walked out into the dining area, then replaced his gun in its holster. He wasn't relieved nor disappointed. He didn't want to kill the woman, nor care if he did. He calculated he had twenty more minutes of work before she returned and that would be plenty of time to do his job and be gone.

He glanced at the uncovered windows and decided to close the blinds again while he worked. He had all the telephones hooked up inside of ten minutes, then gave the apartment a good once over to make sure there were no more hiding anywhere. He placed a few more devices in strategic spots throughout the living area, then walked through the hall to the front door and opened it slowly. Good. No one in the corridors outside.

The blinds.

The cleaning lady would remember if she came back to them closed. He quickly reopened them, then slid along the walls of the apartment to the front door. Once outside, he picked up his earlier jogging pace, making sure to huff and puff in exaggerated tones. In short order he was back over the stone wall, through the woods, and standing next to his rental car.

As he drove off, Avery looked in his rear view mirror and smiled. Finally, this assignment had yielded a few moments of excitement.

There had better be more.

Then an idea. Maybe before the afternoon ended he should check on that dinner guest Thornton had over last night. Turner, Jack Turner. Avery had found out where he was staying.

Though he doubted anything would come of it.

13

JACK WALKED GINGERLY along the banks of the Chambers River, careful to avoid slipping on the smooth stones. The temperature had continued to drop as a cold front moved in. He jammed his gloves in the pockets of his jacket and glanced back at the bridge less than a block away. A man in a jogging suit stood at the midpoint, leaning over the rail staring in Jack's direction.

Jack continued walking; he wanted to be alone. Up ahead, the river made a turn.

Years ago, he loved coming to this spot to think and clear his head. Between the scenery, the solitude, the gently flowing stream, about a half–mile was all it ever took. Today it might take a mile, maybe two. He thought on the drive over, he'd be coming here to sort out his emotions about Gwen. An event that big seemed to warrant at least a few moments reflection. Oddly enough, it felt like he was already over her, mostly.

Still her betrayal stung. How could she treat him with such indifference? Two months she was seeing this other guy. Taking Jack's gifts. Letting him pay her way on dates. When she finally fessed up, she acted like there was something wrong with him, just because he was starting to get serious. What was so wrong about getting serious anyway? Didn't girls mock guys now for running away from commitment? Jack wanted a committed relationship. Weren't there any women left out there who believed in such things?

Maybe Rachel did. She was a general's daughter. She was probably raised conservative. But she was older now, out on her own. Maybe she had chucked all that.

A gust of wind and a loud crack interrupted his thoughts. He looked up in time to watch a limb from a nearby oak fall into the creek, so close Jack had to jump back to avoid the splash. The sky toward the west was growing darker from a building storm. The brunt of it was still miles away. But as he looked toward the other end of the cloud mass, he noticed a dark formation rising high like columns of smoke. It reminded him of the *USS Arizona* receiving her mortal blow at Pearl. Suddenly, he could see it all again. The explosions, Sal, the mess hall, the B–17's…all there in full color. The headache had finally left, but the emotions generated by The Dream were alive and well.

He could chalk the physical symptoms off to anxiety, but how do you account for the memories? They were not like dream–memories at all. More like he had been there, saw everything as it happened. Planes by the hundreds dropping bombs. Men being blown apart, debris falling like rain. Nothing he'd read or studied about Pearl Harbor came close to the reality of being there.

But he hadn't been there; it was a dream. *Get it through your head—it was just a dream.*

The fear was beginning to return. His hands were trembling. Sweat had formed on his brow. He picked up his pace as though he could get away.

Think of something else. How about Rachel?

But getting mixed up with her could be a serious mistake. He was on the rebound. He needed time. It would be a major distraction from his book. On the other hand, she was really beautiful. And she was interested. More than just interested, she was nursing a girlhood crush, which wasn't necessarily a plus. How could Jack live up to whatever lofty image she'd created of him since his days in Ramstein? Especially the way he felt now.

He suddenly felt a chill running through him. Somewhere along the way he'd stopped and sat on a large boulder. The icy rock had seeped through his jeans. He got up and headed back for the bridge, soon passing the remnant of a mud and stone dam, obviously built by children. He remembered building dams just like it in a creek four blocks from his childhood home. Funny the way kids think. *Let's build a dam*, as though they could stop the water from getting through. Still, some part of their imagination had urged them to try.

Jack was one of those kids who always had to try, and his mom always said he had a strong imagination. It was that imagination that had drawn him into the arena of history and, he believed, the reason why he connected so well with others when explaining it. When he studied history, it was so much more than facts and dates of battles or big events. Jack could actually imagine himself living back then, going through the very experiences he read about.

He stopped walking. Was that it? Was that why The Dream happened? Was there some deep desire in his heart to go back in time and see Pearl Harbor for himself, and it just broke through last night?

But that didn't make sense. Pearl Harbor had always fascinated him, but so had every other major event of World War II. Last night he thought about Pearl more than usual because he'd read that old article Thornton had given him, and earlier that day he had lectured on it.

But pick any other day, and Jack might be reading about and teaching some other significant military event. That's what he did for a living. And he'd never had a dream like that before.

As he rounded the curve, the bridge came into view. He closed the gap to fifty yards and noticed the jogger was still there, still leaning on the railing looking down in his direction. When the man noticed Jack looking up at him, he looked away then started walking.

Jack reached the bridge and looked up the hillside, eyeballing the footholds he'd need to grab. Looking downstream, he sighed. He hadn't really sorted anything out on this walk. Had the river lost its magic? Or were his problems now just far too complex?

*

Nigel Avery hurried off the bridge before this guy Turner made his way back up to the street. He had parked on a road off to the side about a block ahead, in the opposite direction Turner's car was parked. He couldn't get there fast enough to ditch this disguise. He knew it was cold out but he was burning up with this thing on.

Just as he figured, this looked to be just another boring dead–end. He had hoped maybe Turner was meeting up with someone in a secret rendezvous. Who takes a walk by a creek in weather like this? But it looked like Turner was just out there by himself the whole time.

Probably one of those wound–too–tight philosophical types, Avery thought, trying to find himself or solve some big riddle of life.

Another waste of time was all it was.

14

PATROLMAN HANK JENSEN walked past the water cooler toward Sgt. Joe Boyd's desk. Boyd could feel him coming, though his face was buried in a proposal. He had asked Hank to block for him awhile so he could get through this thing.

"Say, Joe."

Boyd didn't react.

"Yo, Joe. Sorry to interrupt you, but I got to on this." Boyd swiveled in the chair, but his head stayed focused on the desk. "It's the dead kid's father on line two," Hank said.

"What?" He looked up.

"Ralph Riesner, Senior. Remember they were vacationing in Florida? He finally got the message from the neighbors to call in. You know, the dead kid with the scary face. His dad's on line two."

"Oh, Geez."

"That's why you get paid the big bucks, right?" Hank said smiling.

"Tell him I'll pick it right up. I gotta dig out his file here. Does he know yet?"

"He knows something's up. Seems a little on edge. But I don't think he knows."

Boyd let out a deep sigh. Should he use the can first? He waited a moment to let the rumbling settle, took a sip of his coffee. Cold as ice. "Thanks, Hank. I'll take care of it."

He had been dreading this call all weekend. He knew why. The problem was he cared too much. Death didn't seem to bother him before he and Kate had kids. Now he looked at everything like a father. How do you tell another father his boy is dead? *"Sorry, sir, but we regret to inform you that your son is dead. How? He died in his sleep. We need you to come down to the morgue at your earliest convenience."* You just say something like that and hang up. You don't sit around let the family cry all over you. Boyd looked at the blinking light on his phone. Okay, here goes. "Hello, Mr. Riesner?"

"Yes." His voice already sounded shaky.

"This is Sergeant Joe Boyd, from the Culpepper PD. Has anyone told you why we called?"

"Well, no. My wife and I are still in Florida. She was worried a bit about our dog back home, so she called our next–door neighbor. They've been watching him for us. They said you've been trying to reach us since Saturday but wouldn't say why."

Great, thought Boyd. He had asked the neighbors to please not discuss the case if the parents called but hoped they would anyway, save him the trouble. He figured most people can't sit on a thing like that.

"Has Ralph gotten into some kind of trouble?"

Boyd sighed. Yeah, the worst kind. "Sir, I don't know how to tell you this. You aren't driving are you?"

"No, we're at our hotel."

"Is your wife there with you?"

"Standing right beside me. Please, what's wrong? Is Ralph all right?"

"No, he's not Mr. Riesner. I'm very sorry, but your son passed away, looks like it happened Friday night."

"Oh God, no—" He began to sob. "But how? Are you certain it's Ralph?"

"I'm afraid so. We obtained medical records from the school, the autopsy confirmed—."

"Autopsy?" He was crying uncontrollably now. "There's been an autopsy?" Boyd let Mr. Riesner have a few moments. He heard him tearfully relate what he'd said to his wife. She immediately erupted into sobs.

Boyd sighed, and waited.

"I'm sorry, what did you say your name was?"

"Boyd, Sgt. Boyd."

"Sgt. Boyd, as you can imagine, this is a terrible shock."

"I'm sure it is. I'm very sorry. We didn't know how to reach you."

"You said Ralph passed away. How…how did he die?" He was obviously trying to regain his composure.

"There was no evidence of foul play, Mr. Riesner. The medical examiner said he died of cardiac arrest."

"A heart attack? Ralph?"

"It happened in his sleep. The ME said it happened quite suddenly."

"But how? He was only twenty–two years old. It doesn't make any sense. I'm fifty, and I don't even have high blood pressure."

"Apparently, he had some kind of congenital heart defect, and it kinda just snapped. Listen, I'll tell you what…if you give me your email address, I'll send you a copy of the report. I'm sure you'll be wanting to get up here—"

"Right away," Mr. Riesner said. "We're near Miami. We'll take the first plane out."

"I'll also email you the address, where they're keeping your son. If you call ahead, you might be able to talk to the medical examiner in person."

"Thank you."

"Hey listen, I hate having to do this. I'm really sorry for your loss."

"Thank you, you've been very kind."

After taking down Mr. Riesner's email address, Boyd hung up and gave Hank the assignment to email him the autopsy report and address to the morgue. With a fresh cup of coffee in his hand, he sat back down to his proposal, glad the ordeal was over, glad he hadn't let the word *cadaver* slip out with the boy's father, confident the Riesner case was now closed.

Only one detail remained, and Boyd would have to carry it out carefully. He'd have to inform the press. The press release would have to be in all points unexceptional, mundane. Nothing to arouse suspicions. A poor lad dies in his sleep from a congenital heart defect, the grieving parents arrive today to escort his body back to Charlotte. Along those lines. If he was lucky, it would be buried in the local paper, maybe not even make it to the local TV news.

15

WHEN JACK ARRIVED back at his apartment, he set his keys and cell phone on the desk and noticed he had three voicemails. He took off his jacket and laid his gloves over the corner of the radiator to let them defrost. Then he listened to the messages.

"*Hi, Jack. Thomas here.*" It was Thornton's voice. "*Just checking in, see how you made out your first night. Hope you slept well. I mean it, you don't have to stay there. If you're having second thoughts about it, let me know. I'll set you up right. Sometimes we have these sentimental notions and they don't turn out like we planned. If I don't hear back from you, I'll assume the lecture is on for Wednesday morning. Enjoy your writing. Bye.*"

Writing. It was the last thing on Jack's mind. The second message began.

"*Hey, Jack. Hope I got this number right. I know you told me not to call, but I've got a hot one in the oven.*" It was Judy Butler, Jack's agent and business manager, the exaggerated Boston accent a dead giveaway. "*You watching the news at all? Something's breaking loose in Germany. Some riots about something, not sure what. Anyway, I sent around that demo we made and I just got a call from a producer at*

Fox News, says she liked what she saw, could use you to give some back-ground on a story they're working on. What do you say? I could fly you in tonight, have you back before morning. This is the big time, Jack. I'm serious. She called me. I didn't call her. Getting your name splashed across the airwaves couldn't hurt your book when it comes out, either. Think of it that way, it's not really a distraction. And with your gift of gab and those good looks, you're a cinch to become a regular. They'll get thousands of Tweets from young ladies all across the land with a new-found love of history. They'd have to have you back. I've seen it happen. Call me. The window's open, Jack. Who knows for how long?"

The way Jack felt now, he would probably mangle a live TV interview. Come off looking like anything but an expert. The third message played.

"Mr. Turner... I'm sorry, Jack. Rachel Cook here. Just calling to see how you're feeling. I'm sorry for dropping in on you like that. I really should have called first. There's a flu going around, so you get your rest. Call me if you need anything. Well... bye."

Jack smiled. The smile lingered. He didn't even know he was still smiling until he walked into the bathroom and saw his face in the mirror. Guess a girlhood crush is a pretty hard thing to break, he thought. But now what should he do?

He picked up his phone, deciding to return only one of the calls.

*

Jack looked at his watch. Six–forty five. He had told Rachel he'd pick her up at seven. Plenty of time. It was just dinner, he reminded himself, not a date. To insulate himself further, when he'd called a few hours ago he decided to tell her he was just getting over a bad relationship and wasn't up to starting something new so soon. Rachel insisted she understood.

Turning now into her apartment complex, he knew there was more going on inside than that. He had spent way too much time in the mirror. He'd ironed his shirt and slacks, brushed his teeth for the second time. And he'd picked the River Bend restaurant for dinner. When he attended Culpepper, he couldn't afford a place like River Bend. Salesmen took clients they wanted to impress there; husbands took their wives for big anniversaries.

He smiled as he pulled into a parking spot near the front door of her apartment. Nice place. Way nicer than he could have afforded as Thornton's teaching assistant. Maybe Daddy was helping. He buttoned the top button of his cashmere coat and dipped his head down against the wind. Not a good night to be out. He was glad he found a spot so close to her front door. He rang the glowing orange doorbell, then stepped back to appreciate the attractive border of Italian tile. When the door opened, Jack was stunned. Had a red dress ever looked so fine on a woman before?

This is not a date.

"Come in. Quick. It's freezing." She smiled as she reached out and yanked him in by the arm, closing the door behind him. "I'm almost ready. Give me a minute." She turned and walked toward the hall, tugging at her ear.

"Rachel, you look…very dressed up."

She flashed him a smile as she disappeared into the shadows. "And you're not dressed up, either. Right?"

Touché.

He walked into the living room, big overstuffed sofa and chairs, a white brick fireplace, pillows that matched the pictures on the walls and totally out of place a hideous cat sprawled across a glass coffee table.

"Jack, meet Tuffguy. Tuffguy, meet Jack," Rachel said as she moved from the dining area into the kitchen.

Tuffguy honored Jack by lifting his head about an inch. His expression said, "Get lost." Rachel walked back into the living room, her purse on one arm, a black overcoat on the other. Jack reached out to scratch Tuffguy's head, for Rachel's sake. The cat yanked his head back like a boxer ducking a jab. "Not interested? Fine with me." The thing looked like it had been run through a blender: one ear gone, scalp full of lumps and bald spots, a feline Quasimodo.

"He treats me the same way," she said. "He let me save his life about two years ago. Found him all limping and bloody by the dumpster out back. Took fifty stitches to patch him up, over six hundred dollars in vet bills."

"And for that he won't even let you pet him?"

"He'll let me, but he gets to choose when. It's not a pleasant experience, so I don't mind the gaps in between."

"I can't even look at him."

Rachel laughed. "Tuffguy understands me. I can tell him anything. So where are we going?" She put on her coat.

"How's River Bend sound?"

"Nice place to get caught up," she said. She opened the coat closet and reached for a hat. He noticed two pairs of ladies boots, clearly different sizes. "You have a roommate?"

"How did you know?"

He pointed to the boots with his eyes.

"Very perceptive. Her name's Mary. She's out of town for a

little while. She's checking out a job offer at Purdue. Don't know what I'll do if she takes it. I can't afford this place without her."

So Daddy wasn't helping. Independent type. "You ready?" Jack's hand was on the front door knob.

"Let's do it." They headed out.

Rachel seemed to like Jack's BMW. And why shouldn't she? The car heated up before they were two blocks down the road. Jack did his best to keep his eyes on the road. She was very distracting.

The ride to the restaurant was pleasant. As they drove, the conversation was mostly small talk with a little catching up. Her parents had retired to the Charlotte suburbs, their hometown before the military had moved them all around the world. Jack said he was from the suburbs of Philly. He had just started to travel, loved the chance to see places he'd only read about, hated living out of a suitcase. Germany was still the only country he'd been to outside the US, unless you counted a few weekend visits to Austria and Switzerland while stationed there. He'd been invited to speak later this year at Oxford. He couldn't wait for that, had his agent setting up a tour of World War II sites. She was mid-sentence when they arrived, something about her older brother, the doctor, just getting married.

A valet greeted them at the door and offered to park the car. They walked past a small crowd sipping cocktails and up to the hostess. He had made reservations and was relieved when they were seated after a few minutes.

"I've always loved this place," Rachel said, gazing out the window toward the river. A few well-dressed couples meandered about on a lower level, enclosed in a glass room. Beyond it, the boundaries of the river were just visible by the light of a three-quarter moon.

"Have you been here often?" Jack asked.

"I've *never* been," she replied, "but I've wanted to come for a while. I've read articles about it in the paper, and Mary's been here a couple of times. She said it's wonderful."

The hostess led them to their table. Her eyes roamed around the table, taking in the elegant setting. She turned those eyes on him as she picked up the menu. "Do you know what's good here?"

"From the reviews I've read, everything. And it's my treat, I insist. If you're a vegetarian, they've got an incredible salad bar." Gwen was a vegetarian, always the lecture. The look on Rachel's face brought instant relief.

"I love a good salad, but I come from a long line of carnivores. My father would disown me if I ever stopped eating meat. How about you?"

"Salad has its place, but I like a good steak."

She looked at a platter going by. "Or crab."

"Surf and turf, they've got that. Crab legs or lobster."

A handsome black guy in a tux appeared out of nowhere and stood at their table, asked what they'd like to drink. Jack ordered the house blush wine, Rachel the same. No appetizers, thank you. Moments later, the waiter reappeared with the wine and a basket of delicious smelling rolls. This was all very pleasant, maybe too pleasant. Gwen had barely made an appearance in his mind. What was the proper length of time to grieve over a betrayal anyway?

They studied the menus. Jack went with the salmon, broiled with a lemon dill glaze, Rachel the surf and turf, with crab. They both took a trip to the salad bar.

While eating the salad, Rachel said rather abruptly. "Can we get something on the table?"

16

J ACK LOOKED THE table over, wondering what was missing.

"It's been bothering me since I left your apartment today," she continued. "You're no fool, and neither am I. I'm sure by now you've figured out I've had a crush on you ever since Germany. It slipped out. I don't know what I was thinking coming over like that. It was anything but subtle. Normally, I don't chase men—"

Nor should you have to, Jack thought.

"—and I'm not chasing you. It was just too much of a coincidence, you coming to Culpepper like this. I was curious, and I don't know where I'm going with all this, but I'm glad you told me about you not being in the market, just getting over your Jenn."

"Gwen."

"Sorry, Gwen." She took in a deep breath. "So we're just talking friendship here, no pressure. I've thought about it, and think any reasonable woman would have done the same thing I did, given these circumstances."

"I agree."

"Good." It was settled, she seemed relieved.

"I'm glad you were curious," he said. "And I'm glad you're here, and even glad you cleared the air. So now, we can move on. Tell me about your dad, the General."

"Well, for one thing, he loves your work."

"You're kidding."

"Why? You are a fabulous history writer. And an even better speaker."

"Were you disappointed?"

"What?"

Jack realized, he'd reverted back to the subject of her curiosity. But he had to know. "When you finally saw me after all these years, were you disappointed?"

She smiled, shaking her head in mock disgust. "I thought we were moving on."

"We are—we will. I just—"

"No, I was not disappointed. I'm surprised you had to ask. I came over this morning. I'm here now."

"That could just be curiosity."

"I thought we were talking about my dad."

"Okay, I'm sorry. You were saying…"

Rachel started to talk about a conversation she'd had with her father last night but was interrupted by the arrival of the meal. Jack was glad. The conversation was about Jack's Pearl Harbor conspiracy lecture. She said her father had some interesting questions he wanted her to ask. Jack tried to change the subject as they ate, asking other things about her father, her family, how she had come to take Thornton's class.

She said she was the baby in the family, had two older brothers, one a doctor, the other— taking after her father—a colonel in the Air Force. She had finished her BA in political science a couple of years ago, had worked on the unsuccessful congressional campaign of a conservative Republican she admired, was offered this teaching assistant post and was now slowly making her way through her master's as she debated about what to do with her career.

She talked about how much she'd come to appreciate her parents' relationship in recent years, how they stuck it out through all the ups and downs of a military career, and now enjoyed a great friendship. They still held hands when they walked, still complimented each other, went dancing once a week. Most of her married friends from high school were already divorced, some twice.

Jack had to ask…no, she had never been married, had never really come close. But it was becoming clear, she was holding out for someone like dear old dad. High stakes, Jack thought. But he liked this about her. He liked everything about her, everything she said, even the way she said it.

"You seem to be really taken with the forties, Jack. I mean more than just for a guy who teaches history. The music you listen to, the magazines in your apartment, the gleam you get in your eye during your lectures, almost like a preacher."

Jack wondered, was that an approving or disapproving tone in her voice? "I guess you could say that."

"Don't feel bad. I think it's…" She fumbled for an adjective. "Well, I'm not sure what it is, but I like it. It was such a romantic time. I love watching movies from that period. That's what you kinda remind me of. Like you could have stepped right out of one of them. Of course, your hair doesn't work at all for that time. But other than that…"

"I'm not sure how I became so enamored with the period. It just sucks me in for some reason. Everything about it. It was such a totally different world. So innocent compared to now, even with the craziness of the war. People lived by a code. Right and wrong were clearly defined. Families stayed together. People went to church. The streets were safe. I know that's all a bit oversimplified, but I think you get what I mean. To me, the only drawback of the period was the racial discrimination issue… which was really bad."

"And the way they treated women," Rachel added.

"Right," Jack said, "Those two things and…the musicals."

"What?"

"Musicals. I can't stand the musicals. People breaking forth into song and dance right in the middle of a dramatic scene. Everybody knows the words. Way too hokey."

She laughed and took a sip of iced tea. "So, I get why you like that time period. How did you wind up as a military history major?"

"Well, in a way Professor Thornton had something to do with it."

"He did?"

"I was reading his first—I guess his *only* book on military aviation at a time when I was searching for a career path. I had just come out of the Air Force. Then it dawned on me. I had all these military history books on my shelf, had read every one. I noticed in Thornton's bio he taught military history at Culpepper. I'd never realized this might be something I could do for a living. One thing led to another and the rest as they say…"

"—is history," she said.

"All I know is whenever I read history—especially the World War II era—it comes alive to me. I can almost feel what it was like to be there. A part of me wishes I could go back in time somehow, see it all for myself. See what it really—"

He froze.

"What's the matter?"

"Maybe that's it."

"Maybe that's *what?*"

"Maybe that's what caused The Dream."

"What dream?"

"The dream I had last night."

"The dream, was it some kind of nightmare? You said you had a rough night."

"Yeah, it was." Jack had partially disengaged. Rachel said something else. Jack didn't hear.

"Jack?" She waved her hand in front of his eyes.

"I'm sorry."

"What's going on?"

"I don't know. All day I've been trying to figure out how I could have had such a crazy dream. I think I might have just said it."

"What did you say?"

"I don't know." He looked back into her eyes. "It's just this dream was like nothing I ever experienced before. So intense, so real."

"Why don't you tell me about it?"

"No. Let's don't talk about this. Here we are at River Bend—"

"Jack, I don't mind. I really don't. Tell me about it."

Jack thought a moment. "All right."

He relayed the highlights of his visit to Pearl Harbor and Hickam Field. In seconds, the atmosphere at the table was electrified. At times, Rachel shuddered. Several couples within earshot were unconsciously drawn into the story. Playing it all back made Jack realize just how bizarre it was.

When he finished, she sat there for a few seconds in stunned silence. "That's a tad more exciting than your lectures."

"That's what I meant when I said how a part of me wanted to

go back to the forties and see it for myself. Maybe that desire was more powerful than I realized. Maybe something kind of snapped in my brain." Jack immediately regretted saying that.

"Have you had…many of these dreams?"

Look at her face, Jack thought. I shouldn't have brought this up. "No, only this one. But it's no big deal. I'm sure it was just some freak thing. Look, your food's getting cold." The last thing he wanted was for her to think he was some kind of nutcase.

17

JACK AND RACHEL stood at the doorway of her apartment. "Sorry about the moths," she said, watching Jack flick one from his hair.

"It's all right. Hey look, I better get going." He really was in no hurry, but this date wasn't a date, and he didn't know what either one would do if he stayed there a moment more.

She turned toward the door, pulling the keys out of her purse. "Thanks again for dinner." A pause. "I don't know if you're interested, but there's a theater downtown that replays old movies on Sunday nights, big screen, digital sound."

A good sign. Talking about The Dream mustn't have done any permanent damage. But why get together again in such a setting? The pretext of getting caught up and returning favors would be gone.

"You don't have to," she said.

"No, I want to, and that's the problem. I'm supposed to be grieving over a broken relationship. And I'm supposed to be burying myself in this book project to help me get over it." He smiled, then so did she. "Rachel, I...I need a little time to sort this out. Can I get back to you on the movie idea?"

"Sure. And don't feel strange about saying no."

They returned smiles again. Jack felt the gravitational pull of a goodnight kiss. But it shouldn't happen. Not now. "Good night," he said, pulling back.

"Good night." The door closed behind her.

As he drove off, the distraction Rachel offered began to fade. His mind soon slipped into the torment he'd moved in and out of all day. From the moment Jack noticed the darkness setting in, a restless feeling had come over him. Now that Rachel was gone, he felt it keenly. He knew what it was.

At night people have to sleep.

His car must have remembered its way home. Jack couldn't recall making a single traffic decision as he pulled into the driveway. Different scenes from The Dream replayed in his mind. It still felt as if he'd actually spent those hours at Pearl.

He walked up the rickety steps, carefully closing the screen door so the whapping sound wouldn't wake his landlords. The overhead light in the screen porch was out. He let himself in. The apartment was dark, cold as ice, and silent.

Within the first fifteen minutes, he had the heat on, the lights on, coffee brewing, and the remnants of a store–bought pecan pie heating in the microwave. He sat at his dinette table and started to eat. He was so tired. He tried forcing the dread of sleep out of his mind with thoughts of his first outing with Rachel. Next he tried thinking about the book he was supposed to be writing.

But it was no use.

He finished his pie and walked into the bedroom, flicked on the light. As he emptied his pockets on the dresser, he glared down at the bed.

Where would it take him tonight?

18

JACK AWOKE THE next morning, the only sound a gentle hissing from the radiator. He glanced around the room. Everything was in its proper place. The Norman Rockwell calendar on the far wall, just above it, the floral wallpaper curled and peeled back at the ceiling. Through the window to the right, a sliver of sunlight squeezed through the blinds.

The evidence confirmed; he was at 433 Rambling Road.

He sat up. As he scratched his head, images of a fading dream were quickly disappearing. The only thing he recalled was a woman with big flaming red hair, dressed like a country western singer, bright red rouge on her cheeks and ruby red lipstick. He had no idea who she was.

Just like dreams should be. Stupid, nonsensical.

Maybe she represented Gwen.

By the time he made it to the kitchen, even these images were beginning to fade. The Pearl Harbor dream had been a fluke, not the beginning of a trend. The smell of fresh coffee made the morning complete. He looked at the clock on the microwave as he pulled a mug out of the cabinet.

After finishing off a pop–tart and a cup of coffee, his phone rang. "Hello?"

"Is that you, Jack?"

"Professor?"

"Yes. Did I catch you at a bad time?"

"No," Jack said, "just finishing up breakfast. But I'm glad you called. I was going to call you before I headed in."

"Oh? What about?"

"I just wanted to give a little heads up on my lecture this morning. I've decided to cover the controversies surrounding Doolittle's Raid."

"Oh? I didn't think you had finished with Pearl Harbor yet."

"Well, I almost did. I'd just like to change gears this morning if you don't mind."

"That's fine, Jack. Do you mind if I ask why? I know some of the students will?"

What should he say? *I had a bad dream about Pearl Harbor and I'm scared to even think about it?* "It's just I went a little further on Monday than I planned, got a little lost on the time. I don't have enough material for another full lecture."

"All right, Doolittle it is. I'm sure it will be wonderful. Are you feeling all right?"

"What?"

"Nothing. I just wondered if everything is all right. I called and left a message on your voicemail. Wanted to know if you were having any second thoughts about staying at the apartment. Have any trouble sleeping? That bed looked like something from another era."

Have any trouble sleeping? "I'm fine. Class is still at ten, right?"

"Ten, yes."

"See you there."

"Say Jack, have any dinner plans tonight?"

How he wished he had. "No, I don't. But I couldn't stay late; I really need to get to work on this book."

"Man's gotta eat," Thornton said. "I won't keep you. There's a great gourmet Italian place on my way home. Makes incredible take–out. Lasagna, Veal Scaloppini, Crab Alfredo…"

"Okay, you talked me into it."

"You pick the time."

They decided on a time and what Jack would order and hung up.

*

A few minutes after ten, Professor Thornton looked over the rim of his bifocals at the class. Standing off to the side, Jack noticed Thornton's eyes scanning each row as though taking roll call in his head. Thornton stopped briefly at a lone empty chair by the door. A frown appeared, then he smiled widely, took a deep breath and said, "We're honored once again to have Mr. Jack Turner as our guest lecturer. Today I understand he's going to shift our attention to one of the most dramatic and heroic missions of World War II, our first chance to strike back at Japan after Pearl Harbor. I'll let Jack explain."

Jack arose to light applause. As he made his way to the lectern, his eyes scanned the crowd as well. He paused when he saw Rachel's face. Their eyes met, a quick smile, then he looked down at his notes. He really didn't need them. He knew every detail about the Doolittle Raid by heart.

"Thank you, Professor. I'm sure as fourth–year military history students you're all familiar with Doolittle's Raid on Tokyo. But I've done some checking and, unless you've looked into it on your own, it was the Fall of last year since it's been covered here in class. So I've got this excellent little twenty–five–minute video to refresh your memories. When it's over, we'll look at some of the things the history books rarely discuss. Someone get the lights?"

Most of the class looked toward the front door, but no one got up to flick the switch. "Looks like Mr. Riesner is absent today," Thornton said. "He usually gets the lights. Mr. Holton, would you do the honors?"

A well–dressed kid in the front row dutifully obeyed. Jack turned back to the screen as the lights dimmed. Patriotic music began to play, and the deep voice of an excited announcer began to speak:

On April 18, 1942, just four months after Japan's devastating attack on Pearl Harbor, eighty brave Americans launched sixteen large B–25 bombers off the deck of the USS Hornet. A feat never attempted, before or since. Their destination? Tokyo! Between Pearl Harbor and this fateful day, things could not have gone any worse for the Allies in the Pacific. It seemed nothing could halt the aggression of the Imperial Forces of the Empire of Japan. After Pearl Harbor, there was Corregidor and Bataan, the fall of the Philippines. Then, Wake Island fell and Guam. Malaya, Singapore, and Burma. The Allies seemed powerless to stop the Japanese. Morale was at an all–time low. Something had to be done. That something turned out to be…Doolittle's Raiders. Colonel James Doolittle was given the top–secret assignment of training a squadron of bombers to take the war right back to the Japanese. To do something the emperor of Japan vowed would never occur—the bombing of Japan's capital city—Tokyo.

Jack settled back in his chair. He'd seen the video many times but got sucked in again. There was something so magnetic about the courage of these young men. Every moment of their mission must have been filled with non–stop adrenaline and adventure.

He glanced over at Rachel. She was looking at the screen. She actually seemed interested in this. Gwen hated anything in black and white. Jack turned back to the screen. For the moment, unconcerned about Pearl Harbor and bad dreams.

*

Across town, Nigel Avery walked carefully down the wooden steps of Jack's apartment after gently closing the screen door. Today he was a termite inspector, gray overalls, baseball cap with the company logo, the whole bit. He enjoyed the irony; instead of making bugs go away, he was installing them. But it was a good daytime cover. If anyone asked, he was sorry, he just had the wrong house. He knew Jack was giving a lecture at the University right now, and that would give him plenty of time.

He was less sure anything would come of it. There was still nothing to show for all his time with the Professor. As he slipped across the street into his van, he looked back at the place. What a dump. He had done some checking into Turner's story. It didn't make sense, a guy with Turner's money and position staying at a place like that.

After looking at his watch he drove off toward downtown to grab an early lunch.

19

WHEN JACK RETURNED to his apartment later that night, he had to admit the dinner with Thornton hadn't gone that badly. The Professor seemed in a much better mood, full of superlatives about Jack's lecture that day, the angles Jack had taken about the risks of the Doolittle mission verses its gains. They had talked like peers.

A few nights ago, Jack had wondered if Thornton had become resentful of his success. If so, no signs of it tonight. And the food was delicious. Once again, Thornton had served white zinfandel, and had given Jack another fresh bottle to take home. Jack left shortly after dinner. Thornton said he understood. Besides, he had an important phone call to make.

Maybe Jack should give this second bottle to Rachel. After class that afternoon, he got the feeling she'd hoped they might have lunch together, but he felt the need to make a dent in his book. He had made some progress before getting ready to leave for dinner.

At the moment, Jack was sitting in the stuffed armchair of his apartment living room, holding a new book Thornton had given him at dinner. It was a pictorial essay about the Doolittle Raid, published earlier in the year. It was supposed to include a number of previously unpublished photos, provided by a widow of one of the sailors on board the USS Hornet, the aircraft carrier used to escort Doolittle's bombers to Japan.

He took a sip of coffee and opened the book. It was one of those over–sized, coffee table affairs, big on pictures, short on text. But he didn't care. In no time at all he was drawn in. He reread the highlights of the mission, the personal accounts of some of the survivors. The first set of pictures showed each of Doolittle's sixteen crews on the Hornet's deck, just days before the raid. Each five–man crew had taken their turn, standing proudly in front of a B–25 Mitchell, the bomber used in the raid.

As Jack stared at the men's faces, his thoughts turned toward those who didn't make it back, the ones killed or captured. A list at the end of the chapter paid tribute to these fallen heroes. Jack went back and forth, comparing the list to the faces in the group photos. It struck him how young they were, full of confidence and courage, standing there smiling at the camera without a care in the world. They had no idea this trip would not go as planned. They wouldn't be having that party in Chunking Colonel Doolittle had promised. Some would shortly fall into the hands of the Japanese and be tortured and starved for the duration of the war. Others would be cruelly beheaded. Some would die as their B–25's sputtered out of fuel in mid–air or crashed into the sea. The survivors would never view life quite the same.

But not on the day of these pictures. Here they were all alive and well. A team united against a common foe, ready to risk everything for their country. He knew he should put the book down and work on his book, but he didn't want to stop.

Even after downing two cups of coffee, though, Jack found himself nodding off to sleep. He tried fighting it with a glass of Diet

Coke, but it didn't work. He could hardly keep his eyes open. He finally surrendered, got up, turned out the lights, and turned in.

He was fast asleep before the clock struck ten.

*

Jack awoke to a low rumbling sound, a sound that didn't belong.

It seemed to fill the darkened room. He felt the sensation of his bed swaying slowly and gently beneath him. His mattress was harder than usual, bowing a little in the center, like a hammock. His soft, cottony comforter felt more like a scratchy woolen blanket. Occasionally, he heard a creaking metal sound.

He opened his eyes, squinting at first. They adjusted to a dim red glow coming from somewhere below him in the center of the room. He had the strange sensation the ceiling was just inches above his head. Reaching out his fingertips, he felt a thick canvas–like material. It was hard and curved from one side to the other.

Oh, God, he thought, where am I now? He pounded twice on the surface above him to see if it would give way.

"O–o–w!" someone yelled. "Geez, Jack. What'd you do that for?"

Jack froze. Not again.

"It took me forever to fall asleep," the voice said.

"I'm sorry," Jack replied. "I, uh—"

"Save it for the Japs. I'm on your side."

The Japs again. *I'm back in World War II. Oh, God, no.*

He panned the room. It was larger than his bedroom, big enough to hold fifteen or twenty bunks, stacked in threes. Definitely not the barracks at Hickam field. *Okay, slow down. Get it together. This is just a dream. Somehow, it's happening again. But it's only a dream.*

"You say something, Jack?" the voice from above inquired.

He must have been thinking aloud. But what difference should that make? This wasn't really happening. He was asleep. There wasn't anybody above him. None of this was real, just a figment of his overactive imagination.

"What's the matter, Jack? Can't sleep?" the voice asked, pausing briefly for Jack's response. "Now that we're getting close to the target, I'm the same way."

He wanted to ask what target.

"Jack?" the voice persisted.

"No, I can't sleep," Jack said. He was talking to a phantom, but it seemed impolite not to answer.

"Whatta you think about all this?" the voice whispered. "Think we're gonna make it?"

What should he say?

"It's okay, Jack, you don't wanna talk about it. I keep trying to put it outta my mind, too. I was doing pretty good when we first got on this tub, but the last couple a nights…knowing tomorrow night's the big night and all. I guess it's startin' to get to me."

Jack just listened.

"It's not I'm afraid. You know? Not like I want to back out or nothing. When I heard we were hitting Tokyo I was as excited as everybody else. But after hearing the Colonel talk about some of us not coming home, and that Navy lieutenant telling us what to expect from the Japs if we're captured…I realized that could be me. You know? That could be me not coming home."

Tokyo? Bunks, swaying bed? It had to be…

Somehow he was on the Doolittle Raid to Tokyo.

20

J ACK WONDERED HOW he could possibly be aboard the USS Hornet, back in April of 1942. The video and lecture this morning. The book he was reading tonight.

"You don't wanna talk, Jack. That's okay."

"I'm sure you'll be fine," Jack said. But would they be fine? It was already becoming difficult to remember he was dreaming. The fear and danger he was starting to feel, the uncertainty, was so real.

"Would you guys cut out the racket?" an angry voice yelled from across the room.

"Yeah!" another said. "Prima–donna flyboys."

Suddenly, the silhouette of an upside down face and head appeared from above. "Since you can't sleep and I can't, what say we go topside, get some fresh air?"

"I say—do it," groaned one of the others.

"All right," Jack whispered. "You lead the way."

The young man flipped over, landed on the floor with a thump, then walked down the aisle toward the far end of the room, fading into the darkness. Jack slid off trying not to step on the sailor below and followed after his dream friend. He found him sitting on a bench getting dressed and found a locker and uniform with his own name on it.

The uniform was similar to the one he wore at Pearl. Then he remembered: Doolittle's men were also in the Army Air Force. They had come aboard this navy carrier bunking down with the sailors for the two–week trip out to the target area. The mission was intended to be a payback for Pearl Harbor. Everyone knew sixteen bombers could hardly even the score for the damage caused by hundreds of Japanese planes. This was intended to be a moral victory, like a punch in the nose. The Japanese government had vowed to its citizens that American planes would never attack the home islands.

As Jack dressed, he started figuring out some other things. That he was bunking in a compartment with so many men meant he was not an officer. As an enlisted man, Jack was probably an engineer/gunner. He finished dressing as his new friend made his way out of the room, ducking under the low–hanging doorway. Jack put on a brown leather flight jacket and quickly followed.

The hallway provided a little better visibility. Jack saw his imaginary friend clearly now. He had a boyish face and energetic smile, wore an odd khaki–colored baseball cap, pulled tightly over his head. He was a few inches shorter than Jack, slender and well built. Jack couldn't readily identify him from any of the photographs in the Doolittle book he'd read. He read the name on his jacket: Fitzmaurice, Sgt. Donald. The name sounded familiar. He knew he'd read something about him.

"You ready?" Fitzmaurice asked.

"I'll follow you."

The two walked down a wide hallway with a low ceiling, covered with white hoses and pipes. At either end were oval hatchways with thick steel doors hanging open to one side. Beyond the hatchways, the halls went on for a full city block both ways, dotted every fifty or sixty feet by dim lights fixed to the ceiling. Without breaking stride, Fitzmaurice ducked his head through the first hatchway. Jack followed carefully. He eyed a steep ladder connecting to the deck above.

"With the kind of schedule we've been keeping lately," Fitzmaurice said, "you'd think I'd be dogged tired right now. But I'm wide awake."

"Me, too," Jack said. He followed Fitzmaurice up the ladder steps. He was just about to climb to a third deck when Jack halted. Through a hatchway to his left, he caught a glimpse of the hangar deck. "Hey, Fitz. Hold up!"

Jack stepped into the hangar deck and stood mesmerized, drawn by the irresistible sight of dozens of vintage Navy planes, all in mint condition. Wildcats, Devastators and Dauntlesses were crowded together, their wings folded to conserve space. A small group of men in gray jumpsuits were strapping down five-hundred pound bombs on dollies. Jack heard the whirling sound of a large elevator drop out of the ceiling. When it stopped, four men hurried off with empty dollies, replaced by four others with full ones. The elevator rose. Jack realized this flurry of activity was for their mission to Tokyo.

"What's up, Jack?" Fitzmaurice asked, finally catching up.

"Huh? Oh, I'm sorry. It's just…" Jack stumbled for words. How could he tell Fitzmaurice he'd never seen planes like this before and just wanted to stand here a few minutes taking it in?

"Gawkin' at these Navy birds? They ain't nothin' compared to what we got!"

"No. It's just…I realized all these bombs are for us, for our mission."

"Oh, yeah," Fitzmaurice said. "Hard to think every one of those bombs are going to explode in a million pieces tomorrow. Hopefully they'll blow up a lot of Japs along with them."

Jack looked at Fitzmaurice, so young and naive. He had no idea what to expect, but Jack knew almost every detail.

"If we hurry we can catch the sun coming up. The last one we'll see on the ocean for a while. Tomorrow we'll watch her come up in China!"

Jack looked at his watch. It was 6:15am. He tried to recall the exact time everything would start breaking loose. He followed Fitzmaurice back to the stairs. After passing through several more decks, they came out a hatchway into the chilly morning air.

The wind was strong out on deck. The dark sky had begun to fade as the sun pushed its way into the day. Jack looked toward the rear of the ship and saw the outlines of the sixteen B–25 Mitchells bunched together. Both men huddled against the wall of the carrier's island as the wind baptized them in a biting spray of saltwater.

"Maybe this wasn't such a good idea," Fitzmaurice yelled, stuffing his hands in his pockets. "Let's go up the island a few more decks, get out of this mist."

"I'll go where you go."

Further up, the wind was still raging, but at least they escaped the saltwater bath. "I'm gonna miss this ol' crate, you know?" Fitzmaurice said. "I never thought when I joined the Air Force I'd ever be out to sea on a carrier. I'm gonna have some stories to tell my kids, when I have them. Lieutenant Hallmark said this mission's gonna be one for the books. It'll be something to say we was on it. Won't it?"

Hallmark…Hallmark. That name rang a bell.

"Wouldn't it be great," continued Fitzmaurice, gazing toward the horizon, "if we got to shoot down a Zero or two?"

Jack remembered from reading the book last night. Lieutenant Dean Hallmark. Flight number six. That's one of the crews that gets captured. That's where he'd heard of Fitzmaurice. Jack looked at his gleaming face. A young warrior all ready for battle, a battle Jack now knew would be his first and last. He was one of the seven who died in the raid. Lieutenant Hallmark was his pilot. Their plane would ditch just off the China coast in a storm. Two of the crew, Fitzmaurice and another man, were so seriously injured they couldn't swim out of the surf. The three remaining men, all officers, would be captured. Two of them would die at the hands of the Japanese; one would just barely survive four years as a POW.

A sinking depression overcame him.

"You all right, Jack?"

"No, I'm fine. It's just like you said. Knowing this is the big day."

"You mean big *night*," corrected Fitzmaurice.

No, *big day*, thought Jack. Fitzmaurice was technically correct. The original plan called for the bombers to lift off the deck later that night when the task force would be within four hundred miles of Tokyo. The Mitchells had to be this close to ensure they'd have enough fuel to land safely on mainland China after dropping their bombs.

Jack knew history recorded a different scenario.

"Big night if we're lucky," Jack said.

"Whatta you talking about?"

"Nothing. It's just that being, what, six hundred miles away from Japan now, it's possible we'll get spotted before nightfall and have to launch sooner, that's all."

"Hope you're wrong," Fitzmaurice said. "We're gonna be tight for gas as it is."

Jack decided, at least for now, not to divulge any of his inside information. It didn't seem to alter anything in his last dream, and he didn't see what good could come of it now. He looked down at the crowded bombers below.

B–25's were land–based bombers better than twice the size of an average carrier plane. They looked so out of place on the carrier deck, like a teenager riding on a tricycle. As his eyes traced the distance from the first bomber to the bow of the ship, he was amazed that *any* of these big birds got airborne, let alone all of them. He wondered which plane was supposed to be his.

"You hungry, Jack? I think we can hit the chow line now if we want."

Jack looked at his watch. Twenty minutes had passed. Jack knew the action would begin early that morning. The Navy spotters would see a Japanese trawler, and the big plan would immediately fall apart. He thought it happened around 7:45. "Sure. I'm game," he replied.

"You're *what*?"

"Uh, sure. Let's go eat."

The galley was one deck below the sleeping quarters. All of shiny glistening steel. It was noisy, the lights were too bright, food in massive quantities were piled high in metal tubs, sleepy young men stood bumper to bumper pushing trays along a narrow shelf. A big–bellied guy in a sleeveless T–shirt sloshed scrambled eggs down on metal plates in between puffs of a bent cigarette dangling from his mouth.

Jack looked down at the food on his platter. It was a better looking than the food at Hickam Field. Besides the eggs, which looked real, there was a healthy stack of pancakes and four links of sausage. It even smelled good.

"Dig in," Fitzmaurice said, "starting tomorrow it's rice, rice, and more rice."

Jack began to eat. It even tasted good. He didn't stop to think it was just dream food. Other things brewed in his mind. It was almost 7:00am. He had forty–five minutes to uncover which plane and flight crew were his.

"Say Jack, how did your guns work yesterday in the test? Any problems with the turret? Thatcher said his were stickin'. He can't get the turret to spin without auxiliary power from the cockpit."

Thatcher, thought Jack. He remembered Thatcher. He was Ted Lawson's engineer/gunner. Lawson wrote the book–turned–movie, *"Thirty Seconds Over Tokyo."* The movie that starred Spencer Tracy and Van Johnson.

"Uh…no problems," Jack said. "Everything seemed to be working fine."

"Lieutenant Hallmark said he wanted me to go over every inch of that plane again, being our last full day. You get the same from Manch?"

Lieutenant Manch—that was Jack's answer. "Uh, yeah. Sure did. Going to be a busy day." Jack must be the engineer/gunner in Manch's crew. Jack remembered Manch, because he was so tall. He'd also been mentioned several times in the movie and even more often in Lawson's book. At least that part of the riddle was solved. If Jack could only find out which plane Manch was on.

Jack remembered something else: Manch was a co–pilot. The pilot's name was Lieutenant Gray. Gray would have his name stenciled under the plane's window. A simple stroll to the deck should put the last piece of the puzzle together.

Suddenly, an elusive, unsettled feeling began to trouble him. He pulled on the thread. He remembered Manch's plane had made it through the Raid, so he should be fine. A black and white photograph from the book popped into his mind. Five men stood together in front of a B–25. Manch stood out from the others because of his height. Then, almost peeking out from behind Manch, over his left shoulder, Jack saw in his mind's eye a small figure of a man.

That's when he remembered.

The man standing behind Manch was Corporal Leland Faktor, Manch's engineer/gunner. The way Fitzmaurice had been talking, Jack must be taking Faktor's place on the plane.

Faktor. Wait a minute, thought Jack.

Faktor dies.

21

J ACK WALKED CAREFULLY along the flight deck of the USS Hornet past the second plane, trying to avoid an embarrassing fall. Sailors and bomber crews hurried about doing their various duties. The constant pitching up and down didn't seem to bother them at all. He'd left Fitzmaurice in the galley with some lame excuse about double–checking the ammo boxes. What he really wanted was a firsthand look at his plane.

There it was.

Under the window, painted in white letters he read the name: "Lt. Robert Gray." He took a few steps back to get a better look and almost tripped over some tie–down cords, lashing the underside of the wing to the deck. As big as these bombers were, the sea could toss them off the deck as easily as a woman sweeping leaves from a porch.

The wind had begun to kick up, maybe fifteen to twenty knots now. He glanced up at the plane's top gun turret, its two fifty–caliber guns pointing skyward. This is where he'd spend the majority of the flight searching for enemy planes.

Suddenly, a loud siren pierced the air. A commanding voice thundered over the ship's klaxon, *"General Quarters! Man your battle stations! Man your battle stations!"* The siren continued to wail. Men began running in different directions. They all seemed to know exactly what to do and where to go. Jack didn't have a clue.

Sailors poured out of hatchways, hastily strapping on helmets and life vests. Every anti–aircraft gun buzzed with activity. Some men rolled the guns into position, others loaded ammo. Everyone shifted their gaze between the sky and the horizon. They probably think this is just a drill, Jack thought. General Quarter drills had been called twice a day since the mission began. But Jack knew this time was no drill. He looked at his watch.

It was 7:45am. Right on time.

The ship shuddered as a deafening boom thundered over Jack's left shoulder. He dropped to all fours. He turned toward the sound in time to catch a nearby cruiser, the USS Nashville, as she let go of another fiery blast from her broadsides. Jack followed the direction of the gunbursts. In seconds, a loud explosion to the south signaled the guns had found their mark. A small Japanese fishing trawler now billowed thick plumes of black smoke. Several Dauntless dive bombers circled the sky above like buzzards.

All over the ship, jubilant warriors hollered out their unanimous approval, the first taste of combat for the men of the Hornet. The officers on board had no way of knowing if this fishing trawler alerted the Japanese military to their presence. Jack knew they would decide to launch the B–25s now, not later, even though they were still two–hundred miles farther out than planned. The element of surprise meant everything.

Jack heard the turbines churn faster deep within the belly of the ship and felt the carrier lurch forward. They were positioning the ship to launch the bombers. He suddenly realized how unprepared he was. Over the ship's intercom, the same voice that cried battle stations spoke again: "Army pilots, man your planes! Army pilots, man your planes! This is not a drill. I repeat, this is not a drill."

Instantly, Army Air Force personnel raced out of the main hatchway strapping on their yellow life vests. Jack ran against the flow of traffic as he made his way downstairs. He had no vest and no idea where to get one. Through the steady stream of Doolittle's Raiders making their way up the ladders, Jack saw Fitzmaurice.

"Hey Fitz," cried Jack.

"Jack, this is it! You were right! We're *not* going tonight."

"I know, I know."

"I wish you were wrong," Fitz said near the top of the steps.

"Fitz, where do I get a vest?"

"Right, Jack," he said sarcastically as he made his way onto the deck with the others. "See you in Chunking."

It was the last time Jack would see Fitzmaurice. Fitzmaurice was rushing off to die. But he was too young, Jack thought, too innocent. He should be somebody's kid brother, some little boy's favorite uncle.

Jack waited on the landing for a break in the flow of men, then hurried one deck below. He watched a guy coming out of a room strapping on a vest. He grabbed one then hurried back up the ladder.

As he came onto the flight deck the bow of the ship dipped low, sending a wall of icy saltwater spray across the deck, covering Jack in its mist. He turned toward the bombers, amazed at the transformation that had already taken place in a few short minutes. A powerful little buggy had rearranged the planes in a criss–cross fashion toward the rear of the ship, freeing up several precious yards of deck space for the planes to use during takeoff.

Most of the crews were already in their planes. He made his way toward his but stopped briefly to stare into the cockpit of plane number one.

There was the legend himself.

Colonel Jimmy Doolittle was seated on the far side in the captain's chair. He turned toward his co–pilot and said something Jack could not understand, then glanced down at Jack. Jack felt Doolittle's fierce, determined eyes pierce right through him. Doolittle gestured with his head for Jack to get a move on it, then smiled.

Jack hustled toward plane three, already in takeoff position. As he approached, Lieutenant Manch leaned out his window on the left side and yelled over the noise. "Glad you decided to join us, Jack."

It was so crazy that this guy knew his name. But his warm, Virginian accent and smile relieved some of Jack's tension. "Sorry, Lieutenant. I'll be right up." Why hadn't Lt. Manch called him 'Leland' or 'Faktor'?

He ducked low along the belly of the plane until he came to a small opening. There, waiting like a hotel doorman, a sailor bent down on one knee holding a wheel chock in his left hand. "All ready, Sergeant?" the sailor asked.

"Uh, yeah. Thanks."

"Don't worry. Just go on in. I'll close her up," he said with a grin. "Good luck."

"Thanks," Jack answered as he climbed through the hatch.

"You made it, Jack."

Jack looked up to see the face of Lieutenant Charles Ozuk, poking out from a narrow opening like a badger. He remembered Ozuk from the book Thornton had given him last night. Ozuk was the navigator on plane three. He had dark hair and a round pleasant face.

"I was beginning to worry about you," Ozuk said. "Better get this on. Lieutenant Gray's going to want a communication check any minute." Ozuk handed Jack a set of headphones, then crawled backward into his station and out of sight.

Jack set the headphones aside a moment. He had to see what was going on inside the plane. He followed Ozuk back through the passageway toward the front. After crawling on his belly for a minute or two, he looked down at Ozuk sitting in a small seat behind the cockpit. Next to Ozuk was the bombardier, Sergeant Aden Jones. His cap, set back on his wide forehead, revealed a receding hairline. He looked nervous. He nodded to Jack but said nothing. Looking beyond Ozuk and Jones, Jack saw Lieutenants' Gray and Manch in the cockpit going through their pre–flight checklist.

"Sergeant?" Lieutenant Gray yelled over his shoulder. "What are you doing?"

"Just checking out the scenery, sir," Jack replied.

"Well get back in position. We're gonna take off any minute."

"Sorry, sir."

Jack wiggled backward to his compartment. He had the back half of the plane to himself, but he didn't like it. He put on the headset then turned to survey his surroundings. The fuselage offered little comforts. Jack had toured a few B–17's at various air shows but had never been inside a Mitchell. It was much smaller. His compartment was dark and dreary with only a small porthole. Some extra light came in through the top gun turret. Jack thought about checking it out but decided it was too risky to sit there during takeoff.

It was frustrating. Here he was inside a B–25 Mitchell about to take off an aircraft carrier in World War II, on one of the most historic missions of all time…but he couldn't see a thing. Suddenly, the roar of an airplane engine up ahead sputtered to life. A wisp of exhaust fumes whipped down the flight deck. Jack knew it was Doolittle's plane.

"There goes the Colonel!" Manch shouted. "Come on, sir. Show us how it's done!"

The second engine kicked on. Both engines revved to full throttle, blaring until they sounded like they might explode. No one had ever tried to fly big bombers like the Mitchell off an aircraft carrier before. Doolittle's Raiders had practiced at Eglin AFB, but no one knew for certain if it could be done on a pitching carrier deck.

No one but Jack.

Jack longed to catch a glimpse of Doolittle's plane taking off. He strained his eyes out his little porthole, but the left engine obstructed his view.

"Let's go, let's go, you can do it," Jack heard someone yell from the front of the plane.

"He made it!" shouted Manch as flight number one lifted off the carrier deck with several yards to spare. "Just like back at Eglin. Piece–a–cake!"

Jack sat back in resignation, closed his eyes, and let the black–and–white video of this historic occasion replay through his mind. At least he had the added bonus of hearing the engines roar and could feel the wheels rumble down the wooden deck.

"Pilot to gunner. Pilot to gunner."

Jack grabbed his headset, frantically searching for the mouthpiece.

"Turner, you read me?" It was Lieutenant Gray.

Jack's eyes ricocheted off every item in his little room, finally resting on a hand–held microphone hanging on a hook. He lunged for it, mashing down the button with his thumb. "I read you, Lieutenant. Sorry, sir."

"You having problems, Turner? We're about to sail out of here."

"No problems, sir."

"I'm closing the bombay doors," Gray said. "Do you confirm?"

Jack heard the doors closing, and a *kerchunk* as they locked into place. "Check. Bombay doors secure."

"You got those extra fuel cans strapped down, yet? Don't want to see those things flying through my window when we lift off."

"Right away, sir." Jack found a bundle of canvas straps lying on the floor and quickly secured five big cans to each other, then jerry–rigged them to at least ten others nearby.

"Pilot to gunner."

"Yessir, Lieutenant?"

"Just double–checking. The interphone working properly? Got to be able to connect with you at all times on this."

"Seems fine, sir. The delay before was my fault."

"There goes, Travis," Gray said into the interphone, as another set of engines kicked into action. Plane Number Two. "Okay, boys. We're next. You get those cans squared away, Jack?"

"All set, Lieutenant." The excitement of the moment had temporarily blocked his fears of death and doom. This was a genuine thrill. He looked out his window just beyond the right engine and noticed a sailor wearing a black reefer coat holding a fire extinguisher in his hands.

"Right engine clear?" Manch shouted out his window.

"Right engine clear!" the sailor shouted back.

Suddenly, the plane began to rumble and vibrate as the right engine burst to life.

"Left engine clear?" shouted Gray out his window.

"Left engine clear!" yelled the sailor. The left engine fired up. Even through his headset, the noise from the engines filled the fuselage. The pulsating plane lurched forward and began to taxi into position.

The plane turned slightly to the left. As it turned, Jack caught a glimpse of the second bomber lifting off the carrier deck. It was a breathtaking sight. Not a scratchy, black and white video image but living color.

Jack's plane swung around and faced dead ahead. Gray started revving his engines. The B–25 shuddered then shook violently as the brakes resisted the engine's aggression. After fifteen or twenty seconds, Gray received the all clear. The wheel blocks were jerked away, the brakes released.

The nose gear lifted slightly like a horse shedding its rider, then bounced on the deck and started to roll forward. Jack closed his eyes and braced himself. He tried to focus on the fact that none of Doolittle's planes crashed on takeoff. He wondered how long this dream would play out. How far would the realism go?

Genuine fear, the kind that bullies every other thought stirred inside him. He'd been fighting it since the moment he'd figured out he was sitting in the same spot Leland Faktor occupied during the original mission. What would that mean for him? He thought about his first dream. Was he ever in any real danger? If he hadn't ducked behind those sandbags in that instant, would the bullets that killed Sal have killed him also or would he have just woken up? If he were seriously hurt or killed in this raid on Tokyo, would his body react in character?

How could he know?

His brain was in charge of this illusion, and he had no wish to die. But why had his brain chosen the role of Leland Faktor for him to play? What was the significance of that? He remembered a sermon he'd heard at a funeral a few months ago. The pastor was quoting some passage in the Bible, talking about death being an appointment set by God, not something that just happens by itself.

God couldn't want him to die like this, could he?

Jack tried to reassure himself, then suddenly felt the rear wall of the fuselage sucking him backwards. The plane picked up speed as the carrier deck lifted high upon the tilting sea.

In the next moment, they were off.

22

THE PLANE DROPPED slightly at first, giving Jack the sensation of an elevator falling several flights. She slowly regained altitude then climbed slightly. Jack heard the landing gear retract then the bomber banked to the right. His eyes snapped to the cans he had just strapped in. They were holding. He held on tightly to avoid sliding across the floor himself. Within minutes Lt. Gray leveled the plane out and brought her into cruising altitude, a scant fifty feet above sea level.

"Pilot to gunner. Jack, you read me?"

"I'm here, Lieutenant."

"How's everything holding up back there?"

"Everything's fine, sir."

"Better get started on the fuel cans," Gray said. "Keep topping them off while we're far from the coast. Before long we're gonna need your hawk eyes in that turret scanning the skies."

"Okay, Lieutenant." Jack sized up his assignment. He guessed he was supposed to pour the fuel from the cans into the large tank sitting in front of him. But he knew, in the end, it wouldn't matter. A few extra cans of fuel would never close the two–hundred mile gap created by taking off this early.

Jack knew a pilot of Gray's caliber would have already figured this out. They weren't going to make it to any airfield on the Chinese mainland today after dropping their bombs on Tokyo. Gray had probably already started forming a plan for bailing out.

Jack found a wide–mouthed funnel upside down beside the fuel tank. He carefully poured in the first can. It drank down the entire can like a cowboy swigging a whiskey shot.

When he finished, Jack squeezed into the plexiglass turret. He squirmed around on the seat until he got comfortable then kicked the footrests into place. When he looked up, his eyes contracted from the brightness of the mid–morning sun. The dreary weather near the carrier had evaporated.

After a few minutes, his stomach began to rumble and he felt lightheaded. Sinking below the rim of the turret, he closed his eyes. He'd flown many times before but never at such a low altitude. It seemed they were only inches above the water, skipping over the waves like a stone.

Slowly, he regained his composure and sat up again. A few minutes more, and his system began adjusting to the speed of the passing scenery. There was no land in sight, just the sporadic tufts of stratus clouds floating by and the undulating whitecaps of the sea rolling beneath the belly of the plane. They flew like this for over an hour. Every five minutes or so, Jack went below to add more fuel to the tanks.

"Pilot to gunner."

Jack reached for the interphone. "Go ahead, Lieutenant."

"How we doing with the spare cans?"

"Just loaded the last one about five minutes ago, sir."

"About what I figured," Gray said.

"What do you think?" he heard Lieutenant Manch say to Gray. "Think we'll make it?"

"I think we *have* to," Gray replied. "Okay, Jack. Why don't you give those guns a try? Give the turret a good once over."

"And try not to shoot down Holstrum in the plane behind us," Manch said.

Jack scanned the turret walls for controls. He gave one of the footrests a push with his boot. Nothing. He found what looked to be a control lever below the guns. He moved it back and forth. The twin guns instantly moved up and down. He maneuvered the handle horizontally. It didn't respond. This thing's gotta move sideways, Jack thought.

"I'm not hearing those guns," Lieutenant Gray said.

Jack gave the handle a hard shove. Suddenly, the turret jerked wildly to his right. A loud burst of machine gun fire blasted into the air. He had accidentally squeezed the trigger. In shock and horror he glanced up at the right side of the tail section. A ribbon–like piece of sheet metal dangled helplessly in the wind. One of the stray bullets had torn a hole right through it. Jack watched anxiously for the next few moments but nothing happened. As he stared more closely at the damage, he could see his stupid mistake hadn't affected the rudder's operation. A few second later, the small piece of tail section ripped away and fluttered out of sight.

"Pilot to gunner. Report in. Everything check out back there?"

"So far, so good," Jack said. "I'd like to give it another short burst, if it's okay."

"Negative," came the reply. "Sounds like it's working fine to me. We don't know what we're gonna be up against out here. Better conserve ammo."

"Yes sir."

"Keep your eyes peeled, Jack," Ozuk interjected. "We could be seeing bad guys anytime now."

"Roger," Jack said.

"I see land, Lieutenant Gray," announced Jones, the bombardier. "Coming up fast. Dead ahead."

"I see it," answered Gray. "I'll take her up a few feet just to be safe."

Jack turned in the turret as the plane climbed slightly upwards. So far so good. Except for the occasional fishing boat and cabin cruiser, they'd seen no one else to this point. Although the vessels were harmless, it was still unnerving to see the Rising Sun flag, waving in the breeze atop their masts. Almost everyone on board the boats had waved as they flew by.

"Bogies. I see bogies. Twelve o'clock high. Three of them. No, six of them. Two sets of three," Manch shouted from the cockpit.

"Jack, do you see—"

Gray's voice cut off. Jack flicked on the interphone and hailed Gray. "Lieutenant? Lieutenant Gray?"

No answer.

Jack pushed the control lever to the left until the turret swung to the front. He looked up in the sky and, sure enough, two V–formations of planes were coming their way, about four to five thousand feet up. He raised the twin guns toward the planes, then cracked his knuckles and stretched his fingers. He let them rest, carefully, on the trigger. His heart began to pounce. Beads of sweat started to pool on his forehead.

The enemy planes traveled slowly, maybe two hundred knots. So far, they made no attempt to change course. Jack looked at his watch for an instant, trying to remember from his studies exactly what time Doolittle dropped his bombs on Tokyo. Once the explosions began, the Japanese would know something was up and be on the lookout for others.

"Pilot to gunner. Pilot to—" Again nothing.

Jack tried frantically to respond. "Lieutenant?" he shouted. "Do you hear me? You keep getting cut off. Something must be wrong with the intercom. If you *can* hear me, I *do* see those bogies overhead."

Jack felt a tug on his pant leg. He looked down.

"Jack!" It was Ozuk, the navigator standing below him. "Gray sent me to ask if you saw that formation."

"I'm watching them right now."

"Well, keep your eyes peeled for more. Doolittle's bombs should be hitting Tokyo any minute now."

Jack looked back at the plane formation. They were still there but heading away from them. "I understand. But tell him I can't hear him. He keeps getting cut off."

"I don't know what to tell you, Jack. I'm gonna have my hands full from here on out getting us to the target. Just keep your eyes open." Ozuk headed back toward his station.

This wasn't good. Jack wondered…was this how Faktor died? Did it have something to do with the radio?

*

For the next fifteen minutes Jack remained in his turret, perched in silence. He rotated it every so often. Occasionally, he spotted a lone aircraft here and there, but thankfully they were civilian. He was amazed no one had come after them yet. Surely, Doolittle and Hoover, in plane number two, had dropped their bombs by now.

As he reached the six o'clock position, he heard a loud mechanical noise grinding beneath him, just forward in the fuselage. The bombay doors were opening. A great rushing wind. He stood and turned the turret forward. Tokyo was in sight. To the north, smoke billowed from several buildings, marking the spots where the first two bombers had blazed their trail.

Jack saw strange little black clouds up ahead, although the sky was completely clear in every other direction. Then he realized they weren't clouds. It was flak. They were flying straight into anti–aircraft fire. In moments, the strange little black clouds were all around them. Several rounds exploded close enough to shake the plane. "Okay, okay," he muttered to himself. No one gets shot down on this raid. Stay focused.

Suddenly, the plane banked heavily to the left, then straightened out. Jack felt the back end of the bomber swerve as Gray made a few corrections with the rudder. For the first time on their journey, the plane began to climb dramatically. Jack stiffened to avoid sliding forward into the gun sight.

They were making their bombing run.

The first bomb released from its hold and fell away. He stood in the turret in time to hear the explosion and catch the small mushroom cloud erupt behind them. The plane banked again to the left, only slightly. The tail swerved again in response to the rudder, as Gray brought the plane on course for bomb number two. Jack watched again with amazement as the second 500–pound bomb dropped from the plane's belly. Two large smokestacks disintegrated behind them. A mass of smoke, flame, and flying debris.

Jack was shocked at how low to the ground they were.

In similar intervals, bombs number three and four dropped in quick succession. The fourth bomb was an incendiary, actually dozens of little bomblets that broke apart as it dropped into the wind, raining fire down from the sky. In a city like Tokyo, made of mostly wooden structures, this bomb could cause the most destruction of all.

The whole episode seemed to move in slow motion. When it was over, Jack looked at his watch. The whole run took less than two minutes. The plane dove and turned again, this time south-west, toward the coast of China.

He breathed a sigh of relief. Perhaps the worst was over. For a moment he stared back as the city of Tokyo began to fade in the distance. Then he smiled. As frightening as this had been, it had been proportionately as thrilling. Fear and fascination in equal parts. They flew on for several more minutes without incident.

The quiet was interrupted by the sound of a single-engine plane buzzing overhead. His head snapped in its direction. Under both wings Jack saw the 'red meatballs' the Japanese painted on all their military aircraft. He grabbed the control lever firmly and swiv-eled the turret into position. The Japanese plane turned around.

It had spotted them.

Remember, he thought, lead the plane. Fire where it's going. Don't shoot at it.

He squeezed hard on the trigger and felt the powerful jolt of the twin fifty-caliber guns roaring into action. Tracer bullets quickly formed dotted lines of smoke racing upwards toward the enemy plane. The plane inverted and dropped to the left. Jack followed it as far as he could until the fuselage blocked his view.

No smoke. Must've missed. Okay little guy, where are you?

He swung the turret slowly toward the front, then back to the rear, searching the skies, hoping the plane would *not* reappear. He was just beginning to repeat his loop when tracer bullets started whizzing by no more than ten feet above his head. They were fol-lowed by the rapid staccato of machine gun fire. The plane came right at them, guns blazing, from the starboard side. But Jack was facing port. He needed to get his guns turned around.

Jack whipped the control lever around, trying to force the guns toward the incoming plane. Tracers from the Japanese plane moved steadily downward, just a few feet above the B–25. Soon they'd be hitting their mark. The turret motor whined and spun. Suddenly, Jack lost his balance as his foot slipped off the footrest. He banged his head against the steel sidewall of the turret and was knocked out cold.

*

When Jack awoke, the right side of his head ached and throbbed. He opened his eyes. Everything was all wrong. Where was the Japanese plane? Had he shot it down? Was the dream finally over?

As he looked around, he could tell he wasn't back in his bedroom yet. The sky was dark and stormy again, even worse than that morning. Rain pelted against the plexiglass dome of his turret. He could see streaks of lightning in the distance and hear peals of thunder. Even the plane engine's sounds were different. They were sputtering, choking. What was happening?

Jack dropped down into the fuselage.

He picked up the microphone and yelled into it. "Lieutenant Gray? Lieutenant Manch? Jones? Ozuk? Can anybody here me?" The plane bucked up and down violently in the turbulence created by the storm and the faltering engines. He ran toward the front of his compartment and screamed into the passageway, "Is *anybody* on this plane?"

No reply.

I've gotta get outta here. Everyone's bailed out.

He felt the plane start to gradually descend.

Frantically, he groped along the dark walls of the fuselage until he located a parachute. He strapped it on in frenzied fashion, hoping against hope that it would hold when he pulled the cord. He yanked and tugged at the straps. They seemed secure.

He dropped on all fours, fumbling for the hatch. When he found it, he opened it without hesitation. Chilly wind and rain slapped him in the face. He lay on his stomach, his legs now suspended in the open air. With a deep breath, and a brief, fearful prayer, he flung himself into the elements.

He tumbled for what seemed like an eternity, falling end over end. He started to regain control after he extended his limbs as far as they would go. When he finally stopped spinning, he yanked hard on his ripcord and felt the sensation of all his insides lunging up into his throat.

The sound of the plane's engines faded. He looked up into the darkness for one last glance but couldn't see it. He could barely see his parachute above his head. The cold rain spat on him, drenching his hair and face, even his clothes.

His insides started to settle down after a few seconds, and he even began to feel quite peaceful floating through the air. As his head began to clear, he tried to sort out what must have happened. He remembered shooting at the Japanese plane, then slipping and hitting his head. The rest of the crew could not have known this because the intercom wasn't working. They must have flown on toward China until they ran out of fuel and bailed out. Jack imagined somebody must have yelled back for him to bail out, but he couldn't hear them. Now he was floating through the air over who knows where. He hoped he'd find the rest of the crew when he landed. Or better yet, that he would wake up.

He looked in the direction of the ground below, but it was

much too dark to see. He figured he must be landing far from any towns or villages because there was no ground lighting anywhere in sight.

Then he realized with great relief…he had beaten the curse of Leland Faktor.

He was alive.

A question was just beginning to form in his mind about how much farther he had to fall before landing when a searing pain shot up from his legs. His whole body crumpled and seemed to break apart inside him. The air thrust out of his lungs with terrific force as he smacked into the ground with an impact far too great for anyone to survive.

Then there was nothing.

23

I T WAS THURSDAY morning. Rachel Cook rushed across the campus, trying to make it to class on time. She was responding to an odd request, a favor from Professor Thornton. He'd asked if she would be willing to take over his classes for the day.

She was surprised he'd even thought of her. She was a teaching assistant, not a professor, and her forte was political science, not military history. He said she had nothing to worry about. It was more of a babysitting assignment, presiding over a steady diet of video documentaries, perhaps fake her way through a few class discussions.

Still she was flattered. And a bit nervous.

When he'd called earlier that morning, he'd sounded a little edgy. He said he was just fighting a stomach virus or something. He'd tried calling Jack several times, hoping he might do it but only got his answering machine.

As she climbed the steps of Thornton's building, she didn't notice the large young man running up behind her, didn't hear him call out her name.

"Rachel," the man yelled again. "You hear what happened?"

She almost tripped on a step. A strong arm reached out to steady her.

"I'm sorry. I didn't mean to startle you."

She turned to see a visibly shaken Jed Lucas. He was at Culpepper on a wrestling scholarship. Rachel thought he might be described as handsome if his face hadn't hit the mat so many times. "Hear what?" she asked.

"It's Riesner, he's dead."

Riesner, Rachel thought, the name briefly escaped her.

"You know…Ralph," he said.

"Ralph Riesner?" Now she remembered.

Lucas nodded. "Yeah, he's dead."

Rachel had only one connection with Riesner, Thornton's class. He was an annoying little weasel, although she felt terrible thinking about him like that now. She remembered he sat right by the door, the guy who always dimmed the lights during media presentations. He kept trying to hit on her. She finally had to insult him to get him to back off. "How'd he die?"

"I don't know exactly," Lucas said. "I saw it on the news last night. The police said they're ruling out foul play. They said it was natural causes."

"Natural causes? But he wasn't sick. Was he?"

"I don't think so. Maybe he was, and he didn't want us to know."

"He must've had *something* wrong with him," she said. "Twenty–two year olds don't just up and die from natural causes."

"He always did seem kind of thin…and pale, you know?"

"I still can't believe it. Ralph Riesner is dead. Did they say anything else?"

"Not much. Just flashed a picture of him on the screen—I

about choked on my pizza. They said a student at Culpepper died last Friday evening or early Saturday night. They said his body was discovered by a friend."

"So he's been dead since Friday? Wonder why they're just reporting it now?"

He held the door open for her. "It had something to do with notifying the next of kin."

They walked through the double wooden doors and down several hallways until they reached Thornton's classroom. Rachel noticed the mood inside was not unlike a funeral home.

"I wonder where the Professor is," Lucas whispered.

"Actually, that's why I'm here. I'm kind of subbing for him. He came down with some kind of bug."

Just then, along the wall behind Thornton's desk, the door joining his office to the classroom opened with an audible creak. A noticeably disturbed and subdued Thornton shuffled in. "Good morning class," he began in a shaky voice. "I guess it really is *not* a good morning, is it?"

Rachel was shocked. She assumed he'd called her from home. He must be really sick. He looked like he had aged ten years.

He walked over to his desk, cleared his throat and continued. "I'm sure you've all heard by now the tragic news about our young colleague, Ralph Riesner. He was a fine young man. I believe he had a bright future ahead of him. I'm saddened we will not get the chance to see what his contribution might have been." He paused a few moments, shifted some paper around his desk. He seemed to be trying to regain his composure. Jed Lucas took his normal seat in the third row. Rachel stood off to the side, waiting for Thornton to introduce her as the sub for today.

Lucas spoke up, breaking through the pall. "Professor, do you know anything more about how he died than what they said on the news? He have some disease we didn't know about? He seemed fine last week."

"I'm sorry, Jed. I don't know anything more than you all do about this. As far as I know, he was in good health. I had a brief conversation with his father this morning. He said the family is in a state of shock. That doesn't sound like he had some well–known affliction to me. He didn't offer any additional information, and I didn't pry. He only called to apologize to any of Ralph's friends who might have wanted to go to the funeral. They're shipping his body home to Charlotte today. His father left an address if any of you care to write. I put it on the bulletin board." Thornton took out a white handkerchief and wiped the sweat off his forehead. His voice, though stronger, was still trembling.

Rachel was surprised by how badly Thornton seemed to be taking this. Thornton and Riesner weren't close as far as she knew.

"Guess when your number's up, it's up," Lucas said. He didn't notice the disapproving stares.

"Class, if you'll excuse me…I feel we must keep on track with our plans—as trying as that may seem with this news. It might even help to take our minds off of—excuse me." Thornton wiped his brow again and the sides of his mouth.

He motioned for Rachel to come closer. "I'm actually not feeling very well," he said. "I've asked Miss Cook if she'd be kind enough to sit in for me. We'll be picking up on our study of the Doolittle Raid by watching the classic movie *Thirty Seconds Over Tokyo*. Has anyone seen it?" Several hands went up. "You'll enjoy it, I'm sure," he said. "It is a rather long movie, so you'll have to watch it over two classes. But Miss Cook will be passing out a list of questions I'd like you to answer and turn in on Monday. I should be back in time for our class then. Now, if you'll excuse me."

"Hope you feel better," one of the students yelled.

The mood in the room was understandably unsettled. Rachel watched as Thornton turned and walked away, slipping into the side door leading to his inner office behind the lecture hall.

"Okay class, get comfortable," she announced, trying to sound authoritative. "I've read the book and seen the movie. Pretty close to history for an old Hollywood flick. Not as realistic as more modern war movies like Saving Private Ryan or Band of Brothers, but it should help open the Doolittle Raid up a bit. Could someone get the lights?"

Several students turned toward the empty chair where Ralph Riesner used to sit. "I'll get 'em," Joe Lucas said.

*

Professor Thornton did feel sick to his stomach, but it was no bug or virus.

He drove by Jack's apartment, an extra fifteen minutes out of his way, and parked across the street. He saw Jack's car, but wished he hadn't. If it had been gone, that would mean Jack was at least alive and well somewhere.

He hoped Jack hadn't met the same fate as young Riesner.

The thought of Jack sitting up there, dead in his bed, made him shudder. Jack hadn't answered his calls. He'd left at least one clear message. He felt sure Jack would have responded to it if he could, if only to tell Thornton he didn't want to be disturbed. Should he go up? If Jack was fine, how would he explain the interruption?

The car was still on, the heat turned up, but still Thornton felt cold as ice. He was thrumming his fingers on the dashboard, trying to grasp the enormity, the severity, of what he had done.

What was he thinking?

Over the last week he had set his reputation, his career, everything he'd worked for in the last thirty years, leaning on a teetering ledge. He hadn't slept all night after seeing the news report about Riesner, couldn't eat a thing this morning. Here he was, a never-married, fifty–six–year–old man with a shiny bald head, living all alone with some of the finest furniture money can buy.

All he had was his work. What if he'd lost that now?

Or worse, what if he had to spend the rest of his life in jail?

24

THORNTON HAD ARRIVED home at his condo fifteen minutes ago. Now he sat staring at the telephone on his desk. He finally worked up the nerve to call the private number of Dr. Curtis Jameison in McLean, Virginia, a neurologist who specialized in sleep disorders. He knew Jameison probably wouldn't pick up. He'd be down at his clinic, The Sleep Center in Falls Church, but Thornton wanted to leave a voicemail in case he couldn't get through at his clinic.

As he picked up the phone, he tried to remember the stupid security procedures Jameison had insisted on. After the beep, he said as calmly as he could: "Jameison, Thomas Thornton here. I won't say too much on the phone, but suffice it to say *Bre'r Fox* is dead. That's right, dead. Died in his sleep last Friday, very likely after his dinner appointment with me. Well, that's all I should say for now...call me as soon as you get this. I'll try to reach your office. If I don't hear from you in a couple of hours, I'm flying up there to see you. We've got to talk about this...this wasn't supposed to happen."

He hung up and looked for Jack's cell number. He'd written it on Jack's card yesterday. He had to know if Jack was all right. If Jack didn't answer, Thornton would drive by his place again, only this time he'd get out and knock on the door.

He looked down at the phone. What if Jack did answer, what would he say? He had to think of some reason for the call and say it as calmly as he could.

*

For the last ten minutes, Sergeant Joe Boyd had sweated through another difficult phone call. He should have just let the thing ring; he was almost out the door. "Yes sir, I will call you back as soon as I hear back from the coroner. I understand. No, it's no trouble. Good bye." He hung up the receiver and swiveled in his chair. Hank Jensen was standing by the door with his overcoat slung over his forearm. They were about to head to an appointment with a city councilman, to pitch a request for a better communication system for the department.

"Hear back from the coroner?" Hank repeated. "What was that about?"

"That, my friend, was Ralph Riesner, Senior."

"The father of the dead kid?" Hank said.

"The same."

"What'd he want from Dr. Hargrove? I thought the case was closed."

"I'm sure it still is. He's just a grieving dad looking to make some sense of losing his boy. Can't fault him for that."

"He doesn't buy the heart attack?"

"No, it's not that." Boyd took a sip of his morning coffee, which was awful. "Who made this? Somebody's got to learn how to make coffee around here besides me."

Hank leaned back to catch a glimpse of the coffeemaker sitting just beyond the water cooler. "I don't know, Joe, but there's two more cups worth in the pot. You want me to make a fresh pot before we go?" He looked at his watch, a respectful hint.

Boyd poured his mug into a potted ficus tree next to his desk, its yellowing leaves offering silent protest to its steady diet of caffeine. "No, I know we gotta go."

"So why'd the father call?"

Boyd stood up. "He says he'd been studying the autopsy report, and he noticed something he didn't understand."

"What's to understand about a heart attack?"

"Let me look at this thing a minute." Boyd held Hargrove's autopsy report at arm's length. He had glasses but hated to wear them. "Here it is. There's a section detailing foreign substances found in the bloodstream and Hargrove mentions here finding slight traces of something called *Temazepam*—if that's how you pronounce it. He's made a note next to it that says '*a benzo–diaz-epine*'. Anyway, Mr. Riesner says he's looked it up on the internet and it's some kind of insomnia drug—a prescription–only insomnia drug. He says Ralph wasn't taking anything like that."

"Wow, that is odd," Hank said sarcastically. "A college student taking an insomnia prescription. And without his father's permission."

"I know. But he wants me to call Hargrove and ask him if that could have sparked his son's heart attack."

"I don't think Hargrove would have missed something that obvious."

"Me neither," Boyd agreed. "But, hey…what can I say? It's his kid, it's the least I can do. You remember if we took any prescription bottles from the kid's apartment?"

Hank's eyes rolled back slightly as his brain scanned its files.

"Can't say as I do. But when it started looking like natural causes, I don't think we got so picky about what we brought back."

"Did we turn over all the kid's effects to the dad?"

"I'm sure we did," Hank said, "since we were closing the case. But I can look when we get back and make sure. If we don't have anything left, I'll check our paperwork, see if we made any mention of a prescription for—what's it called again?"

"Here." Boyd handed the report to Hank. "I can't pronounce it."

"But Joe, you know this is going to be a dead end."

"I know. Let's just do it so we can say we did. I'm going to make myself a note here to call Dr. Hargrove when we get back. He'll probably just restate the obvious, but at least his father will know we tried. Maybe then he'll be able to let it go. "

"Poor guy," Hank said. "Can't imagine losing your kid like that. All those years taking care of them, day in and day out, watching 'em grow up, saving all that money for college…he makes it all the way to his senior year and then—bam—dies of a heart attack at twenty–two. They must be falling apart right now. I don't have any kids, but I can imagine."

"Could we not talk about this right now?" Boyd asked. "I do have kids."

"Sorry, Joe. At least when we get done with this little exercise, we can put this thing to rest for good."

25

AFTER WHAT SEEMED like the longest time, Jack's eyes finally opened. His breathing was deep and labored. He felt the syncopation of his heartbeat inside his throat, temples and ears. He lay on his back perfectly still, his arms by his sides, palms facing down. Without moving his head, he allowed his eyes to roam about, surveying his surroundings.

Clearly, he wasn't in heaven.

He looked up at a fixed spot on the wall. The *Norman Rockwell* calendar was hanging right where it belonged, right month, right year. He glanced at the digital clock on his nightstand. It said 10:20 am. He had slept for over twelve hours.

He rolled on his side. His sheets were drenched in sweat. Slowly, he forced himself out of bed. After the Pearl Harbor dream, he had almost danced to the bathroom. This morning he shuffled like a tottering old man. On the way, he noticed the library book about Doolittle's Raid sitting on the desk. He was tempted to open it. After last night, he wouldn't be surprised to find himself in one of the pictures inside.

Suddenly, Jack's heart began to race. He felt lightheaded. Was he about to pass out? He made it back to the bed and sat on the edge. It was hard to breathe. He lay down for several minutes, his eyes closed.

A little calmer now, he took a slow, deep breath. Then another. He sat up slowly. He had to use the bed to help him to his feet.

What was that? He'd never had heart problems before. His blood pressure had always been perfect. It must just be fear brought on by The Dream. Maybe a panic attack. He walked back toward the bathroom, using the wall to steady himself.

Bending over the tub, he turned the knobs to let the water begin to heat up. Just then his phone rang. He peeked into the living room toward the sound. He should just let it go to voicemail. He couldn't talk to anyone right now. He listened as it rang twice, three times. He walked over to check the caller ID. Thornton. No way he could talk to the Professor now. He walked back to the bathroom.

Twenty minutes and a hot shower later, he was actually feeling a little better. He put his robe on and decided to listen to Thornton's message.

"*Hi, Jack. Thomas here. I…uh, just wanted to call and let you know, I've come down with a stomach bug. I was going to ask you to sub for me, but uh…couldn't get you on the phone. I know that's not why you came back to Culpepper. You need time to write your book, I understand. Rachel Cook is subbing for me instead. Hope…hope you're doing well. Bye.*"

Jack finished drying off and got dressed in hangout clothes. He didn't plan on going out today. He walked out to the kitchen. The smell of burned coffee filled the air. He'd put it on a timer last night, must have been smoldering there for hours. He washed it out and set it to brew a fresh pot.

Better get this callback to Thornton over with, he decided.

Maybe he'd just get his voicemail. The phone rang twice and Thornton picked up.

Rats. "Hello, Professor."

＊

"Jack." Thank God, thought Thornton. "You're all right."

"You could say that."

Thornton wondered, was he really? He sounded weak; his voice, was it trembling? "Is something wrong?"

"You see the time?" Jack asked.

"Are you just getting up?"

"I'm afraid so. I didn't even hear your calls earlier."

"But you're okay."

"Got a pounding headache; I'm a bit groggy—"

"Did you hear my message a little while ago?"

"Sounds like you're not feeling too well, either."

Jack's voice was beginning to sound more normal. He was okay. "It's just a stomach bug of some kind. I think I'll be fine in a day or two."

"You said something about Rachel Cook?"

"She's kindly agreed to take my classes today. She'll really just be moderating a number of videos. But I'm very grateful for her help. Are you planning on doing your next lecture tomorrow?"

"I'm not sure I can get back in before Monday."

"Well, Monday will be fine. I've given Rachel plenty of things to fill the time. I'm just glad you're okay."

There was a long pause, then Jack said, "Well, guess I'll see you on Monday, if not sooner."

"Bye, Jack."

They hung up.

So Jack was okay. That was something. Thornton had already seen the others on campus that morning. It was from a distance, but they seemed fine, too. But it didn't alter his plans. One death is too many. He tried to steel his nerve for the confrontation that awaited him when Jameison called back.

Thornton was a coward; he knew that. A stronger man would have never allowed himself to be put in such a predicament. He hated Jameison for this, for everything he had put him through.

Thornton made his way through his condominium corridors and out to the parking lot. He drove up to the security booth and waved to the guard as the gate lifted to let him through. *Smile the way you always do*, he thought. *Not like a guilty man with something to hide.* As he drove off toward the gas station, he remembered the details of his bitter reunion with Jameison three months earlier in Atlantic City, the genesis of this whole sordid affair.

Many years ago, Jameison had spent his first three years at Culpepper and had taken two of Thornton's classes. Thornton had heard he'd left the school after that and switched to pre–med somewhere else. Thornton didn't recognize him across the blackjack table in Atlantic City that night, but Jameison recognized him. He introduced himself. Thornton felt almost apologetic. He told Jameison he had just come here to relax, urged on by a colleague. He hadn't taken a real vacation in three years.

Now he wished he'd made it four.

Once the gambling started it was like some kind of demon had taken hold of him. The debts began to mount. Before the end of the week, it was well into the thousands. And the drinking, every night to excess. It was like he had tripped and fallen down a mossy river bank, with no hold to grab. To make matters worse, a beautiful woman in a tight black dress, easily half Thornton's age, had approached him in the hotel lounge on night four. He should have seen it coming; no one who looks like that had ever given him a second glance. When he found out what she was about and the price—it must have been the drinks—he actually agreed to take her up into his room, something he had never done. The next morning he'd spent twice that sum getting out of jail.

She was a policewoman.

Somehow, Jameison had learned all about this. Thornton found this out when he'd accepted a dinner invitation from Jameison the following day. The dinner started out very cordial and friendly, Jameison acting as if Thornton had been one of his favorite professors, going on about how Thornton had turned him into such a fan of military history. Somewhere between the rolls and the salad, Jameison began to make his pitch.

"So, Professor, I didn't figure you to be such a wild and crazy guy."

"I beg your pardon?"

"The gambling, the girls, that sort of thing. I didn't see that side of you when I attended Culpepper. You were the picture of dignity and refinement as I recall, the stereotypical professor in every respect."

Thornton sighed.

"Here I am at this rather boring medical convention, and I've got to tell you, you might be the very last person I'd expect to see in Atlantic City. And here you are…in it up to your eyeballs."

Thornton looked out the window, hoping Jameison would change the subject. It was already getting dark, he could see his own reflection more than the streetscape outside. The bald head, the droopy ears, the bags under his eyes.

"I'm sorry. I'm making you uncomfortable. Let me shift into

something I think you'll find more pleasant." Jameison then began talking about how Thornton could earn a great deal of money in a short period of time. Thornton had heard enough and interrupted him.

"Please, let me finish," Jameison said. He stuck his fork into a tomato wedge and plopped it in his mouth. He didn't seem to mind talking while chewing. He spent the next fifteen minutes explaining his scheme.

Although parts of it sounded fascinating, Thornton knew from the start he could never get involved. When Jameison finished, he said, "I'm sorry, that sort of thing wouldn't be right for me."

"Oh, but it would, Professor."

"No, really. It would not. I've got my hands quite full at the moment."

"Yes you have," Jameison said. "Full of gambling debts, fifteen–thousand's what I hear, maybe more."

Thornton almost choked on a roll.

"There, there, Professor. Are you all right?"

How had Jameison found out? Was it really that much? He'd been afraid to find out the total. He should have never come to this place. How could he have been so foolish? He wanted to get up that instant, run back to his hotel room and pack his bags.

From there, the visit went from bad to worse.

"And then there's the matter of your little encounter with that female officer in the sleek black dress," Jameison continued. "You old dog. I guess that's another thing I'd never imagine a man of your stature would be involved in. But hey, you're just a man, right Professor? Nothing wrong with having a bit of fun."

Thornton couldn't believe his ears.

"I've done some further checking about how such things would be viewed at Culpepper. Don't worry. I was discreet... for now. But what I learned confirmed something I suspected about an institution as upstanding as Culpepper. A certain document they ask every faculty member to sign, something that even transcends a man's tenure." Jameison paused, seemingly for effect. "I can tell by your eyes you know exactly what I'm referring to. That's right, the moral turpitude clause. How very unfortunate for you. If the Board of Regents found out what a bad little boy you've been this week, you'd not only lose your life's dream of becoming Dean; you'd be out of a job. You'd be lucky to get hired on at a local community college. Isn't that right, Professor?"

Thornton hung his head. To top off the worst week of his life, he was about to be blackmailed into Jameison's scheme.

This had all happened three months ago. After Thornton returned to Culpepper, Jameison had met with him two more times to lay out the plan, always cloak–and–dagger, a different place every time. Jameison had looked over his shoulder every few minutes, as if spies were just around the bend. He never brought up the blackmail issue again, but it was always understood.

Thornton was to do what he was told. Jameison said he'd pay off his gambling debts and keep Thornton's moral lapses between them.

Thornton pulled into the gas station, a dark sense of foreboding surrounded him like a cloud. His life was slowly beginning to unravel. He could feel it. He used to read about people like this, or hear their tragic story played out on the news.

Now he was becoming one of them.

26

I T WAS 1:30 in the afternoon. Jack still had no appetite. He sat at his desk, his laptop open. He'd formatted the page, set the margins, double–spaced the lines. Words were supposed to be flowing now. Brilliant, incisive words with just a touch of cynicism and wit. That's what his editor wanted. "Jack, I've heard your lectures. I want the book to read just the way you speak. Can you do that?"

Apparently, he could not. Not today anyway.

It was all he could do to keep from drifting back to the Doolittle Raid. As with the Pearl Harbor dream, the memories were as vivid as if he'd traveled back in time. The flashbacks weren't just visual things; they came packed with emotion…all the fears, the anxieties, the confusion he felt during The Dream were all right there clutching at the surface. Especially the last few moments as he tumbled in the darkness, then floated almost pleasantly in the air just before smacking the ground. He winced, reliving the moment.

He thought he had died.

He thumbed quickly through the stack of papers to his right, outlines from his lectures. Now just black marks on white pages. He had to force his eyes to focus, to turn the shapes into words, then connect the words to their meaning. He forced himself to remember the excellent premise for the book. He really did believe in this material. This was going to be a breakaway book. The kind people read even if they don't like military history.

He pushed his chair away from the desk, unable to get in touch with any part of him that cared. He leaned back and stretched. His heartbeat felt back to normal. What bothered him more than anything else was the thought that he might somehow be going mad.

Was there such a thing as reading one too many books, seeing one too many documentaries? Had the lines between acquiring knowledge and the real world broken down in his brain? Ever since he was a kid he'd read things at this level; it never bothered him before. Would he have to fear going to bed every night, afraid of where he might end up the next time?

Next time.

He didn't want there to be a next time. He slid his chair back and stood up. He had to get out of there, get some fresh air. Do something. Anything.

After finishing the last swig of coffee, he picked up his phone. One thought had percolated several times in the last hour since his call with Thornton. *Rachel.* He really wanted to see her. She was subbing for Thornton today. He looked at his watch. She'd probably already taken her lunch break. Maybe he could catch her in between classes. He grabbed his overcoat and headed out the door.

*

He pulled into the first faculty parking spot near the Murray Building. As he rounded a corner, a steady stream of students poured out from the ancient cathedral–style doors, all bundled and wrapped in coats and scarves. As he walked toward them, he tried to reassure himself that she would still want to see him. She hadn't called again, but then he realized, she wouldn't do that. She wasn't the desperate type, didn't need to be.

As his eyes scanned the disbursing crowd, he finally saw her, the beautiful face, the brunette hair gleaming in the sun, falling gently on her shoulders. She wore a tan cashmere raincoat, tied at the waist.

This was a good idea.

She saw him and smiled, then looked around as if to assure herself Jack was really looking at her. That touch of insecurity made her all the more appealing. She turned and looked at him again. He waved and pointed to a stone bench under a brightly colored maple tree, about midway between them. She nodded and headed that way.

"Well, this is a surprise," she said. "Professor Thornton told me he tried to reach you earlier but couldn't." She sat down on the bench, tucking her coat beneath her legs. "This bench is freezing."

"Did you get any time for lunch?"

She looked at her watch. "No I didn't. It's been nonstop since I got here."

"The Professor told me he asked you to sub for him today. Have any time now?"

"Maybe an hour."

"C'mon, we'll take my car. It's right over here." He reached for her hand to help her up and lingered a moment before letting it go. "Have you ever taught a class before?"

"I've led some discussions for a group about a third this size. I'm just a teaching assistant in the political science department. But the professor I work for treats me more like a secretary. I'd have loved to see the look on his face when Professor Thornton asked to borrow me for a couple of days."

"Well, here we are." Jack opened the door for her. One of those old fashioned things Gwen had said embarrassed her.

"Why thank you, kind sir." Rachel got in. "Where to?"

"I was thinking Ye Olde Coffee Shoppe. It's a few blocks from here. Know it?"

"I love it. They make great Reubens there."

Jack called in two Reubens on rye so they'd be ready when they arrived. As they drove, he asked her why she was taking Thornton's class. She said it was for her father. Since he'd retired he loved to talk about two things: sports and military history. Since she knew nothing about sports and the school would pick up the tab for any classes she wanted to take, she decided to learn more about military history. After the first month or so, she actually began to like it. Jack liked that she would go to all this trouble to connect with her dad.

The coffee shop was a quaint place, aged bricks and low–hanging oak beams, little round tables. A counter ran the length of it, where all the regulars sat. A rich coffee aroma filled the room. Soon the Reubens were served, along with a dill wedge and chips. "This is just what I needed," Rachel said, rubbing her coffee cup.

"You know, I wouldn't be surprised if it snowed out there," Jack said.

"Weatherman said it might."

A long, silent pause followed.

Jack picked up half his sandwich. "So how'd your time go so far? Any big surprises?"

"Oh my gosh, yes! Did you hear about the student who died in his sleep last week?"

"What?"

"We found out about it this morning. A kid named Ralph Riesner. He was in Thornton's class. I've seen him but didn't really know him. Anyway, I guess he died in his sleep. Some of the kids were saying he must have had a terrible nightmare."

Jack couldn't believe his ears. "Really? A nightmare killed him?"

"I'm sorry, I shouldn't have said that. They were just joking. I forgot you had a pretty bad dream a few nights ago. Apparently, his heart snapped in the middle of the—Jack? What's wrong?"

"What?"

"Are you all right? I didn't mean to upset you."

Jack looked down at his sandwich, his appetite instantly gone.

"Did you know Ralph?"

Jack let out a sigh. "No, I didn't. Did they say anything else about it, about this kid's death?"

"I didn't hear the story firsthand. A student told me about it on his way in, then Thornton announced it to the class this morning. Everybody was in a fog afterward. Kind of like your reaction. I guess there's something wrong with me."

Jack laughed. "There's nothing wrong with you."

"But I'm not really all that upset. Look at you."

"I'm not upset about this kid's death. I never knew him."

"Then what is it?"

Jack didn't want to tell her about last night but now thought he must. "Believe me, my reaction was totally self-serving."

Rachel took a bite of her Reuben. "I'm listening."

Jack looked away. "I had another bad dream last night."

"Like the Pearl Harbor dream?"

"Pretty much, except last night I was on the Doolittle Raid to Tokyo. I don't mean I dreamt about it, it was like I was there." Jack went on to fill in some details. As before, Rachel's face and eyes reflected the horror and wonder of it as Jack's account ebbed and flowed. Right up to the part when he told about smacking into the ground and all the life being crushed out of him. "I woke up terrified. My heart started to race. I felt dizzy and light–headed. Then I had another bad headache."

"Are you all right?" she asked, reaching her hand across the table and resting it on his forearm.

Jack found it more than comforting. It seemed to pull him back to the present. "I'm fine now. It's just what you said about that kid who died. That it happened in the middle of the night. And that his heart snapped. Just a little too familiar."

"That is weird, the similarities I mean." She softly slid her hand back in place.

"I'm sure there's nothing to it. But…"

"Have you ever had dreams like this before?"

"Never."

"I've got to admit, I haven't either. I don't even know anyone who has."

Jack shook his head. "I don't know what to do. I've been racking my brain trying to make some sense of it."

"I've got an idea."

"I'm open to anything."

"My mother has been seeing a sleep specialist in Charlotte, at least she was a month ago. She said he's supposed to be the best in the state. I could call her, see if she could get you in."

Jack smiled, enjoying the sympathy. "I don't know Rachel. I think those guys are all about things like snoring and insomnia. Maybe narcolepsy. Not what's happening to me."

"Narca–what?"

"Narcolepsy. You know, people who fall asleep in the middle of the day, even in the middle of a conversation."

Rachel laughed. "That would be about half of the students in my professor's classes. But Jack, I think these doctors also care for people with chronic nightmares."

"These aren't really nightmares, though. Not in the classic sense. Rachel, I don't know if it comes through when I explain it, but if you told me I traveled back in time last night, I'd believe it. It was that real."

"Yeah, that's what it sounded like. But I still think you should try seeing a doctor. It can't hurt."

"What was your mom seeing him for?"

"Just insomnia."

"I could use a little insomnia right now. Could you call her without telling her it was me?"

"Sure, I can say it's for a colleague at school. But they won't care about something like that. They're not nosy types. You could just say you're having some trouble sleeping."

"All right, I guess I'll see him. But isn't Charlotte quite a drive from here?"

"Three hours. I know some scenic roads."

It sounded like she was thinking of going with him. "Three hours up and back, that's a lot of driving for one day. Maybe I should make the appointment in the afternoon and get a hotel room for the night."

"Or…" She was smiling.

"Or what?"

"Or, we could stay at my parent's house. They've got a huge place. My folks would love to meet you, especially my dad. Well, you guys already met years ago."

"You want to go with me?"

"Sure. Besides, I'm overdue for a trip back home."

They finished their sandwiches and coffee. The remaining conversation was light and airy. They got on the subject of old movies and, to Jack's delight she repeated the invitation to see a movie together this Sunday night in the downtown area, the theater that played old movies on the big screen.

He happily agreed. They got up and put on their coats. Jack helped Rachel into hers. "Guys do this kind of thing in old movies," he said.

As they walked out into the chilly wind, Rachel said. "You know Jack, I wouldn't let this dream thing get me down. If you think about it, it's almost like a gift for an historian, if you could control it somehow. Some people would pay a lot of money to have experiences like that."

27

PROFESSOR THORNTON SAT in the parking lot of The Sleep Center in Falls Church, waiting for the staff to leave. He had come to confront Jameison but didn't want to make a scene. Before deciding to do this, he'd waited almost two hours at home but Jameison never called him back. He couldn't wait any longer, so he went on the internet and found there were a few seats left on a direct flight from Atlanta to Dulles. It cost a fortune, but he booked it anyway. Right now Thornton didn't care about money.

He'd rented a car, braved the bumper–to–bumper traffic and made it here a few minutes before five. As he sat watching the last minutes of sunlight fade, he tried to extinguish any thoughts that he was an accomplice to murder. They came anyway. He had invited Ralph Riesner over for dinner the night before he died, had given him a dose of Jameison's "revolutionary" new drug—just like he had done with Jack last night, and Jared Markum the night before that. And now Ralph was dead. That much was indisputable. A young man cut down in the prime of life. Someone's beloved son.

Thornton had arranged to pick up a copy of the coroner's report on his way out of town. Georgia happened to be a state that allowed such a thing. The report was difficult to read, but it did seem to rule out anything beyond the heart attack already reported. But Thornton couldn't sit idly by as his worries and fears consumed him. He *had* to find out if he was responsible. He had to talk to Jameison himself.

Scenes leading up to this moment replayed in his mind. He could genuinely empathize with people who had committed crimes of passion, convinced a stronger man would have brought a gun. Thornton, on the other hand, ushered spiders out of his apartment on a napkin.

Out of the corner of his eye, he noticed a middle–aged woman wearing a large overcoat and carrying a purse walking out of Jameison's building. Finally. The Sleep Center was beginning to close. It was an attractive single–story facility, sleek and modern, resting comfortably at the base of a small hill. It was part of a larger complex and, judging by the sign out by the road, they were mostly other medical offices. The entire area was very upscale.

He was unsure of himself now that the moment of truth had arrived. How could he have allowed himself to be drawn into such a mess? But what could he do about it now? Losing everything he'd worked for all these years wouldn't bring young Riesner back. And there was at least a chance there was no connection between the drug and Ralph's death. The coroner's report seemed to indicate this. Maybe he should leave, just go back to the airport and fly back home.

He hated his double–mindedness.

No, he must stay and confront Jameison. He had to know for sure. He got out of the car and walked somberly toward the front door. Reaching for the handle on the glass door, he pulled and found it was locked. He cupped his hands and looked inside. Vague shapes of an empty waiting room came into view but no signs of life. He stepped back to look for a doorbell. There was none. He dreaded banging on the door and was just about to, when a young blonde stepped into the reception area. She looked up, startled to see him.

"I'm sorry," Thornton yelled. "But I need to speak with Dr. Jameison."

She came near the glass door but didn't unlock it. "We're closed," she yelled back. "We reopen at 9am. You'll have to come back then."

"I'm not a patient. I'm a...business associate."

"I do all of Dr. Jameison's scheduling. He didn't tell me about this."

"Please just go get him. I'm sure the minute he sees me, he'll let me in."

The woman paused a moment. "Wait right here."

She disappeared down a hallway and returned in a few minutes with Jameison in tow. Jameison was clearly shocked to see Thornton. He mumbled something to the young woman that she didn't seem to appreciate, and she went back down the hall. Jameison hurried to the door then unlocked it. "Thornton, what are you doing here?" His head swiveled nervously as he ushered Thornton into the reception area, locking the door behind them.

"Jameison, we need to talk," Thornton said. His hands were shaking.

"Not here. Come back to my office." Jameison walked down the hall. Thornton followed.

"Don't you check your messages?" Thornton said, trying to sound in charge.

"Not in the hallway. We can talk in here." Jameison opened a paneled mahogany door leading into his office and locked it behind them.

Thornton rubbed his sweaty palms on his slacks as Jameison made his way around the desk.

"Sit down. What's all this about?"

Thornton wondered where to begin. Where was all the hatred he could so easily tap into just a few moments before? Why couldn't he muster the strength to lay into Jameison now that he had him sitting right here? All he felt was fear and intimidation.

"Jameison, Ralph Riesner is dead," Thornton announced.

"Who is Riesner? What are you talking about?"

"*Bre'r Fox. Bre'r Fox* is dead," Thornton said, referring to Jameison's silly code names.

Jameison's face instantly grew serious. He looked away from Thornton, then steepled his fingers and raised them to his lips. After a lengthy pause, straight–faced and emotionless, he said, "All right, tell me about it."

"You said this drug was safe! You said nothing could go wrong. You said—"

"I didn't say lecture me, Thornton. I said tell me about it. Calm down old man and tell me what happened?"

"There's not much to tell," Thornton said, returning to his intimidated, shaky voice. "I gave the drug to him, and to the others. I did everything just the way you said, and Riesner died that same night of massive heart failure."

"Is that what the coroner's report said?"

"Yes. It said he had something called a septal defect, something congenital. Some unexplainable trauma may have triggered it bringing on a massive cardiac arrest. Something like that."

"No mention of any foreign substances?"

"I didn't see any."

Jameison let out a pent–up sigh. "Well then, why the panic?" The news had brought obvious relief.

"Jameison, we killed him!" Thornton shouted. "You know it. And I know it. It was your drug that triggered it. We're the reason for his 'unexplainable trauma.' Didn't you hear? He died in his sleep—the same night I gave him the drug."

"Nonsense," Jameison replied coolly. "And keep your voice down. You said it yourself—he died of heart failure. There's nothing connecting him to us."

"Not legally," Thornton said.

"That's right. And that's what matters. If you keep your head, this thing will blow right over."

"That's not all that matters to me." Thornton looked away, rubbed his forehead.

"Listen, Professor, you're jumping to conclusions. You don't know that my drug caused this kid's death. The report said 'unexplainable trauma,' right? It didn't say 'unexplainable foreign substance.' That means they didn't find any traces of the drug in his system. Anything could have triggered this septal defect. It was just the boy's time."

"Jameison. He was only twenty–two years old." Thornton looked away again.

Jameison did not reply at first, then calmly said, "What makes you think the drug killed him? Think it through. Haven't you given it to four people?"

"Yes."

"And by now, to some of them even twice?"

"Yes, two of them."

"Did any of the *others* die of heart failure?"

"No."

"Have any of the others shown any *signs* of difficulty or distress?"

Thornton thought a moment. He so wanted to give into Jameison's persuasion, to salve his aching conscience. "No. They seem fine."

"There you go. We didn't kill him."

"How can you be so sure?"

"Because I am not a killer," Jameison calmly replied. "And neither are you. I've tested this drug again and again, and I know it's safe." Jameison got up and walked to the door. "Come. I want to show you something."

28

THORNTON GOT UP and followed Jamieson. "Where are we going?"

"Since you're here, I want you to see the animals you've read about in my reports. You did read everything I gave you?"

"Several times," Thornton said. They walked through the door and turned left down the hall. It looked like any other doctor's office. "Shouldn't there be sleeping people lying around in little rooms hooked up to monitors?"

"They're in the adjacent building. This is our administration and research office." They came to a door unlike any of the others: black steel, with a digital security lock beside it. "Here we are." A sign in large red letters: *No Unauthorized Admittance.* Jameison ran a keycard through the lock, punched a few numbers, then opened the door when a buzzer sounded. It slammed behind them with a thud.

Several monkeys immediately began to hoot and howl. They were in a large windowless room, a typical laboratory with stainless steel worktables in the center. To the right was a desk and computer. Beside the desk were bookshelves filled with manuals and notebooks.

"These are *my* students," Jameison said, pointing to the monkeys.

"Students?"

Jameison walked to a row of five cages, each with a different monkey inside. They showed genuine affection for Jameison as he neared, jumping up, reaching for him through the cage openings.

"Professor, these are pygmy chimps. They share ninety–nine percent of our DNA. Each of them has been given a dose of this drug every night for the last two months. Before them, I used it on dogs, and before that, mice. I haven't had one incident in all that time. Not one animal has died or even gotten sick. Not one. Look at them. Do they seem disturbed or deranged? Do they look sick to you?" Jameison reached into the first cage with his fingers and scratched the chin of a grateful chimp.

"No. They look normal to me."

"Whatever happened to your young student happened because it was just his time to go."

Maybe Thornton had overreacted. He desperately hoped so. Jack did say he felt fine. So had the other two students the last time he asked. Maybe it was just a terrible coincidence. Thornton decided right then that it had to be.

"Would you like a cup of coffee?" Jameison asked cordially. He led them back to his office. Thornton nodded. When they reached it, Jameison piped into his intercom, "Kathy, is that coffee ready yet?"

"Yes, Doctor. I'll bring it right in."

Thornton sat in one of the chairs in front of Jameison's desk and tried not to think. Moments later the attractive blonde wheeled a fancy cart through the door and handed fresh cups of coffee to both men.

"Thank you, Kathy." Jameison looked at Thornton. The young girl walked out and closed the door. "I'm sorry you came all this way, Professor. There was really no need. You must let this thing go now. I mean that."

He said this last sentence not as Jameison the comforting friend, but as Jameison the extortionist. And Thornton received it that way.

"It's imperative we stay on schedule with these tests. Some very important plans are resting on your results."

Thornton was so disoriented. How could he go from hating this man to cordial cooperation in a matter of moments? But it seemed he had no other choice. There wasn't any proof connecting Jameison's drug and Riesner's death. And he knew Jameison was entirely serious about ruining his career if he didn't cooperate. More than losing the promotion to Dean, he could lose his job, his tenure, and be unable to find a meaningful position in any decent university. He was too old to start over. "Tell me, Jameison," he finally said, "who else knows about...what you're doing, what we're doing?"

"I'm not at liberty to say. But I'm sure a man with your background and in your position can appreciate the significance of this discovery." Jameison seemed to be trying to charm Thornton now. "When you're through with your testing, I will be putting a proposal together for the military that will be worth millions of dollars. Maybe tens of millions."

"Well, can you at least tell me anything about how this drug works? What it does? You've never explained it."

Jameison eyed Thornton warily. Again, he formed his hands

into a steeple, a slight grin finally appearing. "I can tell you this much, Professor. The drug works with the information most recently stored in our short–term memory. The more that information stirs the imagination, the better." Jameison rose to his feet and stared out the window through deep burgundy drapes. "I envision classrooms of young soldiers one day filling their minds with videos and reading materials on a certain battle or some strategic mission—the possibilities are endless—then my drug is administered. They then get up and go off to sleep in a specially monitored environment."

Jameison looked away from the curtains and turned back toward Thornton. "And here's the wonder of it…they will actually relive the entire event in the safety of their dreams. The drug temporarily links different components of the brain so that all the senses are alive and active in the dream state. I'm not talking about the weird, disjointed kind of dreams you and I and everyone else has."

Jameison sat down again. "These soldiers will see, hear, feel, and touch everything going on in their dream. As if they were right there—flying the strike mission, fighting on the battlefield or house–to–house in the streets of Iraq. No mock city built out in the desert could begin to touch the realism we're talking about here. No computerized simulation system—no matter how powerful—can compete with the human brain for image generation. And when these students awake, they will remember everything. They'll know they have been dreaming, but the drug causes the brain to interpret these images as actual memories, overriding the brain's tendency to delete the dreams once the subject is awake. Think how prepared for action soldiers like

these would be. And all of this for pennies on the dollar compared to the billions now being spent on military training."

Thornton sat in stunned amazement. He had never imagined a military application before. But now it made sense. That's
why Jameison had selected him. "How do you know all this?
Your monkeys can't tell you about their dreams. How do you
know your drug can do all this?"

"Because I've tried it myself, several times. And as you can
see, I've lived to tell the tale. But obviously, my...*clients* will
need more proof than my word on this."

Thornton was confused. "So the military asked you to get
someone to do the field tests this way, secretly using people who
don't even know what's going on? That doesn't make any sense."

Jameison hesitated momentarily, the stern look returning to
his face. "It is a long, drawn–out, and very complicated tale,
Professor. I can't go into it now. I've already told you enough.
What you need to know is this: My drug does everything I've
said it can do. And it is perfectly safe. Of that I'm sure."

"But why hasn't anyone talked to me about their dreams
yet? If your drug was that effective, why hasn't anyone said anything to me?"

"You haven't been asking them any obvious questions, have
you?" Jameison asked.

"No, you said just keep my ears open. Well, I have and
nothing's happening. No one has said a word."

Jameison stood up. "Think about it, Professor. If you started
having wild and crazy dreams, and there was no logical explanation, would you confide in your history professor of all people?
Unless you've been to some personality classes since the days I

29

AFTER RETURNING FROM the bathroom, Thornton noticed Jameison standing up. He seemed ready for their meeting to end. Thornton was, too. Jameison approached and began shepherding him toward the door. "I know we got off to a rocky start, Professor, but we're both reasonable men. There's no reason our arrangement must remain adversarial." He escorted Thornton as far as the reception area but stayed in the shadows of the hallway. Nighttime had come, most of the lights in the office were off.

Thornton pushed the front door open. He stood in the doorway, trying to think of something clever to say.

Jameison motioned for him to come back. The waiting room was empty, but Jameison talked quietly, almost in a whisper. "One more thing, Professor. Do you have access to the health records of those you are testing, including the one who died?"

"I don't, but I'd think three of them—the three students—are on the school's computer somewhere. I don't have any way of getting Jack Turner's."

"Could you get hold of the ones you can then?"

"I suppose so." It could take a while for him to figure out just how.

"Then please do it as soon as you return to Culpepper. I'd like you to get them to me right away. It would help with my research."

"I suppose I could do that."

"When is your next test taking place?" Jameison asked.

"I have one scheduled for tomorrow night." Thornton looked down at the floor mat, stalling as he waded through his conflicting emotions. He looked up and said, "Jameison, are you absolutely sure—"

"Yes, I'm sure," Jameison interrupted. "You've got nothing to worry about, Professor. I'm sure we will have no more problems from here on out."

"I hope not." Thornton said. He walked into the night back to his car, loathing himself.

His flight home left in two hours. Before driving back toward the airport, he pulled into a 7–Eleven parking lot two blocks away to use his cell phone. He was calling one of his test students, Jared Markum, to invite him over for dinner tomorrow night.

Before he lost his nerve completely.

*

Jameison walked back into his office proud of the way he'd handled the situation. He had no conscience problems with anything he had said or done. Certainly, no remorse for the death of Ralph Riesner, who had already been relegated to the rank of mere data in his ongoing experiment.

Yet, he would have to explore Riesner's death, to some extent. Even a small percentage of fatalities would not be good for business. Of course, no one would fault him for an unknown congenital defect. He had already considered his drug could place undue stress upon certain physical profiles. Perhaps Riesner was just too fragile a specimen. If so, knowing this in advance would be most helpful.

Besides, military personnel routinely place physical restrictions on a host of training assignments. Why should his program be an exception?

The drug was safe. The lad had a congenital heart defect, a miniature time bomb waiting to go off at any time. His heart simply chose that moment to explode. Everything was still on track.

Jameison reached down and pressed his intercom. "Kathy, you can go home now. I've got a few more things to take care of first."

Then he called Nigel Avery in Culpepper. When Avery picked up, Jameison briefed him on his surprise visit with Thornton. If Avery had been a little more stable, Jameison would have chewed him out for not catching this in advance and giving him fair warning. But things seemed to be back under control. He instructed Avery to be extra vigilant with Thornton, and the remaining three test subjects.

*

Rachel was sitting on her sofa, scratching Tuffguy's bumpy head. She had just hung up the phone after talking with her mother in Charlotte. The news was better than she could have imagined. That afternoon she had called to ask her help setting up an appointment for Jack with her sleep disorder doctor. Turned out, tomorrow's last appointment cancelled and, as a favor to her mom, he'd be happy to see her daughter's friend. He would leave it open until he had heard back from Rachel's mom in the morning.

Rachel reached for the phone again to call Jack, then was startled when it rang. She was surprised to see who it was. "Hello?"

"Rachel, I hope I haven't called you too late."

"Not at all, Professor. It's not even nine o'clock."

"I'm glad. Listen, I've got some good news. At least I hope you'll think it's good."

"What is it?"

"Well, I'm actually feeling much better. I think I can take my classes tomorrow."

"That is good news, Professor." In fact, it was perfect.

"Did you have any unusual challenges today?"

"No, not at all. But I'll happily turn the reigns back over to you. Since you'll be back, I think I'll take my mom up on an offer she just made and go visit her tomorrow in Charlotte."

"I really appreciate you covering for me."

"No problem."

After hanging up with him, she dialed Jack's cell phone. *Please pick up.* He did.

"Hello?"

"Jack?"

"Rachel? Is everything okay?"

"I'm fine. Actually, I've got some great news, at least I think it is. I just got off the phone with my mom about her sleep doctor in Charlotte."

"Really? His office is open at night?"

"No. I called her right after we talked this afternoon. I guess she has more clout than I realized. The doctor's office called her back before they closed. This guy usually books out three to four weeks. But they had a cancellation tomorrow at 4pm if we can get you there. I'm supposed to call her back, so she can call them first thing in the morning. But we don't have to do this if that's too short a notice."

There was a long pause. Rachel was just about to jump back in and repeat her offer to drop it.

"That'll work."

"You don't sound too sure."

"Like you said, it's short notice. But I really would like to get someone else's opinion on what's happening to me. Did you mention to her the idea of us staying the night and driving back the next day?"

"Yep. As expected, she's fine with that. We have four guest bedrooms."

"But wait," Jack said. "How can you go? Aren't you subbing for Thornton?"

"He just called me. Apparently, he's feeling better. He's taking his classes back, so I'm free tomorrow. My mom said if you said yes, they'd wait till we're done at the doctor's so we could have dinner together."

"That's nice of them."

Still, he didn't sound all that eager. "Jack?"

"Yes?"

"You don't sound too happy. Am I being too pushy here? I am, aren't I?"

"Really, that's not it."

"I can call her back and tell her it's not going to work out."

"No, don't do that. Call her and tell her I'm grateful she went out of her way to call her doctor and for the dinner invitation, and for putting me up for the night."

"Are you sure?

"Yes."

"Do you mind if I ask what the hesitation is about?"

A brief pause. "To be honest…it's your father."

"My Dad?"

"Yeah, it's your Dad. When I think of your father, I see myself back in Ramstein, Germany, standing at attention, saluting the base commander. Now I'm jumping from that to…he can't wait to meet me, and I'm having dinner and staying overnight at his house?"

"Jack, you're going to do fine. My father will love you."

"How can you be so sure?"

"Because…I just know, that's all." Rachel was just about to say, *Because I love you.* That would have been a disaster. And she wasn't sure this was love anyway. Just that her teenage crush had never gone away, and those feelings had only gotten stronger each day since they reconnected. "You're not the same man who used to salute the big general in Germany. It's time to take a new snapshot of yourself, Jack. You are a brilliant, accomplished historian, lecturer, and soon-to-be bestselling author. That's what he'll see you as, because that's who you are."

"That doesn't sound too bad."

Rachel laughed. "So, we're good?"

"All right. We're good."

"How about I drive over to your place tomorrow by 12:30. I'll leave my car at your place. Can we take your car? It's so much nicer."

"Sure. See you then," Jack said.

And they hung up.

30

I T WAS THE following day. Jack and Rachel carefully made their way down Jack's rickety apartment steps, sidestepping around the ice patterns that had formed over the last thirty minutes. It had finally begun to snow. A full two inches had now staked its claim on the ground below. It crunched softly under their feet as they walked to Jack's car. He scraped off the ice on the door handle and let Rachel in.

"Quick. It's *cold* in here!" she yelled through chattering teeth. A rush of frosty wind blew through the front seat as Jack closed the door.

"I'll get the heat on." He hustled around the front of the car taking short choppy steps to avoid slipping in the snow. He finally got the key in and the car burst to life.

"Turn the heater *way* up," she said, her cheeks and nose reddening from the chill. "I think my ears are gonna fall off."

"The heater in this thing is incredible," he said. "A few minutes and you won't even need that coat." Jack stopped and stared back at the steps.

"What's wrong?"

"My bag," he said, "I left it on the landing. And where's yours?"

"Uh, I left it on the ground by the trunk."

"You stay here. I'll be right back."

*

Three hours later, they were riding on the interstate, about ten minutes west of Charlotte. The conversation getting here was still mostly filling in each other's blanks. Jack had shared a few high-lights about his early years at Culpepper after getting out of the Air Force. Rachel talked about the one congressional campaign she had worked on as an intern, mostly all the disillusionment she felt between the public persona and the behind–the–scenes political games.

As they started seeing more signs for Charlotte, Jack started to feel nervous. For a few awkward moments, neither of them talked. "This is the exit we're supposed to turn on, right?" Rachel nodded. What was left of the snow glistened on either side of the highway, except by the road, where it turned into an ugly slush.

"What are you thinking about," she asked.

When Jack realized what it was, he didn't want to say. "Not much. Different things."

"Like what?"

"I'm not sure I should say."

"Why not?"

"I don't know." He paused.

"Just say what you're feeling, what you're thinking."

"Ok. I can't shake the feeling that I'm going to a shrink, and that you helping me get in to see one might not be the healthiest thing for our relationship." Did he just say that? Were they in a relationship?

Rachel reached over and put her hand on his shoulder. "Dr.

Waters is *not* a shrink, Jack. He's a neurologist. My mom said he is wonderful. You're having some difficult dreams, and he's a sleep specialist. That's all that's going on here. I think we're doing the right thing. To me, it's no different than finding out you've got allergies. You better get in the right lane, here's the turnoff for Dr. Waters' office."

Jack slowed the car as they exited the ramp, a complete loop that wrapped around the interstate then dumped them abruptly onto a busy road below. "Well, thanks for saying that." Feeling her hand on his shoulder wasn't too bad either.

"I can't wait for my parents to meet you," she said excitedly.

Jack sighed quietly. "Did you tell either one of them about me...my dreams?"

"Are you crazy? You think I want them to know I'm getting mixed up with some kind of nut?"

Jack laughed. "So you didn't tell them what the appointment was about?"

"I just told them Jack travels back in time when he sleeps to famous World War II battles, and he'd like it to stop." A long pause. Rachel smiled. Jack laughed again. "They didn't ask why and I didn't volunteer."

He was liking Rachel more every minute.

31

"PLEASE, HAVE A seat," Dr. Waters said, pausing briefly to look down at his folder. "Before I examine first–time patients I like to have a little get–acquainted visit. Sort of break the ice, take the edge off." Jack and Rachel sat down in two comfortably tailored chairs in Waters' personal office. Jack had asked if Rachel could join them, since he'd pretty much told her everything already.

Waters was a tall man in his late forties. He had a slender build except for a potbelly peeking out from behind his white lab coat. He had a kind face and an even kinder smile. Jack couldn't help but stare briefly at a small tuft of brown hair perched just above the forehead on his scalp, like a small island sitting alone in the Pacific. The rest of his hair had balded cleanly down the back and sides, except for this lone brown wad.

"It is a beautiful day outside, don't you think?" Waters asked. "I kind of hate to see the snow leave us so quickly. It always does here."

Jack smiled nervously.

"So, tell me, Jack. You are having some difficulty sleeping, mainly your dreams. Is that right?"

Jack nodded.

"Have you ever been to a sleep disorder specialist before?"

"No, sir. I haven't. Nothing like this has ever happened to me before. Sleep has never been a noticeable factor in my life."

"That's an interesting way to put it," Waters said. "I guess that would best sum up my goal for most of my patients. But please Jack, don't feel bad about coming here. This is a very normal branch of modern medicine. A surprisingly high number of people from all walks of life have difficulty sleeping from time to time, some studies say as high as twenty–five percent. Not all of them come to a clinic like this. But we help lots of people every day. If you think about it, sleep occupies a third of our life. If we're not getting the sleep we need, it can really throw a stick in the spokes of the other two–thirds. Do you follow?"

Jack nodded again.

"So tell me, when did you first experience this difficulty?"

"Just in the last two weeks. It's only happened twice."

"How old are you?"

"Thirty–two."

"Employed?"

"Well, yes. I'm an author and college lecturer. Military history mostly."

"I see." Waters scribbled down some notes. "Would you describe these dreams as nightmares?"

"I guess you would call them that. But not like the standard nightmares I'm aware of."

"In what ways were yours different? Or maybe I should ask, what do you consider *standard* nightmares?"

"These dreams were like real life. I haven't had many nightmares in my life. The ones I can remember were bizarre distortions of reality. Things flashing in and out. Scary things that make no sense."

"And these weren't like that?"

"Not at all."

"Were you afraid in these dreams?"

"At times, but only when appropriate."

The doctor looked puzzled. "I think it might be best, Jack, if you try to remember one of these dreams and play it back for me. Do you remember either one well enough to do that?"

"Doctor, I remember every single detail. From both dreams. Just like you'd remember anything you've gone through in real life, even more. I can forget what I had for breakfast. This was like—" Jack struggled for words. "Have you ever been through something extraordinary, like almost being killed? You remember every little detail. This was like that."

"Okay," Waters said. "So, pick one of the dreams, and tell me what you recall. Let's see where that takes us."

*

Jack unraveled the details of his latest dream with Doolittle's Raiders. Waters nodded and mumbled, "uh–huh," at what appeared to Rachel to be methodical, insincere intervals. She got an uneasy feeling from his eyes and the expression on his face. The dots weren't connecting. At several points in the tale, Waters looked more like a child being read a ghost story than a doctor forming a diagnosis.

When Jack concluded, Waters simply said, "That's…quite amazing." After a long pause, he added, "Was this the first or second dream?"

"Second," Jack said.

"Do you remember the details of the first as vividly?"

"Like it happened yesterday."

"And how long ago was the first?"

"Just over a week ago."

"Did you write the details of the dreams down when you woke up?"

"Excuse me?"

"Sometimes," Waters said, "we remember the details of extraordinary dreams for an extended time if we capture them in a journal or diary soon after they occur. I'm wondering if you wrote yours down. Is that why you have such vivid recall?"

"I didn't write anything down."

"Doctor," Rachel interjected, "have you ever heard of anything like this?"

Waters seemed to regret letting his bewilderment show. He tried to repair the look on his face. She could tell, though, he'd never experienced anything like Jack's dreams before.

"Well, not *exactly* like this," Waters said. "But it's not uncommon for people to vividly recall certain details of a nightmare months, or even years later. This is what we call a *parasomnia*, abnormal events that occur during sleep. But I must admit your level of detail, Jack, is quite astonishing. And you *are* right—most nightmares are not as structured and well–ordered as what you've just described. You sounded like you were relating historical events. Almost like an eyewitness."

"That *is* how I felt, Doctor. I was living it."

"Well, in any case," Waters said, "I think I need to get some more data before we start drawing any firm conclusions." He sat back in his chair, resting Jack's folder in his lap. "Tell me what you were doing immediately prior to going to sleep, on both occasions."

"That's something I was thinking about, Doctor," Rachel said. "On both times we had been studying the subjects Jack dreamed about in great detail. Jack gave lectures on them, and we watched videos."

"Yes," Jack said. "And on both occasions I did some extensive reading about these things before going to bed."

"That certainly could be a factor," Waters noted. "Nightmares are commonly dislodged by things we imbibe extensively just before bed."

"But Doctor, I've been studying extensively about these things for years. And before college, I probably read just as much. I always read before bed. Nothing like this has ever happened to me before. Why? Why now?"

Waters jotted this down. His puzzled expression involuntarily returned. "I'm not sure, Jack. It definitely sounds like you are experiencing some significant irregularity in your last stage of REM sleep."

"What's that?" Rachel asked.

"REM stands for Rapid Eye Movement," Waters said. "When we sleep each night our bodies go through several sleep cycles. REM is the dream phase. As the night progresses, each cycle contains some amount of REM sleep. Our first dream phase could be as little as five minutes in length. But the last phase could be as long as thirty to sixty minutes."

"But these dreams seemed like they went on for hours," Jack said.

"They could have. But that would be abnormal. It might have just seemed like hours. It's pretty hard to judge something like that when you're asleep. But there is one way to verify some of these things."

"What is that?" Rachel asked.

"Well, it would involve you, Jack, coming back to one of our sleeping quarters. We would try to simulate the conditions you've had prior to these dreams, hook you up to an EEG, monitor your brain activity during sleep, and—"

"I'm sorry, Doctor," Jack interrupted. "But that won't work. For one thing, I don't live in Charlotte, and I'd practically have to live here to do that. These dreams were separated by several days. Most of the days in between were spent in extensive study with no dream episodes. I didn't have one last night, and I can't tell you what's made the difference in the nights I had the dreams. I've been racking my brain for an answer, believe me."

"I see." Waters jotted down some more notes. "Well, we'll get to the bottom of this, Jack. I'm very thorough. In a few minutes, I'll do a quick physical exam. Then I'd like to get you to do a little homework for me." He handed Jack a small notebook.

"What kind of homework?"

"It's sort of a diary, a journal, outlining all your activities: what you did, what you ate, if you took any medication—are you on any now?"

"No."

"Well, this journal will hopefully capture any potential connections between your lifestyle and these dreams. If there are any."

"So, you don't have anything you can give him now?" Rachel asked. "Any medication to help stop these dreams?"

*

Jack looked at Rachel. Her question seemed a little tense. It made him uncomfortable.

"Unfortunately, we don't have any drugs to counteract dreams.

Most of the medications we prescribe are for people with varying forms of insomnia." He looked at Jack. "You seem to have no problem falling asleep. But there's no cause for alarm. Let's see if the physical exam tells us something. I'll also order some bloodwork. Perhaps some imbalance in your system might surface. It may be something as simple as a vitamin deficiency. Maybe we'll see something in the journal you're going to keep. If you have any more dreams like these, I'll examine your journal for possible links. But you're going to have to be faithful jotting everything down, Jack, if the journal's going to do any good."

"I will."

Waters looked clearly stumped. They both knew it. He got up, shook their hands warmly, then escorted Jack to an examination room. Rachel smiled and headed down the hall toward the waiting room. Jack tried to discern the look in her eyes.

*

Jack knew the examination would prove inconclusive. He was in superb physical health. But his mental condition had taken a giant step backwards. As he and Rachel made their way out into the parking lot and then down the road, both tried for several minutes to inject some encouraging, optimistic thoughts into the discouraging mood that had set in at the doctor's office.

It was a pointless exercise.

At a red light, Rachel said, "Listen Jack, I don't care what this is. You've got to know I don't blame you or think less of you because of this. I know Dr. Waters didn't offer us much hope, but there are other doctors in this field."

"Do you really think another doctor is going to say anything different?"

Rachel paused. "No, not really."

"Neither do I."

"But Jack, we don't even know if you're going to have another dream."

"I know. But what if I do?"

"Then we'll deal with that when it comes. If it comes."

They drove in silence for a few minutes. Rachel leaned over and kissed Jack softly on the cheek. "You all right?" she asked.

"That helps," he said.

"Hey," Rachel said. "Up ahead, at the next light we need to turn right to get to my parents' house."

32

THE DOORBELL RANG, a pleasant set of English chimes. It was completely dark now. The snow had stopped some time ago.

Jack pulled his shoulders back and stood up straight. They were standing in front of a solid paneled door with two narrow side windows. White sheers partially veiled the view inside. The front of the two-story brick home was covered in ivy. Three dormers pushed out from a high-pitched copper roof, covered with a fine layer of patina and snow. Deep green hedges, trimmed to precision, bordered the curved driveway leading up from the street.

He couldn't be more nervous.

He heard what sounded like footsteps coming down the stairway. From the other side of the door, a woman's muffled voice said, "It's Rachel, Bill. C'mon." Jack stared at the doorknob. His mind rehearsed several ways to greet them. *Hello Mrs. Cook, nice to meet you. Hello, I'm Jack; nice to finally meet you Mrs. Cook. General Cook, what a pleasure. General, sir, Jack Turner, so nice to see you again.*

"Rachel! I'm so glad you're here!" A woman in her late fifties burst through the threshold and embraced Rachel firmly. Mrs. William Cook, or Anna, had kept herself well through the years.

Jack thought she looked very classy; her face beamed with warmth and hospitality. He liked her instantly.

"Hi, Mom," Rachel said through a tight hug. "Hope we didn't ruin your plans."

"Nonsense. What do we ever do on a Friday night anymore? Come in, come in. And you must be Jack."

"That's me," Jack said extending his hand. *That's me?* Was that all he could say? That's me?

She took his hand in both of hers and shook it tenderly. "I have to say you look very different from the young man I remember in Germany. But you look just like Rachel described you. Come in, come in." Still holding his hand, she led him through the doorway.

"Dad!" exclaimed Rachel running past her mom to give a big bear hug to the General as he came into view.

He was much smaller than Jack had remembered. Except for a thickened waistline he appeared in excellent shape. He'd kept most of his hair, now a salt–and–pepper gray, still parted on the left side. He dressed like Fred MacMurray from the old sitcom *My Three Sons*: button down sweater, loafers, pleated slacks. "Hey, Puddin," he said, as he disappeared into Rachel's thick furry coat.

*Hello General…Hello, Mr. Cook…Good evening, sir…*Jack rehearsed his options. Suddenly, he was aware of his hair, much too long for a General.

"Daddy, you remember Jack," Rachel said, walking her father toward him.

"Jack. Great to see you again," the General said in a deep but friendly voice. He held out his hand.

"Nice to see you too, sir. I mean…General…sir."

"Call me Bill, Jack," the General said as they shook hands.

"I think I'm going to have a hard time calling you Bill, sir."

"Bill sir," repeated the General. "Okay. Call me Bill Sir if you like."

"No, no. I mean…"

"I know what you mean," the General said. "At ease, Jack. Any friend of Rachel's is all right with me. And neither one of us are in uniform anymore. Here, let's get those coats off."

Jack reminded himself that there was no need to be nervous. Rachel had said they would have plenty in common. Yeah, Jack thought. I've studied history, and her father had made some.

Mrs. Cook took their coats from her husband and put them in a hall closet. The couples walked into the foyer, across glistening wood floors, and past a finely carved wraparound stairway. The ceilings were high, maybe ten to twelve feet. They turned left into a spacious living room. Centered on the far wall was a brick fireplace. Above the hearth, hung a large oil painting of the Wright Brothers' first flight at Kitty Hawk. A fire danced around a stack of logs.

"You three sit down," Mrs. Cook said. "I'll have dinner out in just a few minutes."

"C'mon in, Jack," the General said. "Warm yourself by the fire. Perfect temperature right now." He sat in an overstuffed recliner.

Jack obeyed. The fire was comforting. Standing there also gave him a few moments to regain his composure. Rachel walked up behind him, put her arms around his waist, and squeezed gently. That felt even better. He didn't know what Mrs. Cook was preparing, but a pleasant aroma filled the room.

"How was your drive over?" the General asked. "Road's pretty slippery?"

"They weren't too bad," Rachel said.

"So, Jack," the General continued, "Anna tells me you're here to see a doctor."

"Yes," Jack said.

"Is it a shrink?"

Jack's heart skipped a beat. He didn't know what to say.

"If not, I suggest you see one soon. Getting mixed up with that crazy dame behind you."

Rachel led him to the sofa.

"Take a load off, Jack," the General said, pointing to the coffee table. "Anna's got her museum collection in the parlor across the hall. You'll wanna watch yourself in there. In here, we get comfortable."

Jack obeyed again. He appreciated the General's efforts at breaking the ice. He didn't know what he'd say if that job had been left to him. Rachel stepped over Jack's legs and sat close beside him.

The General reached over and picked up a pipe from a large ash tray. "Mind?"

"Not at all," Jack said. "I love the smell of a good pipe." In moments, the penetrating scent of the General's pipe complemented the smells coming from the kitchen. Jack stared at the General, smiling, longing to say something impressive, or at least nothing foolish.

"You really like military history, Jack? I mean it's more than just a job to you."

"Very much," Jack answered, trying to refrain from saying *sir*.

"It shows in your writing. I don't mind telling you, I've enjoyed reading your articles in *MHQ* more than almost any military writer I know. When you write, it's like I'm there. That's something special."

"Thank you."

"And Culpepper's a good school. That's why I sent Rachel there. A number of my general buddies took their ROTC there.

The military is one of the few disciplines where a knowledge of history is critical to success." He took another puff of his pipe, releasing a pleasant aroma of blue smoke into the room. "Last time we talked, Rachel and I had an interesting chat about your Pearl Harbor lectures. I'd like to sit in on them someday. I've read quite a bit about the conspiracy theories myself."

"There's a lot there," Jack said, not wanting the conversation to head in that direction. He looked at Rachel, who gave him a reticent nod. Perhaps he could subtly change the subject. "Have you heard I'm writing another book?"

"Yes I have. And I heard someone's paying you to write it."

"That's true, way more than I would have thought it's worth."

"I doubt that. What's the premise?"

"It's based on another series of lectures. Well actually, I'm not allowed to teach them anymore until after the book comes out."

"You can't talk about it at all?"

"I can. Just not publicly." The General was smiling; Jack could see he was curious. The trick now was not to go overboard.

"Would you call this public?"

Jack took a deep breath. "No, we can talk about it. I'm not sure where to begin. I don't want to bore you."

"That would be next to impossible," Rachel said. "Daddy can out–bore just about anybody."

"See?" the General said, smiling. "She's getting me back for the crazy remark."

Jack gave the General an overview of his new book about how radically different World War II would have been if the military leaders had to deal with a hi–tech 24/7 news media. The General sat back in his recliner, puffing on his pipe. Was he bored? Was he angry? Had Jack gone too far? He decided to take a measurement and paused.

For a few moments, the General did not respond. Then he said, "Anna hasn't rung the dinner bell yet, Jack. She won't let us talk shop at the table. Finish what you're saying."

That was a good sign. "Well, let me give you an example of this cover-up attitude that existed in World War II. Ever heard of a little fiasco called Operation Tiger? It was a D–Day exercise that went terribly wrong."

"Can't say I have."

Jack went on to explain the details. When he'd finished, there was a noticeable tension in the room, not unlike the tension he felt after one of his lectures. It seemed appropriate then, even desirable. Not so much here. After a moment, the General sat up, stretched out his hand for a shake. "Jack, I appreciate your passion. And I think you're onto something there. Something that needs to be brought out in the open more. I think your book will make for some lively discussions when it comes out."

Jack shook his hand, relieved.

The General stood and walked to a built–in bookshelf, filled floor–to–ceiling with hardback books. "After dinner you'll have to check out a few of these. They're mostly military history. I've got two more racks in my den upstairs, but these are my favorites."

"I'd love to," Jack said.

"You can take a few home, if you'd like. You won't find some of these babies in a book store anymore. Many are first editions."

Anna Cook walked in from the formal dining room announcing to all that dinner was served. Jack and Rachel got up and followed the General into the dining room.

"He never lets anyone borrow his books," Rachel whispered, pinching Jack's arm playfully.

*

The meal was a true feast. Filet mignon with bordelaise sauce, asparagus, homemade mashed potatoes and homemade sourdough bread. For dessert, they devoured Mrs. Cook's cheesecake over a fresh pot of coffee. Jack enjoyed the atmosphere the most. All his fears of fitting in with the Cook family were washed away by the warmth, charm, and hospitality of Rachel's parents.

His biggest surprise had to be Rachel's father. Jack had expected as much from her mom, but getting to know the General turned out to be a pleasant surprise. He'd even suggested Jack and Rachel stay over another night. Maybe go to church with them on Sunday and head home after Sunday dinner.

By the time he'd turned in for the evening, he felt rejuvenated, like the misery of his dream neurosis lie a million miles behind him.

*

Rachel was delighted with the outcome of the evening. She knew her dad was taken with Jack. That would make him, officially, the first man she'd brought home that he had ever approved of. Her mom registered her approval from the first moment they walked through the front door, raising her eyebrows behind Jack's back as she took his coat. As they cleared the table, she had said as much several times, as her father entertained Jack in the living room.

Later, after a few more pleasant hours of conversation, Jack began to yawn quite a bit. He finally excused himself. Rachel showed him to his room, then returned to spend more time getting caught up with her mom.

33

OYD COULDN'T BELIEVE it…another Saturday
morning ruined. Instead of eating an omelet his wife had
made special for him that morning, Boyd was racing his
unmarked car toward Culpepper University, blue lights blazing.
The call said some student had just taken a flying leap off the tallest building on campus.

What the heck?

As he drove, he thought about a phone call yesterday afternoon with Dr. Hargrove, the Medical Examiner. The call was supposed to put the lid on the first case. As Boyd expected, Hargrove
said the father's drug concerns were no big deal. There were trace
amounts of an insomnia drug in young Riesner's body but not
enough to affect his heart. Hank hadn't found any prescription
bottles in his personal effects, either. All three men agreed there
was no mystery here. Riesner could have picked the pills up from
anyone on campus, day or night.

But now what, Boyd thought, another kid at the school dies in
less than a week?

Boyd turned into the main university parking lot, pulled
his car into the first open faculty spot. He walked up a grassy

embankment onto a double–wide sidewalk. A small crowd of students circled the body of a young man who lay twisted and contorted on the cement walkway. A pool of blood expanded beneath his head and neck.

"Geez," Boyd said as he got his first look.

Hank Jensen pointed. "He jumped from up there." Hank was the first officer on the scene.

Boyd looked straight up the six–storied wall of the Jefferson Administration Building. The morning sun pierced through the gray sky at that moment, blinding his eyes. His head swirled through a brief moment of vertigo. He looked down and refocused on the kid's body. "Could somebody cover him up, Hank?" Boyd looked away. It wasn't a pretty sight.

"Dobbs is getting a sheet from the trunk," Hank said.

"Dobbs?" Boyd said, remembering he was the same kid who screwed up the Ralph Riesner scene.

"I think he can manage fetching a sheet, Joe."

"Where are the others? We need them on this crowd."

"They're on their way, should be here any minute."

"Let's push this perimeter back a bit. I'm feeling a little cramped."

"Sure, Joe. I can do that. Okay folks, let's back it up. This isn't a show."

"Is he…dead?" asked a blond coed.

"Yes ma'am, he's dead. Let's back it up. Why don't you all go back to what you were doing before? We'll handle this."

Of course, no one left. In fact, the crowd grew in size. Amidst the clamoring voices, gasps and sighs added to the mix as new onlookers joined and were updated by the rest. Officer Dobbs pushed his way through the crowd, yellow sheet in tow. He unfolded it and flapped it once in the wind, flinging an eight-inch adjustable wrench through the air. It made a loud clang as it bounced on the sidewalk.

"Watch out!" Boyd yelled. Fortunately, no one got hit.

"Sorry, Sarge," Dobbs said. He ran over and quickly pocketed the wrench. "Must have been inside the sheet."

He draped the sheet reverently over the body. Boyd stood behind him. Dobbs turned to face Boyd, fumbling for something to say. "Two student deaths in a week," he said. "That's gotta be some kind of a record around here."

"Do we know his name?" Boyd asked Dobbs. "Anyone know the kid's name?"

"I'll see," Dobbs said, "Does anybody know this guy's name?" he shouted to the crowd.

Boyd rolled his eyes. "I coulda done that."

The murmuring intensified, but there was no singular response. Finally, a young man said, "I don't know his name, but I know he goes here. I've seen him walking around a lot, going in and out of classes."

"He's definitely a student," Dobbs said, as if Boyd didn't hear.

"Did you think to check for a wallet?" Boyd bent down next to the body.

Dobbs just looked at him dumbly.

Boyd reached under the sheet below the mid-section of the boy's body, patting his back pockets. He instantly recoiled his hand. The body was so twisted, his back pockets weren't where they were supposed to be. His upper half was lying face down, while the lower half was turned, facing upwards. His hip had obviously disintegrated in the fall. Boyd swallowed hard and reached in again, gently lifting the body to reach underneath for the back pockets. He wrestled a wallet free and stood back up.

"Jared Markum," Boyd read aloud, as he stared into the youthful face on his driver's license. His mind immediately flashed to a similar scene in Riesner's apartment.

"That's Jared Markum?" a woman's voice cried out from the crowd. "It can't be! Not Jared!" The woman broke through the crowd line. She was well–dressed, in her late forties or early fifties, possibly of Italian or Greek descent.

"You know this man?" Boyd asked.

"I'm Mrs. Trocolli, one of his teachers. Why would he do such a thing?" She was holding back tears. "He was so bright. He had so much to live for. This doesn't make any sense!"

Police sirens suddenly pierced the air. Boyd looked up in time to see two patrol cars racing into the main parking lot. Several students darted out of their way.

"What are they doing?" Boyd yelled. "The kid's already dead. They wanna kill somebody else?"

Hank Jensen nodded.

"Has the M.E. been called yet?" Boyd asked.

"On his way. It'll be a while, though."

Boyd turned back to the woman. "Excuse me, Ms. Trocolli did you say?"

"That's right."

"This address here on his student ID card," Boyd said. "Isn't that one of the dorms around here?"

She glanced at the card. "Yes. It's that building right over there. Do you see, between those two big trees?"

Boyd looked up. "So, if he's staying in a dorm, guess that

means he's really from out of town. Any idea where? We're gonna need to contact his folks."

"I'm afraid I don't know him that well. But I can find out for you. I'll go look it up right now."

"That would be very helpful, Ma'am."

"This is so terrible," she said as she turned and walked away.

"Hank?"

Hank gave a few parting instructions to the patrol officers and came over to Boyd. "Yeah, Joe?"

"Anyone been up on the roof yet? How do we know he didn't jump out of a window?"

"I don't think it was a window—judging by where he landed." Both men looked up at the even rows of windows in the various floors of the building, each forming geometric diagrams in their heads.

"You're right. It's the roof," Boyd said. "Anyone been up there yet? Do we have a suicide note?"

"I'll go up right now," Hank said.

"I'll go up with you. Do you think these guys can handle things down here?"

"I think so."

"Hey, Dobbs?" Boyd yelled.

"Yessir, Sergeant?"

"Hank and I are going up on the roof. Come get me if the M.E. shows up."

"I will, Sergeant."

As Boyd and Hank walked through the front doors, a handful of students were hanging out in the lobby, whispering and pointing as the two men walked by. "I'm sorry if I seem a bit edgy, Hank. It's just everything's been so quiet around here since I arrived, and now this—two dead kids in a week. And that guy Dobbs is really getting on my nerves."

"It's all right, Joe. But, hey...it could be worse."

"How's that?" Boyd asked.

"At least there's no foul play involved. We got, what, a heart attack with the first kid and now a probable suicide? We could be saddled with two murder investigations."

When they got to the roof, they didn't find a note. No trace that anything had occurred here in the last several years except air conditioning maintenance. Boyd picked the approximate spot where he thought Markum must have jumped and carefully made his way to the edge. He peeked over the short wall. There was the yellow sheet on the sidewalk below, looking like a bull's-eye surrounded by a wide circle of onlookers. He straightened back up and scanned the view of the campus. It was definitely the tallest structure of the school.

Boyd decided it would be a great place to jump if jumping was your thing.

*

An hour later, Boyd and Hank were searching through Jared Markum's dorm and talking with students who roomed nearby. No suicide note had been found, but Boyd noticed a half–dozen books about the Holocaust stacked on Markum's desk. Several of his friends commented on an unusual depression that had come over Markum in the last two weeks. One friend, a short dark–haired kid who roomed next door, was particularly helpful.

"Sometimes Jared would rattle on and on about the Holocaust," the friend said, "real irrational stuff, as though he somehow blamed himself for what happened to the Jews. He's not even German or Jewish, I asked him. He talked about horrible things the SS guards had done to the Jews, but not like it was sixty–something years ago, like he was one of them. Talking in the present tense. I went into his room a couple of mornings ago—we've got this class together, so we walk together—and he was just sitting on his bed, staring up into the corner. I said, 'Hey Jared, you ready?' I had to say it three times. Then he mumbles on and on about those poor Jews, and what had he done, like he'd just killed one of them himself. It was weird. I tried talking some sense into him, but I couldn't get through. I just left him sitting there."

This was definitely odd. Several other students crowded around, nodding their approvals to what the kid said. One added that he was pretty sure Markum's girlfriend back home had dumped him recently. Boyd wrote all this down, though it seemed incidental to the case. The kid jumped. A big dose of depression, girlfriend gives you the heave–ho. He'd seen a lot of suicides back in Pittsburgh over a lot less.

Just then a hand holding a crumpled half–sheet of paper was shoved in his face. Boyd looked up to see a heavy–set girl with a pleasant smile. "Here," she said. "I think Jared wrote this. Sometimes he wrote poetry. Some of it was pretty good. I found this in the hall yesterday outside his room. I'm sure it's his handwriting, but he didn't sign it. I don't know why I kept it. Maybe it will help."

"Thanks," Boyd said. "I think we've got enough now. Why don't you guys go on? Hank's got your names and numbers. We'll call if we need to."

As Hank herded the students out into the hall, Boyd smoothed out the wrinkles in the piece of paper and held it out to read:

Things in the Night

I no longer watch as one on the sidelines
I'm holding the trigger; I'm giving the word
Today this one lives
Today this one dies
I cannot stop these things in the night
A curse they've become
A race I can no longer run
So I must take my leave
Not just now but evermore
Hoping I go to a better place
In search of peace, an end to this war.

This is poetry? What a load of nonsense. Boyd turned to Hank, holding out the poem. "Take a look at this. I ain't no Emerson or Jack Frost, but it sounds like it might be a suicide note to me."

"You mean Robert Frost?" Hank asked.

"Whatever."

Hank took the note and began to read. Boyd took another slow pan around the room, shaking his head, thinking about the poem, the tall building, the broken up body below, this kid's folks, and about having to make another call.

Then he thought, *Jack Frost, that's the snowman, you idiot.*

34

JUST AFTER LUNCH, Professor Thomas Thornton almost had a heart attack. It came while listening to the local news. The anchorwoman, a dark brunette, had announced to the world that the second death in two weeks had occurred that morning at Culpepper University. This one an apparent suicide. The young junior, Jared Markum, was twenty–one years of age and had been slightly depressed in recent weeks, according to friends. Other than that, he was said to be friendly and well–liked. At this time, police believe there is no connection between the death of Markum and another Culpepper student, Ralph Riesner, who died two weeks ago. She cocked her head to the left, picked up a new camera angle, and transitioned from feigned concern to a petite perkiness as she told of a local high school band raising money for a trip to Cleveland, some kind of marching contest.

Thornton didn't hear that part. A mouthful of hot coffee, fixed just the way he liked it, spilled down the front of his shirt and across the dining room table.

Thornton was gasping for his next breath.

Why didn't he see this coming? He'd told Dr. Jameison they should cut out this covert crap, that no good could come of it.

Jameison was so cocky, so sure of himself. Well, he couldn't smooth talk his way out of this one. Thornton had given Jameison's wonder drug to Markum last night. Which meant they had killed Jared Markum, just as surely as if they held hands and pushed him off the Jefferson Building themselves.

Now what should Thornton do? Go to the police? That's what he should do. But he'd spend the rest of his life in prison. Certainly, they would view this as a murder, manslaughter at the least. They weren't looking for anyone right now. If he confessed, that would be it. No turning back. Was he ready for that?

No, he wasn't. But he had to do something.

He decided to call Dr. Jameison, tell him it's over. No more tests. It stops today. Jameison could do whatever he wanted. It didn't matter. It was time to fight fire with fire. He had enough information to put Jameison behind bars for life. Jameison's only power over him was Thornton's fear of exposure. But this was too much. Now two of the four people he was testing were dead. Jameison had as much to lose as he did.

So, he would call Jameison and terminate their deal. Then he wondered about Jack. Was Jack all right? Two nights ago he had given Jack the drug. Without thinking, he reached for the phone. It rang four times, then Jack's confident, gentle voice told whoever was calling to please leave a message at the sound of the tone. Should Thornton leave a message?

The beep. Thornton hung up.

He sat staring at the television. An energetic sportscaster was telling everybody who did what last night in the world of sports. Thornton didn't care. Young Jared Markum was dead. And Thornton had helped to kill him. "Jameison," he muttered aloud, as he searched for his name on his phone. He looked at his watch.

Jameison should be home. Thornton drummed his fingers on the bar as the telephone rang.

"Hi, you have reached the number of Dr. Curtis Jameison. I'm not attending the phone right now, but I'd like to return your call. Please leave your name and number, and a brief message, after the tone, and I'll call you back first chance I get. Good—bye."

"Jameison," Thornton yelled. "You know who this is. You need to call me. Now." Thornton allowed for a brief pause. "Now two are dead, Jameison. Do you hear me? Two! Bre'r Bear—or whatever codename we called him jumped off a school building this morning. But we both know…we pushed him off. You and I. As soon as you hear this, call me."

Thornton set his phone down when it rang. He looked at the screen. It was Jameison. "Jameison, now another student is dead!"

"Calm down, Professor. Now, what's this all about?"

"I will not calm down! Another of my students is dead. Do you understand? Dead!"

"I heard you. Yelling like this won't change anything. Calm down and tell me what happened."

"I told you all this secrecy would complicate things. Didn't I? But you have all the answers, don't you?"

For a moment, Jameison didn't speak. "All right, Professor. Just tell me what happened. Who died?"

"Markum. Jared Markum. Earlier this morning. He jumped off a six—story building at the university. It was on the news just now." Thornton's voice cracked.

"Pull yourself together, Thornton. Once again, this is not our problem," Jameison said. "So…a poor, depressed young man decides to end his life prematurely. It happens all the time."

"Not this time, Jameison. Have you no conscience at all?

Markum was not a poor, depressed young man! He was a bright, energetic student, well–liked, with a promising future. And we killed him."

"Don't be ridiculous, Thornton. Is that what you want to tell the police?"

"No!" Thornton shouted back.

"Then wise up, old man. Pull yourself together and let's think this thing through."

"There's nothing to think through, Jameison. We are through. No more tests. It's over."

Jameison didn't reply.

"Do you hear me? I said…it's over. You can threaten me. Blackmail me. Do whatever you want to do. Right after I hang up this phone—"

"—all right, Professor. You win."

"What?"

"I said…you win. No more tests."

This was unexpected. He gave in way too easily. "I'm glad to hear you say that."

"Well, Professor. I'm not without compassion here. I'm very saddened by this news."

"Why didn't you listen to me?" pleaded Thornton, his mood more conciliatory. "I told you doing the tests this way would complicate things. Couldn't you see that?"

"Of course, that was a risk."

"A risk? It was more than a risk. You lied to me."

"Professor, we couldn't run the risk of telling our subjects what we were doing. Not at this stage."

"But we could run the risk of some of them *dying*?"

"I'm not happy anyone's dead, Professor. But millions of dollars are at stake here."

"Maybe for you. But I don't care about the money for my gambling debts. I'll take care of them on my own. What I want from you is your assurance that I will never see you, or hear from you again."

"Professor, why so nasty? I said we could end our little tests."

"Just to make sure we understand each other here," Thornton said, "I am taking some…precautions."

"What do you mean?"

Thornton didn't want to say.

"What are you going to do, Professor?"

"Are you worried, Doctor?" Thornton enjoyed the uncertainty in Jameison's voice. It was the first time he had heard it. "You needn't be. That is, unless you intend to ever bother me again. Because if you do, it will set a chain of events in motion that will end your lavish lifestyle. You'll spend the rest of your life in an orange jumpsuit." Thornton surprised himself with his audacity. "All I want is my name off of this… project. And if you breathe a word to the Board of Regents, I'll go straight to the police. I swear I will. I'll go to jail, but so will you."

"I don't know what you're planning, Professor. But, I don't think it's a good idea to—"

"I don't care what you think, Jameison. And you shouldn't care what I think, remember? This is our last conversation."

"Well if this is our last conversation, then there's something you should know."

"Such as?"

"You're not the only one who's taken some precautions."

*

Jameison sat in his leather upholstered chair and quickly composed himself. He set his phone down on the end table and began to plot his recovery from this unplanned event. He already had enough data to convince himself that the drug was fine. Really, there were no setbacks here. You have a wimpy kid who dies from a heart defect and another kid who commits suicide. The drug, by itself, didn't hurt anyone. Jameison would simply specify in his proposal that the soldiers who would use this drug must meet the same physical criteria required for pilots and combat–ready troops. And of course, all of them would be fully aware of what they were about to experience before taking the drug.

He could do this. It could still work.

The real question now was…what to do with Thornton, and all these loose ends.

35

I T WAS MONDAY morning. Last night, it happened again.
Yesterday afternoon, Jack and Rachel had driven back to
Culpepper after a great visit with her folks. As planned, they
attended the church her parents belonged to, ate lunch at a bar-
beque restaurant, then arrived back in Culpepper shortly after five.

Jack had mentioned he really needed to spend time getting ready
for his lecture today, so after a very pleasant goodbye kiss they'd
parted. Jack had gone into his apartment, laid his study materials
out on the coffee table, poured a glass of white zinfandel from that
bottle of wine Thornton had given him, and started reading. This
next lecture surrounded the events on the infamous WW2 raid on
the ball–bearing plants of Schweinfurt and Regensburg in Germany.
A daylight raid where over sixty B–17 bombers were shot down and
dozens more damaged beyond repair.

The problem was…Jack didn't just read about the raid; he fell
asleep and woke up inside one of the bombers, just as it was being
attacked by a swarm of German fighters.

It was the most terrifying and, in some ways, most exhilarat-
ing experience of his life. More intense than the first two dreams
combined.

But why had this happened? He hadn't had one of these dreams for several nights and thought the spell had been broken. Why did it happen again?

What makes one historic event more magnetic to his subconscious than another, or is that even a factor? As with the other two dreams, Jack had been reading intensely about a history topic before bed. But the truth was, he'd been reading that intensely since the age of twelve. How could it matter? Why was it happening now?

There had to be an explanation.

He got out of bed, walked straight to his little four–footed bathtub, and turned on the shower. After, he got dressed and went into the kitchen. Two cups of black coffee were sitting in the pot. He sat on the sofa with his mug and noticed the last magazine he'd read last night lying across the armrest. "Fateful Armada," he said aloud. It was fateful all right. Holding it up, he looked at the colorful print of the B–17 formation on the cover. It looked so pale compared to the real thing. In frustration, he tossed the magazine across the room.

It landed on the journal he'd received from Dr. Waters. He felt a strong impression just then to do what the Doctor had ordered. He was desperate for answers. It couldn't hurt. He got up halfway and leaned forward, nipping it in his fingertips. As he opened the journal, he looked at his watch again. He could spare thirty minutes or so.

He remembered something the pastor had said yesterday in his sermon. He talked about how we often spend hours thinking about our problem but spend only minutes in prayer. So Jack said a quick prayer, asking God to show him something that would help nail down the cause of these dreams, if there was anything here.

The journal proved to be just a cheap three–holed folder with a fancy logo printed on the front. There was a form inside asking for name, date, and the like. The better part of the page was divided into three wide columns labeled morning, afternoon, and evening.

An instruction page told him to put the condition he was tracking in the space provided, then to list everything he did on the day before the condition occurred. And the words: "Please be as specific as possible."

Jack wrote down: "Intense, realistic dreams." Sounded about right. He decided to start with last night's dream episode and the events of the previous day, since they would be the easiest to remember.

For the morning he wrote:

> Got up at 8:00am
>
> Had some bacon and eggs, a cup of coffee with Rachel and her folks.
>
> Drove to church, got there at 10:00
>
> After, ate lunch with them, BBQ pork platter and a diet Coke.

For the afternoon:

> Drove home.
>
> For the evening:
>
> Ate some leftovers.
>
> Prepped for Monday's lecture on Schweinfurt Raid.
>
> Drank a glass of wine.
>
> Went to sleep around 10.
>
> Woke up on a B–17 headed for Schweinfurt

"This isn't getting anywhere."

He was about to close it and give it up. But his sense of discipline nagged him to finish. Reluctantly, he turned to the second page. It took him a while to remember the details of what he did the day of the second dream, the trip to Tokyo with Doolittle's Raiders. But he dutifully wrote it all down, as best he could remember. Still nothing clicked.

On to day three—the Pearl Harbor dream.

This took even a little more time. He could recall the dream with stark clarity. What he ate and drank and did that day was a bit tougher. But he got it all down, as best he could remember. He flipped the pages back and forth a few times, trying to find something that connected them together.

Through a tedious process of elimination, he listed one thing he had done on two of the three occasions.

Had dinner with Thornton

Then two more things he had done on all three:

Spent time with Rachel

Drank a glass of wine.

Jack stared blankly at the items convinced more than ever the exercise was futile. How could there be anything here? He never ate the same things, didn't read the same things. He certainly wasn't allergic to Rachel. That was absurd. And how could a glass of wine trigger these dreams?

His phone rang. He picked it up. "Hello?"

"Just thought I'd call and say good morning." It was Rachel. "And also to tell you, I won't be at your lecture this morning. The professor I work for needs me to do some special project this morning."

He tried to pull himself together. "I'm going to miss you. But it's good to hear your voice."

"It is? You don't sound very good. Is anything wrong?"

A pause. What should he tell her?

"Jack? Let me guess…did you have another dream?"

Man, can she read me. "I did. But, that's not what's bothering me."

"It's not?"

"Not really. I mean I'm not glad it happened. Maybe I'm getting used to it. I don't know, but that's not what's bugging me."

"Where was it this time?"

"Schweinfurt and Regensburg. I was on the raid in a B–17."

"Were you reading before bed again?"

"Yes, but Rachel I had to. It's the lecture I'm speaking on today. Besides, the dream isn't really the thing that's bothering me. Not the big thing."

"Then what is?"

"I've been sitting here the last thirty minutes trying to write down some things. Trying to sort this out. Remember that journal from Dr. Waters?"

"Yeah. You started on it. Good."

"I'm not sure it's going to do any good."

"Dr. Waters seemed to think it was important."

"I don't know, Rachel…"

"What?"

"I got the impression he was just fishing. We spent the time, I spent the money. He had to give me something to take home."

"I don't think it was that, Jack. I agree it wasn't what I was hoping for, either, but I don't think he'd do something like that for nothing. Did you find anything, any pattern after writing it all down?

"I got two things here, the only two things that happened before each of the dreams."

"What are they?"

"There's nothing, Rachel."

"Just tell me. Maybe I'll see something."

"Okay, I saw you each day and drank a glass of wine each day. That's all. I don't know what good I thought it would do…"

"You sure you didn't forget anything?"

"I've been over it and over it."

No one said anything for a moment. "Well, I gotta say one thing."

"What's that?"

"You sound a whole lot better than you did after the other two dreams."

"I guess I do."

"But there's something else you did all three times that you didn't include on your list."

"What?"

"Dr. Waters told you to lay off reading before bed."

"I know. But, Rachel. I don't think that's it. It's gotta be something else."

"When was the last dream? About four days ago, wasn't it?"

"Probably."

"Have you read anything before bed each night since then, besides last night?"

Jack pretended to think a minute. He was just stalling. "No. I didn't."

"That's a pretty big coincidence if you ask me."

"All right. Maybe there's a connection. It's just so hard to accept. I've been reading like this as long as I can remember. Why should it matter all of a sudden like this?"

"I don't know, Jack. But it seems like it does. Don't you want these dreams to end?"

Jack hesitated. "Yeah, I do."

"You don't sound too sure."

"No. I do. It's just…"

"Just what?"

"I've been thinking… maybe these dreams aren't so bad. You even said it…some people might pay big money to have experiences like these. Here I am seeing things, hearing things, and talking to people—like traveling back in time, like being there when it first happened. I was thinking, if I could just get over the fear of it, maybe I could live with it. I don't know." Jack really didn't know. Nothing he said represented how he felt for more than a few moments at a time.

"I hope so," Rachel said, "but either way, there's something I wanted to tell you."

Jack paused.

"I've been doing some thinking myself lately…" Rachel began.

"About what?"

"About your dreams."

"Oh?"

"I just want you to know, I don't care about these dreams. I don't care if you have them till you're old and gray. It doesn't matter. They're not a big deal to me. They won't affect…how I feel about you."

That was a relief. For the moment, these crazy dreams, even their cause, didn't seem to matter.

"Well," she said, "I've got to go. I should be done about the time you finish up. Want to have lunch together?"

"I'd like that."

"Okay, call me."

36

NIGEL AVERY SAT in his surveillance van parked on a side street in downtown Culpepper. It was time to call Jameison. He'd taken the weekend off since so little was happening. And hey, a guy needs to unwind every now and then. He had just finished reviewing the audio files recorded during his absence. He couldn't believe his ears. Things were officially unraveling.

It was time to start shooting people. He was sure Jameison would feel the same way.

The phone rang a half–dozen times. "Hello?"

"Jameison, it's me."

"Avery?"

"It's all hit the fan, Doc. Big cow paddies. But I guess you know that."

"I know. I tried calling you. Where've you been?"

"Had some misbehaving to catch up on. But everything's still under control, for a little while anyway. Sounds like our Professor is losing it. Heard the last conversation between you two."

"Then you heard him threaten me at the end. If I ever contacted him again, he said I'd be sorry. That he'd taken some precautions. What do you make of that?"

"I'm guessing he's made duplicate files on everything, something he could send to the police in a flash. Might have even recorded a video, if he knows how. Something he could upload to YouTube?"

"I was thinking the same thing."

"There's more," Avery said. "We got two of your guinea pigs still breathing. One of them, the lecture guy, was just talking with his girlfriend. It's serious."

"How so?"

"Sounds to me like they're in love." Avery laughed out loud.

"Nigel."

Avery continued. "I'm not kidding. I think they're getting pretty tight. Anyway, this guy—Jack Turner—he's really scoping this thing out. Sounds like he's been to a sleep doctor. Think somewhere out of town. He and this chick were talking all about what's been causing these dreams. He's filled out some kind of journal trying to isolate the cause."

"Does he sound close?"

"He's not there yet, but he's a thinker. It's just a matter of time." Both men paused. "Time to pull some weeds, Doctor."

"For now, just the one, Nigel."

Avery knew he was talking about the Professor. "Just one? Not a good move, Doc. You getting soft on me?"

"I'm not getting soft. Think about it. Think about the publicity. You just got done telling me we've had another dead student. Thornton said he heard it on the local news?"

"Yeah," Avery said. "It made the news."

"And so did the first death, less than two weeks ago," Jameison said. "When you get rid of the Professor, you've got a third sudden death. Then you want to add two more? This is a little college town, Nigel. The local police haven't picked up the scent yet, but you start dropping that many people—"

"Doc, no one would be able to connect the dots if I do it."

"Nigel, you're not listening. I can't take a chance on the publicity. You take out the Professor, get whatever material he's gathered on this, and the students will stop having crazy dreams. Time goes by and, for a little while, everyone'll wonder what all this was about. More time goes by, and it's a fading memory. If you get wind of something that shows imminent danger of exposure, I'll reconsider. But for now, just take care of the Professor."

*

Thornton was considerably relieved after his telephone call to Jameison. A sense of absolution had welled up inside him after the courageous way he'd handled the situation. As he went about the afternoon, he had tried to resist any thoughts or images of Riesner or Markum. They were gone and it was over.

Now, all that remained was to complete the precautions he had mentioned to Jameison and move on with the rest of his life. Walking into his closet, he pulled his camcorder from a small nylon case. He'd hardly ever used it. The sad testament of a man with no memories to make and no one to share them with. In moments, he had the camera set up on his dresser and plugged in.

He decided to film the video in his bedroom and positioned the camera a few feet from a small stuffed chair in the corner. He sat down, set the camera to record and began to speak.

"My name is Professor Thomas Thornton. On this video, I will lay out the evidence I have against a neurologist named Dr. Curtis

Jameison regarding clandestine drug tests he's forced me to help him with…through blackmail. I realize the things I will share will also implicate me in criminal activity. I'm making this video to be used in the event of my sudden death or disappearance."

Why mince words, he thought. If anyone ever watched this video it would be too late to worry about reputations. He retold the entire affair, incident by incident, for the next twenty minutes.

At the end, he left a final word for Jack. "Jack, if you're watching this then you already know the terrible things I've done. I know you think highly of me, at least you did before this terrible mess. But you shouldn't, Jack. I'm just a pathetic coward. An old fool. I became jealous of your success. And I cared more about my reputation than the lives of my students. What hurts the most though, I think, is how I have betrayed you. But all the encouraging words I've said to you, Jack, they're all true. I really do wish you the best. You can do whatever you set your mind to do. Well, goodbye."

Thornton shut off the camera and shut down the emotions it had stirred up inside him. Obviously, he hoped no one would ever see this, that his life could go on now to better things. He felt almost clean inside after his confession, as if telling all this to a camera somehow set things right.

He uploaded the file to his computer and created a DVD. Then he called the school, feigning illness then left a message on Jack's voicemail letting him know he wouldn't be at school. Jack could easily handle things on his own. After writing "Evidence against Dr. Jameison" on the DVD with a marker, he got in his car and drove to his local bank. There he placed the DVD in his safe deposit box. Later, after his class had ended, he would drive to his office and pick up the file he'd been creating on Jameison's project and put it in the safe deposit box also. He kept a copy of the key in his bill drawer with all his important papers.

If it came to that, someone would find it.

He decided to head to the university now instead of going straight home. How could he relax until he'd put everything behind him. Perhaps he could get in and out of his office without anyone noticing him.

It seemed like a solid plan.

37

JACK WAS ABOUT to drive to the University when he noticed a voicemail on his phone. He'd better listen to it.

"Hi, Jack. I…I'm not feeling well this morning. Must be that bug showing up again. I don't think I'll be coming in today. At least not this morning. But, I'm sure you'll handle things just fine. I hope… everything is okay. With you, I mean…well, bye."

Jack thought Thornton sounded strange. Different than sick. More like…afraid. And why did he keep asking Jack if everything was okay? That must have been the fifth time Thornton had inquired about Jack's well being, each time sounding a few notches above small talk. Jack picked up Dr. Waters' journal and put it in his brief bag, grabbed his coat and gloves, and headed out the door.

On the drive there, he began thinking through the loop that had gripped him all morning, trying to nail down the cause of these dreams. As he pulled into the parking lot he was mumbling the three things each dream experience had in common. *"Saw Rachel—drank a glass of wine—read before bed."* Over and over again. He stopped the car and stared at the dashboard, both hands on the wheel. Something was brewing inside. He repeated the phrases again, but more slowly, *"Saw Rachel—drank a glass of wine—read before bed…"*

What was he expecting? Okay, there was no way Rachel was provoking these dreams. And he'd been reading before bed for years without incident. And he'd only had a single glass of wine each time.

Something started breaking loose, deep down, like a levee slowly giving way. A thought that formed all on its own. *Maybe it wasn't the quantity of wine but something in the wine that triggered the dreams.* But that was ridiculous. That would mean someone had spiked the wine with some kind of drug, and that *someone* could only be Thornton. The wine had come from him. He'd served it with dinner the first two nights, then last night Jack drank from one of the bottles he'd given Jack to take home.

But why would Thornton do such a thing? Even if he did, what kind of drug could have that effect on someone's dreams? Jack started to get out of the car, but wished he could just sit there until he had sorted this out. But he had to go.

It was time to get in there and give his lecture on the Schweinfurt–Regensburg raid.

*

When the class ended and Jack had chatted with the students who'd hung around a few minutes, he slipped into Thornton's back office. Instantly, the same wrestling match kicked in as before.

He thought about the first dream, the one in Pearl Harbor. He had eaten dinner at Thornton's that night for the first time after all those years of knowing the guy. And why was Thornton drunk? Why had he made such a big deal of having Jack over, only to chase him away right after they had eaten?

The second occasion had come the night after Jack's date with Rachel at River Bend restaurant. This time it was gourmet Italian. And once again, another bottle of wine.

Wait. He remembered. Thornton was drinking from a different bottle. Both times. And last night Jack had drunk from one of those bottles again.

Could that mean something?

But this was foolishness. What was Jack thinking…that Thornton had drugged him or something?

A sick, sinking, anger started to slow–boil inside him. He fought back with it. "This is nonsense!" he said aloud. Professor Thornton wouldn't do something like this. Why would he? How could he?

Jack thought again about the many times over the last two weeks Thornton had asked about his health. Also new behavior for Thornton. If Thornton were drugging Jack, it would make sense to keep asking about his health. He'd want to know how Jack was doing.

A few minutes later, Jack found himself hovering over Thornton's desk. It displayed its usual chaos. Having worked for Thornton years ago, he knew he tended to resist the online world and only cooperated to the extent he had to. Recent conversations confirmed he was still that way. Thornton put his greatest confidence in paper, old fashioned notes in notebooks, documents in file folders.

Jack decided to check his desk drawers and file cabinet. Nothing in the drawers of interest, except the key to the file cabinet, which was locked. He quickly opened it and began thumbing through the folder tabs, looking for folders or tabs that might look crisp and new.

When he got to the J's, one hanging folder caught his eye. It was new and the tab was handwritten in capital letters. He couldn't believe what it said:

JAMEISON DRUG TESTS

*

At the same moment, Professor Thornton's car rounded the last curve into Culpepper's main parking lot. Normally, he would have pulled into the faculty lot. This wasn't a normal occasion. He didn't care to be seen by any of his peers today.

38

STANDING THERE IN Thornton's inner office, Jack's eyes bugged out as he read the words on the tab. He yanked the folder out of the drawer and looked nervously around the room. The door leading to the classroom was slightly ajar. He walked over and closed it, then headed back to Thornton's desk and opened the file. Inside, were several manila folders. The first folder was titled simply:

Code Names

He opened the folder, just a single page inside. Centered on the page, a listing of four names, a set of initials beside each one. He read the names and initials; his palms instantly beginning to sweat.

Bre'r Rabbit = JT

~~Bre'r Fox= RR~~

Bre'r Bear= JM

Bre'r Possum = MT

He recognized his initials next to the name Bre'r Rabbit. Beneath his, the code name Bre'r Fox and the initials 'RR', a line drawn through both. "RR," Jack said aloud. "RR," he repeated. Who is RR? Why is the name crossed out? Then instantly he knew. Ralph Riesner. The kid who died in his sleep. There was a second name crossed out. Bre'r Bear, with the initials JM. Who was JM? A second student had died over the weekend, a suicide. But Jack didn't remember his name. He'd have to check, see if the initials matched.

He looked around the room nervously, then back at the remaining code names and initials. Try as he may, he couldn't figure out who the last two were. Probably just two more students caught in Thornton's scheme. He opened the second manila file, labeled:

Instructions

He pulled out a single sheet with a handwritten note and began to read:

> Pick four students. Must be healthy. No known medical problems. Students should have a passion for military history. Four times, spread several days apart. Use in drinks or with food.
>
> Tasteless, odorless.

This could only mean one thing: Thornton *was* drugging him. Jack's mind seized up. It felt like the force of five G's had suddenly pinned his feet to the floor. Thornton must have killed Riesner. Riesner was being drugged and had died in his sleep. There had to be a connection. Jack sat in Thornton's chair, holding the sheet in front of him, and read it again.

*

After parking his car, Thornton walked toward the Murray Building, stopping briefly under an oak tree to catch his breath and to think through his plan. He looked at the side entrance. A couple of students loitered about, but no one he recognized. And he wasn't worried about students anyway. He looked at his watch. This was a good time, at least twenty–five minutes before the next set of classes let out. He could take the side stairs, be in his office and out before any other teachers saw him. Jack was likely gone. Thornton had observed Jack didn't hang around long after his lectures were through.

*

Jack's initial shock gave way to fear then anger as the scene began to sink in. A man he deeply respected, completely trusted, a man he would do anything for and thought would do anything for him was, in fact, a monster. A sociopathic monster. All this time he believed Thornton actually cared about him. Jack thought he might be going mad with these crazy dreams, and all this time he was being drugged.

By Thornton.

And Riesner, he thought. If Riesner had died from taking this drug, Jack could have, too. Thornton had to have known this, yet he drugged Jack two more times after Riesner's death. Why would Thornton do this? For money? Thornton didn't seem like the greedy type.

No matter the reasons, Jack needed to involve the police. That's all there was to it. But should he confront Thornton first?

He was about to read the rest of the contents of the file when he suddenly remembered Rachel wanted to meet him for lunch. What would he tell her? She'd never believe this. Who would? He had to make copies, to get proof. He grabbed the stack of documents and hurried out the door. The copier room was just down the hall.

Fortunately, the copier room was empty. One–by–one, he slapped the pages down and put the originals back in their proper folders. In minutes, the entire file was reproduced.

He slowly opened the door leading back into the main hallway. The corridor was almost empty. As he rushed back toward Thornton's office, he saw Thornton on the stairway, one landing below, talking to a student.

Thornton saw Jack, too, and called out to him. "Jack. Say, Jack."

Jack pretended not to see or hear. When he got past the stairway, he ran to Thornton's office, slammed the door, and ran to the file cabinet. Whipping the file drawer open, he shoved the original hanging file back in its place, but it wouldn't slide in properly.

"C'mon. C'mon." He finally made some room, got it in place and closed the drawer. He turned around, trying to act nonchalant, expecting Thornton to come in any second.

Wait, he thought, the file cabinet. He had forgotten to lock it.

*

Thornton ended his conversation with a student and made his way up the stairs. If he did run into any of his peers, he would just say he'd come in to get a few things to work on at home, try to look and sound sick as he spoke. That should be easy to fake, looking and feeling the way he did. He hadn't even shaved yet today. He rounded the corner of the stairwell and walked toward his office. Thornton was actually glad Jack hadn't seen him and was reassured that Jack looked all right.

He was so relieved all this was finally over. He longed for things to be normal again.

*

Jack fidgeted with the file drawer keys. After getting it locked, he tossed the keys back in the desk drawer. Just as it closed, Thornton walked in.

"Jack, I'm surprised to find you here. Thought you would have left already. I called you from the steps. Guess you didn't hear me." All business as usual.

Jack turned around. "No, I didn't hear you, Professor." He looked at Thornton and quickly turned away. What should he do? It was like seeing someone he had never met before. He wanted to scream and swear, long and loud—right in the man's face. Then he wanted to pounce on him with his fists, let Thornton feel his rage and frustration.

"You all right, Jack?"

Like you care, thought Jack. "Fine," he forced out. "But, I've gotta go. I'm supposed to meet Rachel for lunch, right now. I just ducked in here to get away from a few students who were hanging around a little too long."

Thornton smiled. "I do that all the time."

Out of the corner of his eye, Jack noticed his freshly–made copies sitting in plain view, face up on Thornton's desk. He backed up and grabbed the files with his right hand and slid them behind his back. Keeping the copies close, his back to the door, he side-stepped away from Thornton.

"By the way, did you get my message this morning, Jack?"

Jack backed up, almost to the door. "Oh, yeah. I did. Hope you feel better soon. Sorry, but I really gotta go."

Out the door he went.

*

Thornton thought Jack was acting strangely, but he didn't spend too much time worrying about it. At least Jack was alive, and he looked healthy.

So Thornton did what he'd come there to do. He pulled the file cabinet key from his desk drawer, unlocked it and slid out his file with Jameison's instructions. He'd feel a lot better getting this into his safe deposit box back at the bank.

Before stepping into the hallway, Thornton peeked through the door. The coast was clear. He slipped out of his office and walked down the stairway, out the way he came.

*

Jack trotted across campus against a frigid wind. Rachel had just texted him, saying she was sitting at the same bench they had met at a few times before. The frigid wind of reality was starting to sink in. He thought through what he should tell her.

There was no way he could hide something like this.

39

"WHAT'S WRONG, JACK?" Rachel asked.

Jack was slightly out of breath.

"You didn't have to run like that," she said. "We've got plenty of time. Come here. Sit down." He joined her on the bench. "Why were you running?" When Jack lifted his face, his eyes must have conveyed something was dreadfully wrong. "Has something happened?"

"Here." He handed her the copies from Thornton's files. They were wrinkled from their journey across campus in his jacket. He looked around but there was no sign of anyone paying them any undue attention.

"What is this?" Rachel said.

"Just read it."

She took the copies, snuggled closer to him then read in silence a few moments. "I don't understand. What am I looking at?"

"Proof," Jack said. His breathing had almost returned to normal.

"Proof of what?"

Where should he begin? Whatever he said would sound ridiculous. Even now, with the files right in front of him, he found it difficult to believe. "Rachel, what you're looking at is the cause of my dreams."

"What?" she said. "How? I don't get it."

"What do you see on the first page?"

"I see...four names. They look like names from those old Disney characters. I don't remember the story."

"They're from the Uncle Remus stories. Bre'r Rabbit and the Briar Patch."

"That's right. And beside them, I see four sets of initials. Two of them are crossed out."

"Read the initials."

She did. "So? What does it mean? What does it have to do with your dreams?"

Jack glanced down at the sheet. He realized the phrase *Code Name* didn't appear anywhere on his copies. "These are code names, Rachel. I pulled these from a file folder in Thornton's cabinet. From a locked drawer. This particular folder had the words *Code Names* written on the tab."

"Code names...what's that supposed to mean?"

"Read the initials again. Whose initials are first?"

She looked again. "JT," she said aloud.

"What are my initials?"

She nodded. "Okay?"

"Now read the second set."

"The first one crossed out?"

"Right."

"RR... RR. Who is RR?"

"What's the name of the student who died last week in his sleep?"

Rachel thought a moment. "Ralph? RR... Ralph Riesner."

"His name's crossed out because he's dead," Jack said. "Do you remember the name of the kid who just committed suicide Saturday?"

"I think his name was Jared Markum. I didn't know him personally."

"Look at the initials on the 2nd crossed out name."

"JM," she read aloud. "Jared Markum."

"Right. I didn't know his name, but that just proves it even more. Thornton crossed his name off, because he's dead, too."

"Who's this other name?"

"I don't know. My guess is it's another student from one of Thornton's other classes. Now skip to the second sheet." Jack watched her eyes as they slid back and forth across the page. At one point, they widened brightly.

"Are you thinking this means—"

"It means he's been drugging me, Rachel." Jack rubbed his forehead. "It means he drugged Ralph. I think it means he also killed Ralph."

"Killed Ralph? Jack, do you hear what you're saying?"

"And he's responsible for the kid who jumped. I'm sure of it. Look at it, Rachel. I know it sounds bizarre, but look at the first page again. The line drawn through Ralph and Jared's code names and initials."

Rachel looked again. "Why would Thornton kill Ralph, or Jared? Why would he drug you?"

"I don't know why, but look at the second page again...*Pick four students. Must be healthy. No medical problems. Four times, spread several days apart.*" Jack could tell it was beginning to sink in. "*Use in drinks, or with food. Tasteless, odorless...*I had to leave them in Thornton's file cabinet, but these sheets were in a handful of manila folders that were all stuck in one hanging folder. The main tab was labeled: *Jameison – Drug Tests.*"

Rachel's shoulders dropped. She looked toward the ground for a moment, shaking her head. "So who is Jameison?"

"I don't know. The point is…everything here has to do with drug tests. That's what we're looking at. Thornton is involved with somebody named Jameison. He's secretly been giving us some kind of drug that affects people's dreams. He's done it to me and to these other two guys. I think these drugs are responsible for Ralph's death. You remember how he died."

"In his sleep."

"And remember Thornton saying his parents didn't know he had anything wrong with him? And how upset he acted about Ralph's death?"

She nodded soberly.

"And remember this morning I told you the three things—the *only* three things—that were the same all three times I had the dreams?"

Rachel nodded, her face full of anxiety.

"On all three occasions I either ate with Professor Thornton, or like last night, drank a glass of wine from a bottle I got from him. Think about it…*Mix in drinks, or with food. Tasteless, odorless…*and I remembered, those two nights I did eat with him, he drank from a separate bottle of wine. He said it was because he wanted me to take it home as a gift." Suddenly, Jack remembered. After getting the second bottle, he'd thought about giving it to Rachel. So glad he never did.

"Oh, Jack."

"Thornton's been drugging me. I know he has. And these other three students. I think Ralph's death, technically, may have been

230

natural causes, like the autopsy said, but I think it was triggered by the dreams he was having. And the kid who jumped? I bet if we dig a little bit, talk to some of his friends, we'd find he was struggling with crazy dreams, too."

The thing that really angered Jack, now that he thought about it was that Thornton knew this, too. But it didn't stop him from drugging Jack two more times."

"Jack, what are we gonna do?"

"We've got to go to the police." He rubbed his temples, trying to ease the headache forming there.

Rachel took his hand. "Then let's go do it. Let's go now. What can they say? We've got the proof right here."

Jack hesitated for a moment. The rage he felt for Thornton sat atop years of deep admiration and respect. This next step meant the end of their relationship. It would change everything, forever.

40

THIS UNSAVORY BUSINESS with Dr. Jameison had ruffled Thornton more than he realized. After Jack had left his office, on the way down the steps toward his car, Thornton had broken into a cold sweat, his heart started to palpitate. It was then he gave up any notions of trying to teach his afternoon classes. He decided to go to his lakeside cabin instead. He had already taken the day off. His cabin had been such a refuge in the past. He counted on its calming effects taking hold of him again. After stopping off at the bank, he'd driven home and packed some things in an overnight bag.

The dirt road leading to the cabin was hard–packed and frozen, rattling Thornton's jaw with every bump. Thornton hardly noticed. Driving along, his mind's eye was riveted to the interior of the cottage and how much better he'd feel once the fireplace was lit. On the passenger seat laid a stack of research files, the beginnings of a new book he'd been meaning to start for some time.

He pulled the steering wheel hard to the right, narrowly missing a pine tree, as the rear end fishtailed across the road. Around one more curve, and there she stood, in a clearing about one hundred yards away. He had bought it several years ago from the proceeds of his one and only book on military aviation.

It had originally been built as a fishing cabin, within plain sight of Lake Sampson. The thought of Thornton fishing was an absurd notion to anyone who knew him. The supply of fishing gear that had come with the place stood quietly in the storage closet rotting away. For Thornton, the cabin stood for two things: peace and quiet. And maybe now a third: a great place to write.

That's what he needed—a diversion. Something to fill the vacant, haunting voids in his mind. Something to snuff out the recurring images of Riesner and Markum's deaths. Something to keep the Jameison affair at bay. He had come so close to losing it all. But it was time to put all that behind him. What better way to start a new chapter in life than to start Chapter One of a new book?

At least he still had his job. His reputation was intact. Becoming Dean of History was at least a possibility someday.

Thanksgiving break was just a month away, not long after that would come Christmas. For someone with no family, both were great seasons for writing. He stepped onto the creaking wooden porch and unlocked the door, glad to be thinking of the future again.

See, he thought, the cabin was already doing its trick.

*

On the campus of Culpepper University, Nigel Avery wandered about the Murray Building. After receiving the go–ahead from Jamieson, Avery had gone to the school in search of his prey, only to find Thornton had called in sick. He had driven to Thornton's residence, but Thornton wasn't there, either. He drove back to the school to see if he'd stopped in here.

He knew Thornton wasn't really sick, not in the physical sense. And he knew Thornton would be a wreck about now. He was probably looking for somewhere to unwind, regain his composure. That's what Avery would do if he were a cowardly drivel like Thornton.

He located Thornton's main classroom and put his ear to the closed door. Total quiet. Opening the door slightly, he peeked in. Empty. He walked to the desk at the head of the class, slid open a few drawers, quickly deciding this wasn't Thornton's *official* desk. Noticing the door in the corner, he edged his way toward it. Again, an ear to the door. Not a sound. Slowly, he opened it and looked in. Also empty. Once inside, he locked both doors and slipped into Thornton's chair.

"Desk just like your stinking house," he mumbled. He stared at the stacks of papers and folders. Who could work like this? At first, he lifted the papers carefully trying not to disturb anything. Then he shoved them aside. What difference did it make?

Thornton wouldn't be coming back here.

"Let's see what we got." He noticed on the corner of his desk, an old fashioned Rolodex. "Who uses these anymore?" He lifted the lid and began thumbing through the cards, hoping something would click. He bypassed any cards that had people's names. "There we go." Under the letter *C*, the word, *Cabin*, and a phone number. No address. Nothing else. Could be anybody's cabin, but Avery had a hunch.

He wrote the number on a post–it note. That's when he noticed the first three numbers were a local exchange, the same exchange for at least one of the student numbers he'd been monitoring. The cabin couldn't be too far away. He put the note in his top shirt pocket and silently slipped out into the hallway, mingling with the student traffic walking by.

He made his way down the steps. Found a nice shady tree and pulled out his smart phone. After selecting the White Pages, he hit the reverse phone option, keyed in the cabin's phone number and a few seconds later had an address. Then he checked local property records to see if Thornton owned this cabin.

It was all going so smooth. Must be Thornton's time.

*

An hour later, Avery had Thornton's little hideaway by Lake Sampson all mapped out. Everything checked. All that remained was to stop at his motel room for a quick change, check on his other wiretaps, then run a little errand in his rental car.

Avery was certain Thornton was at that cabin. He could almost feel him there.

41

JACK AND RACHEL drove toward the Culpepper Police Station.

"What are on these other pages?" Rachel asked, thumbing through the stack of files Jack had handed her.

"I'm not sure. I didn't look at them yet. Why don't you read a few?"

She pulled one out. "This one is about Jameison. Looks like he's some kind of doctor, a neurologist."

"What's it say?"

Rachel read the page, line by line:

Dr. Curtis Jameison

Neurologist, Researcher at The Sleep Center

5300 Turnbay Rd.

Falls Church, Virginia

"Then there's the phone number. Below that it says his home address is in McLean, Virginia. Then it says:

Former student.

Class of '95

Switched to pre–med

Student ID at Culpepper: 342030–01

She stopped reading.

"Is that all there is?" he asked.

"On this page."

"So he's a former student of Thornton's. I wonder what the connection to the drug is."

"It doesn't say. Maybe the professor is getting paid some enormous amount of money."

"Could be," Jack said. "But he doesn't strike me as a man driven by greed. Listen to me, like I know him. What else is there?"

"Let's see…here's a handwritten note…"

Jameison plans to market this to the military, once he's certain the drug is safe. He seems to think it still is. He's certain they'll pay millions for it, says it will eventually become the number one method for military training, replacing the billions spent on hi–tech equipment and computer simulation. So much cheaper and more efficient to do all this in the 'safety' of their dreams, he says.

"You hear that? In their dreams?" There could be no doubt now. "That line about this doctor thinking it still is safe. Thornton must've written this recently, after Ralph's death."

"I think you're right." Rachel's face was anything but enthusiastic.

Jack involuntarily slowed the car. "So he's planning to sell this to the military. Why not? I can definitely see how effective it would be. If they could get the bugs worked out."

"But Jack, two students have died."

"I know, but I'm not sure they would have if they knew what was happening. If they were told what to expect, and could plan for it." Jack thought a minute. "Even my symptoms, the dizziness and headaches. Could have just been generated by fear."

They didn't say anything for a few blocks. Then Rachel said, "Are you sure Thornton doesn't know you know?"

"I don't see how he could." Jack thought a moment, retracing his steps in Thornton's office. "No, he doesn't know."

"Maybe we shouldn't go to the police just yet? If this is a military thing, maybe we should call the FBI or something. Or my father. Maybe he could tell us something."

Jack took hold of her hand as he accelerated through the intersection. The police station was only a few blocks away. "I think we should go to the police first, Rachel. Doesn't sound like the military's even involved yet. And the Culpepper PD will have to get involved anyway because of Ralph and Markum. Even though the drug itself didn't kill them, I'm pretty sure the way this went down, they'd call it a homicide."

*

"Is this an emergency, sir? Are you reporting a crime?" The plump receptionist wrestled a piece of gum in her back molars. She sat behind a half–moon shaped countertop dressed in a police uniform.

"I think it is," Jack said.

"Could we be more specific?" she asked.

"It's not really an emergency. I mean, no one's in any danger. Not at the moment anyway."

"Then how can I help you?"

"I'd like to speak with whoever's in charge of the Ralph Riesner homicide. I mean death."

"I don't recognize the name."

"Ralph Riesner?" Jack repeated.

"Sorry. Doesn't ring any bells."

"He's the student at Culpepper who died a few—"

"You mean the jumper?" she interrupted.

"Jumper?"

"The kid who jumped yesterday. Off the Jefferson Building?"

"This is going to involve him, too. But I'm talking about the student who died a couple of weeks ago…Ralph Riesner," Jack said. "The one who died in his sleep."

"Oh, yeah. The kid with the scary face."

Jack and Rachel looked at each other. "What?" Jack said.

"Never mind. I know who you're talking about now. White kid. Skinny. Dark hair. Senior?"

"That's him," Jack said. "Could you put us in touch with whoever handled that investigation?"

"I could, but that's not an active case anymore. Coroner ruled it natural causes. What was it, a heart attack or some kind of defect."

"I know," Jack replied, holding up the copies. "But we have something here that might shed a different light on it. Could we speak with the chief investigator? Just for a minute? We won't be long."

"I suppose. That'd be Sgt. Boyd. Let me see if he's available." She swiveled in her chair and pushed two buttons on a digital switchboard. Lifting her headset in place, she said: "Hank? Rona here. I got two people out here, a man and a woman who want to talk with Sgt. Boyd on those deaths at the school. Is he back there? No, they're right here. Okay. I'll send 'em back."

Rona faced them and stood up. She grabbed a piece of paper from a plastic bin and slapped it down on the counter top. It was a building layout. "We're here," she pointed with freshly painted nails. "Follow this corridor around to the left, past the water fountain. Just before you get to the ladies' room, it's the first door on the right. Just knock if it's closed. They won't bite." She sat back down and turned her full attention to some paperwork next to the telephone.

42

ARM IN ARM, Jack and Rachel walked through a set of double doors, through the tiled hallways, carefully tracing the steps Rona had marked. The door was closed. Rachel was just about to knock when it suddenly opened.

"Oh, sorry," a young policeman said. "You the two who want to see the Sarge?"

They nodded.

"Sergeant Boyd'll be right out. Have a seat. My name's Jensen, call me Hank." He led them to a small cubicle with shoulder high partitions. They sat in two straight back chairs with green vinyl seat pads. "So, you guys here about the guy who committed suicide yesterday?"

"Yes," Jack said, "and also the one who died almost two weeks ago. Ralph Riesner."

"Want some coffee? A little old, but it's hot. Temperature still dropping out there?"

Jack couldn't answer. He hadn't noticed the weather.

"Seems like it," Rachel said.

Hank took a sip from his mug. "So, you want some?"

"No thank you."

"None for me, either."

From the same doorway Jack and Rachel had entered, a man wearing a coat and tie walked in. Jack noticed Hank stand as he came toward them.

"Just warming your seat, Joe. These are the two Rona sent back."

"Are you Sgt. Boyd?" Jack asked.

"That's me," Boyd said, shaking their hands. "What can I do for you?" He sat in his chair and leaned back. "Say Hank, you put on some fresh coffee? You guys want some?"

They shook their heads no.

"We're here about the Riesner case," Jack began. "And also the—"

"The Riesner case," interjected Boyd. "There is no Riesner case. Not anymore."

"We think there is," Rachel said.

"We've uncovered something here, Sergeant," Jack continued, "and we think it's significant."

Boyd's face shifted from friendly to sour. "I told you there *is* no case. Are you friends of the family? Did the father ask you to come here?"

He wasn't yelling, but his terse remarks set Jack on edge. "I've never met Ralph's father. I'm here because I have evidence that indicates Ralph may have been murdered."

"Murdered?" Boyd looked at Hank, rolling his eyes. "That's not what the coroner says. He says he died of a heart attack. And he's not guessing. Talked with him myself. No doubt about it. A plain and simple heart attack in his sleep. Had some birth defect that snapped. That's all there is to it."

"That's *not* all there is, Sergeant. Here…look at these." Jack handed him the stack of copies.

Boyd leaned forward slightly and took the pile of wrinkled papers. He glanced at them, his face like granite.

Jack continued. "Those documents show an elaborate scheme has been underway with a professor at the university involving experimental drugs. I think Ralph was being drugged by this professor. The student who jumped on Saturday was, too. And…so have I."

"Drugged?" Boyd said sarcastically. "The autopsy checked his blood for drugs. The only drugs in his body was a small dose of some prescription sleeping pills. Dr. Hargrove said it was well within safe limits and couldn't have made any difference in his death." He leaned forward in his seat, his face taking a conciliatory look. "I'm sorry guys, but you're barking up the wrong tree. It's a shame when kids that young suddenly die, but it doesn't do anybody any good to go around making up wild accusations. You're wasting your time."

"It's possible these drugs wouldn't show up in the bloodstream." Jack tried to sound authoritative, looking Boyd straight in the eye.

"Whatta you mean…*not show up in the bloodstream?*" said Boyd. "Course, they would. Drugs do that. Show up in dead people's blood."

"These are experimental drugs. The coroner probably just did some basic tests because no one knew about this. He wouldn't have known what to look for." Jack was purely speculating.

"There were no mystery drugs," Boyd answered. "No experimental drugs. And they didn't show up because they weren't in his body."

Why was this guy giving him such a hard time? Jack thought. "Did you read those documents?"

"No. You and I been talking here. How could I read them?"

Rachel squeezed Jack's forearm, as if to say: *let's get out of here.* Boyd flipped through some of the pages. Except for his blinking eyes, there was no movement in his face.

"What am I supposed to be seeing here?" Boyd asked.

Jack tried to compose himself. "Do you see those code names on the first page?"

"Code names, is that what you think they are?"

"Look at the initials beside them. Mine are the first. *JT.* Do you see it?" Jack pointed to it on the page. "That's my name, Jack Turner."

"Okay...so?"

"Look at the second set. RR. Ralph Riesner's. See how it's crossed out? And the third, JM. Jared...what's his name, Rachel?"

"Jared Markum."

"So what? I see an RR next to a Bre'r Fox and it's crossed out. A JM next to a Bre'r Bear, also crossed out. Maybe it does stand for Riesner and Markum, and maybe it—"

"You don't think that's strange?"

Boyd tried to keep from laughing. "Strange? Let's see...two students die, and somebody crosses their name off a list. What's that tell us? It says we can't use them for this school play, or whatever this Bre'r Rabbit nonsense is about."

"There's no school play about Bre'r Rabbit," Jack said. "This isn't a high school. Ralph was a history major in his senior year. I found this document in a file folder called *Code Names.* In a drawer in a history professor's desk. Those are code names used in this drug deal. Look at the next page."

Boyd quickly flipped through several more. "Gee, this *is* strange…"

Jack perked up, hopeful.

"…I see a handful of student records," Boyd continued. "And you say you found these student records in a teacher's desk drawer? What do you make of that, Hank?"

Jack's face fell.

*

Boyd held the stack of papers in front of him, an exasperated look on his face. "I don't have time for this." He looked into Jack's eyes, trying to detect any signs of sincerity or hoax. The guy looked intelligent. Was he just seeking attention, recognition? A computer geek or a conspiracy freak with way too much time on his hands? He'd seen people like this in Pittsburgh. Dozens of times. Looking for deep dark secrets behind everything they don't understand. Looking for someone important to tell them how clever they are. On the other hand, geeky guys weren't usually able to attract such an attractive girlfriend.

"I don't know what *you* see here," Boyd said. "But I don't see anything that convinces me there's something sinister here. It's gonna take a lot more than this to get me to open up a case that's been closed by the coroner. And the kid who jumped? Everyone who knew him said he'd been real depressed that his girlfriend back home dumped him."

He handed the papers back to Jack.

*

Jack was stunned. Rachel could see it in his face. This wasn't the plan. But sitting there quietly, hearing the story played back from an outsider's viewpoint, she could see how flimsy it sounded.

There was nothing proof–positive in their documents. No clear admission of guilt. It was a small sampling of circumstantial evidence that would only be convincing to those directly involved. It seemed Boyd had nothing further to say. They had failed. Now they were back on their own.

"If you'll excuse me folks," Boyd said, "I got a lot of work to get working on."

Jack and Rachel stood up. Jack turned and walked stiffly toward the door. Rachel followed closely. Jack said nothing. Retracing their steps down the hall, she saw up ahead the original set of double doors that exited to the lobby. Suddenly, Jack stopped beside a doorway on the left.

"What is it, Jack?"

"I've got one last idea. I've got to do this before we leave. Hold on." He walked through the doorway. A copy machine stood in plain view.

"Jack, what are you doing?" Rachel whispered.

"Making copies," he said. He quickly ran the sheets through the machine, Rachel involuntarily serving as the lookout in the hall. When he finished she followed him back down the hall and into Boyd's office without knocking.

"If I may, Sergeant. I think you should have a copy of these." Jack handed Boyd the documents. "Please don't throw them out. A day will come when you'll be glad you have them. I'm not making any of this up. And I'm not crazy. Something very wrong is going on around here, right under your nose."

Boyd leaned forward and took the copies. "Is that all?" he asked.

"For now," Jack answered, then they left.

*

Back in Boyd's office, Hank said, "Kind of hard on 'em, Joe. How come?"

"I wasn't hard. I was firm. You heard him. This guy doesn't know what he's talking about. There's nothing here. I just now got the father to back off and agree to start putting all this behind him. Where do they get off stirring this whole thing up again? Some stupid notion about an experimental drug ring going on under my nose."

"I'm not saying I disagree," Hank said. "Want me to toss those out?" Hank pointed to the copies.

"No. Not yet." Boyd paper–clipped them together and set them in his inbox. "I tell you one thing. They better not call the kid's father about this. If I gotta get back with him 'cause they went snooping around…" Boyd swiveled in his chair. He lifted a report he'd been reading and set it down in the center of his desk. "That coffee ready yet?"

"I'll check."

As Hank got up, Boyd looked over at that thin stack of copies sitting in his inbox. He was sure. There was nothing there.

43

JACK MARCHED ACROSS the police station parking lot toward the car.

"Jack, wait up." Rachel trotted carefully toward him, trying to avoid the icy puddles.

He slowed down.

"What do we do now?" she said.

"Now? I don't know." He opened her car door.

As she got in, she repeated her earlier suggestion. "How about we call my dad?"

Jack walked around the rear end of the car, considered the idea. "We've got to do something," he muttered as he sat behind the wheel.

"Do you have a problem with calling my dad?"

"Yeah, I guess I do."

"Can I ask why? I know he'd help us."

Jack suppressed his anger. It certainly wasn't directed at her. "He might. Or he might respond just like that police sergeant."

"My dad wouldn't react that way."

Jack didn't completely hear her. "I should have been more prepared. I just rushed in there like an idiot." He held up Thornton's papers. "There's not enough here for the police to act on." He turned the car on.

As he pulled to the edge of the parking lot, Rachel said, "I believed it."

"That's only because you care about me. I need enough evidence for people who could care less." He pulled onto the road with a vague sense he was driving toward The Whispering Hills condominium.

"I do care about you, Jack." She took his hand. "But that's not the only thing that convinced me. I know, for example, that Professor Thornton isn't directing any school plays about Bre'r Rabbit. And I think what you explained to me adds up. I think it would to anyone who knew the whole story." She moved her hand to his shoulder. "You know something else this evidence means?"

"What?"

"You're not crazy after all."

"So you thought I was?"

"Maybe a little." She smiled. "But I was okay…with a little."

Jack returned her smile. As he fixed his eyes back on the road, an idea popped into his mind.

"What is it?"

Jack didn't answer, just nodded his head. "That's it."

"What's it?"

"I just need better evidence. Something that will force Sergeant Boyd to reopen the case."

"Okay…so, where are we going to get better evidence? What are you thinking?"

"The way I see it, there's only two sources, Professor Thornton and this Dr. Jameison. I'll start with Thornton, confront him with *this.*" He held up the file. "I'll tell him I've been to the police. He doesn't have to know they brushed me off. What time is it?"

"1:30."

"I'll have to hurry." Jack glanced in his rear view mirror, then swung the car into a left turning lane.

"What are you doing, Jack?"

"I've gotta make a call."

"To who?"

"Thornton." He pulled the car into a store parking lot.

"Right now? Here? What are you going to say?"

"I don't know yet." He pulled out his cell phone and dialed Thornton's home number from memory. "C'mon, Professor."

"Hi. You've reached the home of Thomas Thornton…"

He hung up then dialed Thornton's cell phone. Voicemail again.

"Can't get him?" Rachel asked.

"No."

"Okay, so how about we call my dad?"

"Rachel. I'm not sure that's a good idea. I want your dad to like me."

"He already does."

"And what's he going to think if we start talking about all this?"

"I think he'll hear us out."

"Do you? Okay, let's say he does. Do you think he'll be happy I've involved his daughter in something like this? Do you think he'll want me to keep seeing you? I wouldn't want my daughter mixed up in something where people are being drugged and killed. I think he'll listen like a father, not like a general."

"I think you're wrong. I think he can do both."

Jack took a deep breath. "Once I get more evidence, better

evidence, I promise I'll get your dad involved." He started tapping his phone.

"Who are you calling now?"

"Thornton's extension at the school. Maybe he was feeling better and decided to teach his afternoon sessions." The phone rang several times, then voicemail again. He was about to hang up, then decided against it. At the end of the message, Jack said: "Professor, this is Jack. We've gotta talk. Right away. It's about…it's about the contents of your locked drawer. The file about the drug tests. Call me. I'll try again later." He should have just hung up.

"Voicemail again?" she said. "Think you should have said that much on a voicemail?"

"I don't know what I was thinking. It just came out."

"Maybe it's not so bad. You're going to tell him anyway as soon as you see him."

"No. I screwed up. In person, I could have controlled the situation better. Now I have no idea what he's going to do once he hears this."

"Maybe he won't hear it," she said. "Maybe he's not there."

They sat in silence a few moments. Jack turned the car on and pulled out of the parking lot.

"Where to now?" she asked.

"Thornton's condo is just five minutes away from here. Maybe he's there and just not answering the phone."

44

NIGEL AVERY DROVE along the hilly wooded terrain surrounding Lake Sampson, occasionally glancing down at his GPS, set to what he was sure was Thornton's cabin. Far from nervous, he was pumped.

He was driving a car he'd stolen for this purpose. Had to make one detour on the way, to buy a new set of tires. A cash purchase made some thirty minutes ago. All the roads around Lake Sampson were dirt. For Avery's plan to work, it would be necessary for only one set of tire tracks to go in and out of Thornton's cabin, so he changed out the tires on this car to match Thornton's.

As he rounded a curve, Avery rolled the car window down a few inches. He could never find a middle ground with car heating systems. Part of the problem was this costume. He was bundled up in the latest mountain man wear, deciding that would be the simplest and least conspicuous attire for the occasion. Irritating beads of sweat dripped down his neck and back.

He continued down the bumpy dirt path Thornton must have traveled earlier that afternoon. The GPS said the final curve was directly ahead. Avery stopped the car just before reaching it. He turned the car off and got out, leaving the door open. Closing the gap on foot, he surveyed the scene behind a thick pine for several minutes. There was Thornton's car. He saw no movement at first, then the front door opened. Thornton came out, got something from the front seat of his car and went back inside the cabin.

There you go.

From Avery's earlier casing of the area, he was certain none of the surrounding properties could overhear an indoor gunshot. But he couldn't use a silencer on this anyway. Considering Thornton had zero social life, Avery had also figured no one would discover Thornton's body for days. He reached down and pulled out a nine–millimeter from his leg holster and shoved it into his waistband. Inching forward from his covered position, his eyes roved from side to side.

In seconds, he was at the edge of the front porch. Too many boards would creak, so he walked around the side facing away from the lake, ducking under the lone window.

As he'd anticipated, there was a back door. No porch or walk-way. He turned the knob, slowly. It was unlocked. Holding his breath, he pushed it forward, ever so slightly. No creaks. He paused waiting for any reaction from inside. None came. He stepped into a short hallway, pulling his gun from his waistband. With the other hand, he gently closed the door.

Still, no reaction from Thornton. The cabin was silent. He had to be in here somewhere. There were two doorways on either side of the hall. Avery took one step forward, his gun raised. To the left was an empty bathroom. To the right, a large pantry. Two more steps forward, and he was at the edge of a large big room. He heard the unmistakable sounds of a man snoring.

There you go.

The guy must be exhausted to have fallen asleep that fast. Avery walked into the center of the room. In the front left corner he found Thornton lying on a single bed. The curtains had already been drawn, a dying fire flickered in the fireplace. A laptop lay open on a small desk, the screensaver tossing up a nice aviation picture every few seconds. Leveling his gun at Thornton's head, he reached up with his foot and kicked Thornton's toes.

Thornton moaned. Avery kicked him again, a little harder. Thornton's eyes opened. They focused on the center hole of the gun barrel. His body didn't move. He looked up at Avery, "Please... don't hurt me. Take anything. My wallet...it's over there on the dresser."

"I don't want your money, Professor," Avery said. "I make more in a month than you make all year. Now get up please...*if* you don't mind."

"Do you know me?" Thornton asked, rising slowly from the bed.

"Sure. You and me good buddies." Avery loved toying with his game. "But now, I'm afraid, we must part."

"Where are we going?" Thornton asked, his face in a panic.

"I'm not going anywhere," Avery said. "You are. Problem is...I can't tell you exactly where. That's the stuff for philosophers and preachers."

*

An icy dread filled Thornton's insides. This man had come to kill him. But why? He reached his right hand beneath his pillow, feeling for his micro-recorder. He had started dictating some thoughts for his book before he fell asleep. He clicked it on and slid it forward to the edge of the pillow. "Who are you?"

"Guess it doesn't matter if you know. Not now. The name's Avery. Has been for a while now."

"Who sent you?" he asked. "Dr. Jameison?"

"Jameison?" repeated Avery. "Good guess. He's a little peeved with you. Making those threats to the good Doctor…not a good idea."

"I didn't make any threats. Is that what Jameison told you? He's lying."

"Come now, Professor. Show a little courage here at the end. I got you on tape. It won't do any good to bluff here. There ain't nobody you talked to in the last couple a weeks that I haven't heard. Let's see, this morning you called a Mr. Jack Turner about your stomach ache. Were you faking, Professor? You didn't sound too sincere. Now, get up!" He kicked Thornton's foot. "I didn't come here to chat."

Thornton stood. "What do you want me to do?"

"First, tell me where you've stashed any dirt you have on Jameison. I want all of it."

"And, if I don't?"

"I'll kill you."

"And, if I do?"

Avery didn't respond.

"So, why should I make it easy on you?" Thornton said. "You're going to kill me either way."

*

"Here's one reason." Avery thrust his fist into Thornton's chest, sending him flying back against the bed.

Thornton lay there, breathless, looking terrified. Momentarily unable to move.

"See, nothing says I can't hurt you first. I know how, Professor. Our government spent a good deal to teach me. Got straight A's in that class." Avery was bluffing about torturing Thornton. He had to make this look like a suicide, which would automatically involve an autopsy. Torturing Thornton would leave too many marks.

"How much you figure you can take, Professor? I'm in no hurry."

45

WHEN HIS LUNGS finally rebounded from the blow, Thornton drew in a breath. A strange calm came over him. Thornton resigned himself to his fate. Justice had stepped in and decided he should die. He had betrayed the lives of four young men, men who trusted him, and now two of them were dead. It was only right that he should join them. He lifted himself off the bed. "I don't have much. I was bluffing Jameison to get him to leave me alone."

"I don't care how much you have. I want it all."

Thornton hesitated a moment to give the impression of playing hard to get.

"I mean it, Professor. All of it."

"Over on the dresser, next to my wallet, you'll find my keys. My house key is the round one, with three triangles etched in it. There's a file folder with everything I have in my bill drawer. In the bedroom desk." That was partially true. Thornton had made a set of copies and put them there.

"Shake my hand," Avery said, "if that's all there is. I hear you're a man of your word."

Thornton reached out his hand. It seemed an odd gesture at

the moment. Avery suddenly grabbed his hand and squeezed, hard. Thornton screamed and tried to pull away. "Please I told you the truth."

"We'll see," Avery said, squeezing a little harder.

Thornton somehow found the courage to look Avery straight in the eyes and said, "I *have* told you the truth."

"Fine, Professor." He let go. "I'll get the keys. Move over to the desk. Take out a sheet of paper and a pen. Not a pencil, a pen." Avery held the gun on him as Thornton obeyed.

"What now?" Thornton rubbed his fingers. The pain began to dissipate.

"Sit," Avery said.

Thornton sat. "Now what?"

"Here's how it's going down, Professor. See, you don't know this, but I do. Turns out, you're gay. That's right. You've been in the closet all these years. But you can't take all the hiding anymore. You're old school. You don't have the guts to come out. And you're totally distraught because your partner…what's the name of that kid who jumped last week?"

"Jared Markum?"

"Yeah, that's him. You're distraught because he's gone. So you've come to this cabin to end it all."

"That's absurd. No one will ever believe that!"

"Sure they will. I looked into it. Nobody's seen you date anybody for years. Your faculty buddies don't even know if you like girls."

Thornton's heart sank. It saddened him to realize that Avery was right. The shallow relationships he'd developed at the school could easily believe he was gay. What evidence did he have to offer in his defense?

Then, he remembered. The micro–recorder. It was getting all of this. That was some consolation. And when the authorities had finished going through his possessions, someone would discover the key to the safe deposit box—and the DVD. With that flicker of hope, he turned and began to write.

"Good move, Professor. For that, I'll make it one quick shot to the heart. You won't feel a thing. You might even like it better where you're going…who knows?"

Thornton wrote these words:

To all those who know me, I am teribly sorry for the harm and embarrasment my leaving the world this way will bring. For all these years, I have been a secrit homosexual. I cannot live with the shame any longer. And I'm overcome with grief becaus of Jared Markum's death.

Please, forgiv me, if you can.

Sincerly,

Tomas Thornton

He left his final parting clues in his spelling. Listening to Avery mangle the English language, he decided it was at least possible Avery was also a poor speller. Anyone who knew Thornton would know he had a rich vocabulary and never misspelled even the most complicated words. "Here," Thornton said, handing the note to Avery.

Avery took a step back from Thornton and read the note, still holding the gun pointed at him. "Think you left off an *e* here on the word forgive. Forgive's got an *e* on the end."

Thornton took the note back. "So, I did," he said, and made the correction. He could almost feel the presence of death, as if it existed in the physical presence of this man, Avery. Thornton rummaged through the corridors of his mind, searching for childhood prayers, even pieces of prayers to offer to the Almighty. His hands trembled.

"Okay, Professor. I think we're all set."

"Lord, have mercy on me," he whispered. "I know I deserve this, but please have mercy."

"What'd you say?"

"Nothing," Thornton said. He swiveled in his chair toward Avery, attempting to make a last, hopeless appeal. Before the words formed in his mouth, he looked down. Avery had stepped closer. The gun barrel was inches from his chest. He saw a flash and felt the punch of the bullet strike his chest. He never heard the sound.

Then, darkness.

That fast, Thornton was dead.

*

"Now, that didn't hurt too bad, did it Professor?" Avery smiled, staring at the face of the lifeless corpse. He looked up at the ceiling. "Some say you're hovering over me right now, checking things out." Avery pretended to wave. "Where you at, Professor? Over the bed? Over this laptop here? See, I told you it wouldn't be so bad. You're already seeing things and knowing things philosophers and wise men have argued about for centuries."

Avery thought a moment, then said mockingly: "Run to the light, Professor. Run to the light."

He laughed as he turned and walked out the back door. Walking into the woods, he found a thick log lying on the ground. He picked it up and brought it back into the house, setting it next to Thornton, who was now slumped in his desk chair.

"Now, were you right or left–handed?" He forgot to notice. He glanced down at the slant in Thornton's handwriting. "Same as mine." He placed the gun in Thornton's right hand, positioning his finger on the trigger, and aimed for the heart of the log, firing once.

Splinters of wood spread out from where the bullet entered, littering the floor. The bullet embedded deep into the log. "That'll do," he said to Thornton. "The coroner will be wanting to see this stuff on your hands." He placed the gun in Thornton's hand then right up to the gaping wound in his chest and let go. The gun bounced off Thornton's body then dropped to the floor.

"That looks about right." Avery looked around the small interior of the cabin, noticing again the aviation images changing on the laptop screen. He decided to leave it on. Keep things natural. He carried the log back outside and set it temporarily beside the back door.

He had one last detail to attend inside the cabin. It required him to walk back to his car and fetch his little black pouch of spy goodies. From it he fished out a small rectangular container half–filled with gray putty. It wouldn't do for the police to find Thornton's lone house key missing from his chain.

A few moments later, inside the cabin, with a reasonable facsimile of the key now impressed upon the putty, Avery's mission was complete. On his way out the back door he turned the door knob lock so that it would lock from the inside when closed. Then he grabbed the log and walked it into the woods for several minutes, heaving it into the thick underbrush. The splinters of wood the bullet had sprayed on the cabin floor didn't concern him. Slivers of wood were all over the floor from Thornton's fire–building efforts.

Avery picked up a pine tree branch and used it to sweep away his footprints from the cabin door as he walked backward toward his car. At the car, he took one last look around. The coast was clear. The scene was calm and uninterrupted, inviting even. He opened his car door, sat down, and turned on the ignition. As he drove off, he looked in the rear view mirror and said, smiling, "There you go."

46

"HELLO THERE, YOUNG man." It was the elderly security guard at Thornton's condominium complex.

"We're here to see Professor Thornton?" Jack said. "You might remember me? I've been here twice in the last few weeks."

The guard got out of his office chair, a clipboard at his side. "You do look a little familiar. But Professor Thornton isn't home right now. Left a little while ago."

As the guard stepped closer, Jack saw his nametag above his shirt pocket. "You don't happen to know where he is, do you...Mr. Evers?"

"I do, but I'm not really supposed to say..."

Jack allowed a short pause. "I've got some important papers for him to sign. I work with him at the University. We've been friends for years. I don't think he'll mind if you tell me where he's gone. I'd be willing to sign something, so you can blame me if you get any flak about it."

"Well," said Evers, "I guess it'll be alright. Since you work with him and all. Course, I don't know exactly where he is."

"Do you have *any* idea?"

"He left here a few hours ago, said he was going to his cabin for a few days. I never been there. It's out by Lake Sampson. Or was it Lake Ames? See, I don't even know which lake it's on."

Jack knew Thornton had a cabin, but he'd never been there. Between the two lakes there had to be hundreds of cabins. Many were set back off the main roads on unmarked dirt paths. This wasn't good news.

"What are we going to do now?" Rachel whispered.

"I don't know," Jack said. He looked back out the window. "That's okay, Mr. Evers. You've been a lot of help. If you hear from him, tell him Jack Turner is looking for him, will you?"

"Right–O," said Evers. "Have you tried calling him?"

"I have. He's not picking up. Since he's out at the cabin, maybe he's turned his phone off."

"Could be," the guard said. "Well, you have a nice day now."

Jack turned the car around, drove down the road a little and pulled off to the side. "That didn't help," he said to Rachel. "Guess I've got no choice now." He pulled out his phone.

"What do you mean?" Rachel said.

"Let's see. It's 1:45. That doesn't give me much time." He looked around for a travel app on his phone.

"Jack, what are you thinking?"

He knew Rachel would totally disapprove. "I'm going to drop you off and take the first plane I can get to the DC area. I need to get to Falls Church, Virginia. If possible, before five."

"Falls Church? Jack, isn't that—?" She began scouring through the loose sheets of paper in the front seat.

"Yes, it is," Jack said. "It's where Dr. Jameison's office is."

"Why would you go there?"

"I have to, Rachel."

"Why? If he's the mastermind behind this thing, then he's—"

"There's no other way. I can't just sit on this. We need hard evidence to get the police to believe us. I'm sure I can get a direct flight from Atlanta to DC. If I leave now, I might be able to get to his office before it closes."

"And then what?"

"I don't know. I'll think of something on the way there."

"Jack, please. You don't know what you're getting into. They've already killed Ralph. And without flinching, they kept giving you and Jared Markum these drugs. Now Jared's dead. Let's wait till we get hold of Professor Thornton. We can drive all around Lake Sampson. Maybe his name is on the mailbox."

"Rachel, there are hundreds of cabins up there. We'd be looking for two days. I can fly to Falls Church, check things out, and be back tonight or first thing in the morning. I won't do anything stupid. If I can't think of a safe way to get more information, I promise, I'll let it go and come back."

"I wish you'd let it go now. It's too dangerous."

Jack thought of a concession, "I'll tell you what—I'll drop you off at your place. You get some stuff together and drive to your parents' house. I'll meet you there. I'll make my return flight to Charlotte, and we can tell your dad all about this tomorrow. Hopefully, I'll get something more from Jameison that'll help convince him."

"Why don't I just wait here in Culpepper till you get back? Then we can drive to my parents together first thing in the morning."

"I'm not sure it's safe for you to stay here. What if Thornton checks his messages? He'll know we know what's going on." Jack couldn't imagine Thornton doing anything violent, but then, he could never have imagined the professor being mixed up in this scheme in the first place. "I'd feel a whole lot better if I knew you were safe at your parents' house."

"All right," she said. "Will you at least call me then when you get in tonight?"

"If it's not too late."

"I don't care how late it is. I won't be able to sleep anyway."

"Okay, I'll call."

47

RACHEL HAD BEEN arguing with herself for the last twenty minutes, ever since Jack had dropped her off. She was sitting on her couch, scratching Tuffguy's scabby head, staring at her phone. Jack would be furious if he knew she called her dad, but Jack didn't know him. She was certain her dad would be sympathetic and at least try to understand. He'd never blame Jack for something he had no control over.

She called their home number. It rang several times, too many times. She was disappointed but not surprised when their voicemail responded. Hearing her father's voice, even in digital form, soothed her nerves some. After the beep, she left this message, trying to sound calm:

"Hi Dad, Rachel here. Umm, I was thinking about driving up there tonight, maybe stay there at least through tomorrow. Jack's flying to DC this afternoon and said he'd meet me there tomorrow. Something's come up. We're fine, it's just…it's kind of hard to explain over the phone. I'll tell you all about it when I get there. But I don't want to start driving unless I know for sure you guys will be home. I

don't have a house key. Sorry to be leaving such a crazy message. Call me when you hear this. Love you.”

*

Two hours later, Jack was driving a rental car through the DC traffic toward Falls Church, Virginia. In rush hour. It was bumper to bumper but flowing well. Most doctors' offices stayed open at least until 5:00pm. That was twenty minutes from now. He was cutting things razor close.

The flight here and the drive had given him time to think. He had studied Thornton's files on the plane. There had to be something there, some clue to build on. What was Thornton's involvement? Why had he done this? He found no references to money or any other benefits mentioned. Nothing that spoke to motive. But something had to explain Thornton's aberrant behavior.

Then there was the matter of the records Thornton kept. So scattershot and vague. Like a man guessing, postulating ideas. Jack decided Thornton was being kept in the dark. Maybe he was being blackmailed into this. Jack wanted to believe that. It would take some of the sting out of Thornton's betrayal. Still, any way you looked at it, it was clear Thornton didn't care whether Jack lived or died.

That thought made him angry.

Thornton's job must be to provide the lab rats, Jack decided. For some reason, he and the other three students were selected for testing. He shifted his thoughts to the dreams themselves. The fear that he was losing his mind was gone, the gripping fear that these dreams were uncontrollable anomalies that might spring up at any time. It wasn't about how often he studied or how intensely.

Reading before bed had nothing to do with it. He could return safely to these pastimes whenever he chose.

He began to dwell on the marvel of a drug that could take someone back in time, cause them to experience events as an eyewitness. This was breakthrough technology. Dr. Jameison was a genius. A corrupt sociopath but still a genius.

The GPS lady's voice brought him back to the present. The turnoff to Jameison's clinic was just up ahead. What would Jack say when he saw him? What *could* he say? "*Hello Dr. Jameison, I'm Jack Turner, one of the guys you've been drugging. I'd like to ask you to come back with me and turn yourself in.*"

He was five minutes away from a meeting with a mad scientist, and he still didn't have a clue about what to do or say.

He'd better think of something very soon.

*

Nigel Avery had stopped by the Whispering Hills complex to fetch the copies in Thornton's bill drawer. He had taken the indirect route: through the woods and over the stone wall. Only this time he had a key. Once inside, it didn't take long to find the set of documents and, best of all, no maid to deal with.

How about that? They were right where Thornton said they'd be. He grabbed them and headed for the door. For a moment, he thought about stopping to reclaim all the bugs he'd set up in Thornton's apartment, but changed his mind. It was Jameison's money. Besides, no one would ever find them and, if they did, they'd never connect them to anything real.

Once safely in the car, he picked up his phone to call the good doctor.

*

"Okay, Nigel, what's up?" Jameison looked at his watch. It was ten minutes till five. All his patients had left. The staff was already starting the lockup routine.

"It's a wrap, Kimosabe," Avery said.

"Is everything...taken care of?"

"I got the Professor's papers right here, and he is unable to make any new ones."

Jameison did not reply, but was deeply relieved.

"You want to see this stuff or should I make a campfire?"

"Have you read them?"

"Are you serious?"

"I don't think they matter now, but you better get them to me. You sure you have everything?"

"I am. I persuaded the Professor it was in his best interest to be forthright in this matter."

"Are you sure, Nigel? You know what's going to happen. Even with a suicide, people will be going through his things piece by piece—"

"Now do I ever try to tell you how to be a doctor?"

"Okay," Jameison said. "What are your plans now?"

"Figured I'd stick around a few days, see if they discover the Professor's body. Make sure everything goes the way it's supposed to."

"I agree with that."

"Now, you sure you only want the cleanup to go this far? I'm not sure that's"

"Yes. As long as the lid stays on, I want this thing to be over. I got what I needed out of it. Culpepper's a small town. Too many deaths in a short period of time—even explainable ones—might stir up trouble."

"Okay then. I'll be in touch."

*

Avery drove across town and out to the highway, pulling the van into one of the few motels within Culpepper city limits, the Woodbine Inn. This thing wasn't over yet. In a few days, somebody at the school would miss old Thornton, trace him to his little cabin there by the lake, walk in on the stink.

He had no doubt the subsequent investigation would follow the course he had set in place. But he didn't like walking away from a job with so many loose ends.

Weeds had a way of spreading.

48

JACK SAW THE sign for The Sleep Center. He pulled into the parking lot then sat nervously in the car staring at the front entrance. He went over a plan that had begun to form in the last five minutes. From reading Thornton's documents and considering the way Thornton had conducted these "tests," Jack figured Jameison wasn't that security conscious. Jack's plan hinged on that assumption. If he was wrong, he'd be spending the night in jail as a common thief.

That would be the best case scenario.

It was 4:55pm.

He walked toward the set of glass doors at the entrance. The air was crisp and colder than back in Culpepper. The late afternoon sun had already begun its descent toward the horizon. As he came within ten feet of the doorway, he scanned the doors and windows, looking for signs of a security system. To his amazement, there were none. Then again, this was an upscale area and, really, a medical facility, not some hi–tech government operation.

He stepped over a large rubber mat, opened the right side door, and walked inside as a mild electronic chime sounded. Behind a half wall, Jack saw an attractive, blonde receptionist seated in a small room. She looked up but didn't smile. She continued tapping on her keyboard.

He walked to the right corner of the room and looked down a long hallway. Various doorways branched off on either side. He sat, picked up a magazine and pretended to read as his eyes scanned the perimeter of the room for surveillance cameras. He got up and walked toward the receptionist. "Excuse me, Ma'am," Jack said, feigning a slight southern drawl.

The blonde looked up. "Can I help you?"

"I'd like to see the doctor," Jack said. "He in?"

The look on her face said, *are you out of your mind?* "Do you have an appointment?"

"No. I probably should have called," Jack said. "I'm in from out of town…a pest control conference at a hotel over in Fairfax. But I ain't getting a lick of sleep since I got here."

"I'm very sorry, sir, but we can't help you with that. The Sleep Center's about to close, and we don't take walk-ins. Dr. Jameison's a very busy man. I'm taking appointments now for five to six weeks out."

Jack had counted on that. He had decided not to confront Jameison directly. "I won't be here but a few more days."

"I'm very sorry," she said. "Have you tried any over-the-counter medications? Some of them are pretty strong. There's a pharmacy in the plaza just down the road at the first light. Maybe you can stop in and talk to the pharmacist."

Jack pretended to look discouraged. "Do those things really work? I hear you wake up pretty groggy."

"Why don't you stop by and talk to them? There's no way Dr. Jameison could see you today…I'm sorry."

"Well, I guess that'll have to be it. Thank you just the same."

Jack turned to walk away, then halted after a few steps and turned back to face her again. "I really hate to bother you."

She looked up.

"Could I…would you have a restroom?"

Jack got a feeling she was supposed to turn him down. "Third door on your right, down the hall." She quickly looked down, returning to her keyboard.

Jack walked down the hallway. He stopped at each door, searching for Jameison's office. He walked past the bathroom and finally found it two doors past, on the opposite side. He'd no sooner finished reading the name on the door, when it suddenly opened. He gasped, stepping back. It wasn't Jameison, not even a man, but a middle–aged nurse, dressed in white, carrying a small stack of folders.

"Can I help you, sir?"

"I'm sorry," Jack said. "Looking for the bathroom."

"It's not in here," she said smugly and pointed down the hall.

Jack followed her hand, feigning to notice the restroom sign that hung from the ceiling over the bathroom door. "There it is," he said. "Thank you, Ma'am." He walked in that direction, listening as her footsteps went the opposite way down the hall. He reached for the doorknob, pretending to go in, listening once more. When it seemed she was gone, he glanced over his shoulder. The hallway was empty again.

Walking faster, Jack searched for a closet and found one a few doors up from the bathroom on the same side of the hall. He quietly opened the door, stepped in and closed it. His hand scraped along the wall, searching for a switch. An overhead light revealed a small janitorial room, about the size of his kitchen.

He surveyed the scene for several moments, taking mental

snapshots of each item on the floor. He shut off the light and stepped carefully toward the back of the room. He squatted down behind a metal cabinet, hoping the cleaning duties at The Sleep Center were handled by someone other than the office staff and at some other time than closing.

Sitting there in the pitch black, he wondered what chance did this half–baked scheme have? This was a crazy idea. He shouldn't have come.

Rachel was right.

49

I T FELT LIKE an hour had gone by but it had only been twenty minutes. Jack was still sitting quietly, crouched in the black darkness of the janitor closet. It smelled of stale mops, dust rags, bathroom disinfectants and air fresheners. There hadn't been a noise for ten minutes. Before that, he'd heard a number of *good–nights* and *see–you–tomorrows*, mostly from female voices in the hall.

Jack decided it was time.

As he shuffled his feet forward in the darkness, he tried to remember where everything was on the crowded floor. He reached the door, pressed his ear against the cool metal. Not a sound.

Opening the door slowly, he was relieved to find a darkened hallway. From the reception area he could see nighttime had arrived. He headed back to Jameison's office to hunt for something, anything that could be used as evidence in Jameison's scheme. After looking both ways, he gently turned the brass knob.

As the door opened silently, the presence of lamplight inside startled him. He froze with the door half–opened, half–expecting to hear someone call. After a few moments, he stepped into the room. It was empty. A ceramic lamp glowed softly from an end table next to a leather couch. A thick mahogany desk and credenza were centered against the far wall, which was covered with floor–to–ceiling curtains. He gently closed the door. Where should he begin?

If he were Jameison, guarding a discovery of this magnitude, Jack would have kept it in a vault. Considering Thornton's lack of care with his files, and the absence of any security system in Jameison's office, he hoped he might find something right here.

There was a laptop on the credenza, plugged in with the lid closed. There were probably plenty of incriminating files on it, but Jack didn't know enough about Jameison to even begin guessing passwords.

He walked toward the desk. If Jack had only a minimal concern for security, a locked desk drawer would be just the thing. He sat in Jameison's high–back leather chair and realized how tired he was. He could feel his body beginning to deflate, so he sat up and pulled on the center drawer. It slid open easily. He heard the telltale sounds of keys jingling from the rear of the drawer. He reached in and found a ring with an assortment of keys.

He quietly started pulling drawers in both the desk and credenza, stopping each time he found one locked. He scoured through each drawer but found nothing useful. Frustrated, he leaned back on Jameison's chair. His eyes drifted to the doctor's laptop. He was sure he'd find something on it, but what should he do, steal it? Then what? He was no hacker.

Suddenly, his eyes focused on something sticking out the side of the laptop. He leaned forward. A jump drive.

He pulled it out and stood. This could be something. He couldn't read it here, but in the car he had an iPad in his briefbag, with a little USB adapter. He pocketed the drive, set the keys back in the center drawer then walked back toward the hallway. Turning around, he double–checked that he'd left everything the way he'd found it. Then he hurried down the hall, through the lobby and, after unlocking it, through the front door. As he crossed the sidewalk onto the parking lot, he half–expected an alarm to go off, but none did.

Still, he decided not to hang around. He'd check out this jump drive at a nearby restaurant.

*

Jack was too excited to eat. He ordered coffee and a donut. Opening his iPad, he plugged in the adapter and the jump drive. Once again, he was surprised that it wasn't password protected. In a few minutes, he was scanning the file folders.

Bingo.

He clicked on a folder labeled Thornton.

As he browsed through the files, he was shocked to find medical files about Ralph Riesner, Jared Markum and another student he didn't know. Continuing on, he came to a document that stopped him cold. It was the initial report Jameison had written after reviewing the medical records. Specifically, the frank admission to the possible connection between Jameison's drug and Riesner's death. Then a bulleted list of reasons why Jameison felt the drug was still safe enough to sell to the military.

This was the smoking gun. This was hard evidence.

He found a second document that looked like notes after a meeting with Thornton. It was about Markum's "suicide." Again, after a paragraph explaining things, a bulleted list detailing why the drug was not responsible.

Jack didn't need to read any further. He already had enough to prove what he and Rachel had told the police. He paid his bill and headed out to the car.

As he turned the car on, he still found it hard to see Professor Thornton in this new light. But these new documents offered undeniable proof. Thornton had teamed up with this doctor and had chosen Jack and the others to become their laboratory rats. Jack could no longer hold onto the illusion that Thornton was unaware they were responsible for Ralph's death. Thornton continued drugging him and Jared Markum after Ralph died. All this time Jack had thought so highly of Thornton, and all this time Thornton could care less about him.

How could Jack have so misjudged the man?

He picked up his phone and called the non–emergency number for the Culpepper PD. A woman answered. "Yes, this is Jack Turner calling. I was there to see Sergeant Boyd this morning. Is he in now?"

"I'm sorry. Sergeant Boyd has gone home for the day. Is there someone else you'd like to speak to?"

"Can you give me a number I can reach him? This is kind of an emergency."

"If you're having an emergency, sir, you should hang up and dial 911."

"Well, it's not that kind of an emergency."

"Officer Hank Jensen is still here. He works closely with Sergeant Boyd. I can let you speak to him."

"Thank you," Jack said before she put him on hold. "Can I talk with him?"

*

A few moments later. "Hank Jensen here, can I help you?"

"Hi. This is Jack Turner. I was in to see you a little before lunch with my friend Rachel, about Ralph Riesner's death."

"I remember you," Hank said.

"Do you remember what I told Sergeant Boyd?"

"You mean about the death not being natural causes? I was listening. You've gotta understand, we've been through a lot around here the last couple a weeks."

"Well," Jack said, "I realized after I left, I didn't give you guys too much to go on. But now that's changed."

"How do you mean?"

"I'm sitting here looking at documents that *prove* what I was saying. Beyond a shadow of doubt."

"Hold on, now," Hank said. "You're getting a little ahead of me. Tell me a little more of your story."

"I told Sgt. Boyd that I believed—no, that I *know*—that Riesner's death was *not* from natural causes, not exactly. Riesner, the young man who committed suicide on Saturday, me and one other student were being drugged by a history professor at Culpepper. His name is Thornton."

"Drugged? Okay, I remember now."

"Just hear me out," Jack said. "I don't mean drugged as in meth or heroin. This is an experimental drug. It affects people's dreams. It made our dreams seem like real life. I know that sounds absurd, but I was drugged three times. Ralph Riesner died the same night he was given his first dose. I know the coroner said he died of heart failure. But I'm telling you, the heart failure was caused by this experimental drug."

"A drug that makes dreams seem like real life?" Hank said. "I've never heard of anything like that."

"Nobody has. Some neurologist named Dr. Jameison invented

it. I'm not sure what the connection is yet, but for some reason he's been testing it covertly, using us as human guinea pigs."

"You've gotta know how ridiculous this sounds."

It did to Jack, too. "I know, but I'm looking at documents—not the ones I gave to Sgt. Boyd earlier. New documents—ones that prove everything I'm saying is true."

"How 'bout you bring what you got over right now?" Hank asked. "If you convince me—I'll call Sgt. Boyd at home. Otherwise…"

"I can't bring it over right now," Jack said. How could he explain he was near Washington DC, with documents he'd only gotten by stealing?

"When can you get here?"

"Not for three or four hours, at least."

"Three or four hours? I'll be off duty way before then. This'll just have to wait till the morning."

"You don't understand," Jack said. "These people are dangerous. There is still another student—I can give you his name—Thornton has been drugging. For all we know he could be giving him another dose right now."

50

HANK JENSEN WAS perplexed. The strength of this guy's appeal had convinced him something wrong *might* be going on. But Boyd would rain fire down on his head if he got involved in this again on nothing more than a phone call. Hank had worked so hard to get in Boyd's good graces.

"I'll tell you what," Hank said, "I'll come in first thing in the morning, say 8:00am. You be here with your evidence, and we'll see what gives. That's the best I can do for now."

"Okay," Jack said. "I'll be there. And this will not be a repeat of my first visit. What I have will blow you away. I think Sergeant Boyd would want to be there tomorrow. You guys may even need to get the FBI involved."

Hank rolled his eyes. This was almost too bizarre to take seriously. "I'll think about it," he said. "See you at 8:00."

"I'll be there," Jack said.

*

Jameison was about to order his favorite dish at Amoo's House of Kabob, a fine restaurant in McLean featuring the best of Persian cuisine, when an app on his smart phone chimed. Curious, he took it out and looked. Hmmm. It was a brand–new security app that tied to a hidden camera in his office.

He had been planning on investing in a comprehensive security system after he'd finished getting all the results from Thornton's tests. Before submitting his proposal to the military. A security salesman had come by a few weeks ago tempting him to try out their system. He'd even offered to install a single camera, free for thirty days, to show Jameison how easy it was to use. He could check on any of the installed cameras from his smart phone. The cameras didn't have to run all the time; they had built–in motion detectors.

Jameison clicked on the app and saw that it had been activated almost thirty minutes ago. The chime he had just heard must have gone off then, but he missed it. He was even more curious now, because the office was closed. He'd locked the front door himself.

Tapping on the app, he found his way to the button that played back a copy of a video taken inside his office. His eyes almost popped out of his head, as he watched a young man with long-ish hair walking in. The picture wasn't as clear as it could be, since Jameison had only left the desk lamp on, and the intruder hadn't turned on the lights.

The man sat in his chair and quickly found his keys in the back of the center drawer. A few moments later, he was rummaging through all the drawers in both the desk and credenza. What was he looking for? Jameison didn't keep any drugs in his office. No money or valuables, either.

After looking through the drawers, the man leaned back on Jameison's chair. His face became more visible in the light. He looked very familiar. Jameison could also tell by looking at his clothes: this was no drug addict.

Who was he?

The man now set his attention on Jameison's laptop. He should have never left it there. As the man reached for the laptop, Jameison realized who he was. It was Turner, one of Thornton's four guinea pigs. The oldest one. The guy who was teaching one of Thornton's classes. What was he doing here, in Jameison's office?

This wasn't good.

The next thing Jameison saw was even worse. Turner pulled his jump drive out of Jameison's laptop, looked at it then put it in his pocket. A few moments later, he hurried out the door. Jameison remembered...all his files for the project were on that jump drive.

He stood and hurried out of the restaurant. Once inside his car, he called Nigel Avery.

Avery picked up after the second ring. "What's up, Doc?"

"Avery listen. This is serious. I just watched a video of that guy Turner breaking into my office."

"You mean one of the guys the professor was drugging? That Turner?"

"Yes, that Turner. He must've figured everything out."

"He's there in DC?"

"That's what I'm telling you. But that's not the worst of it."

"How did he break into your office?"

"I have no idea, but will you listen to me? The point is, he did. And he stole a jump drive from my laptop. All my files on this project are on that jump drive."

"You've got to be kidding me," Avery said. "You put all your files about this dream thing on a jump drive? And you leave that jump drive in your laptop out in the open where anybody can see it? Or steal it?"

"It was a stupid thing to do, but we've never had a security issue before. I was looking into getting a better system. Look, I don't want to get into that now. We've got a big problem."

"Any of those files say anything about me?" Avery said. "About you and me?"

"No."

"Then *you've* got a big problem, Doc. Nothing I've done back here ties back to me. I don't work that sloppy."

"Avery, I will pay you twice what I've already paid you to take care of this. You've got to find this guy Turner and take care of this. I need to get that jump drive before he takes it to the police."

"If I'm taking care of him, I'm also gonna have to take care of that girl he's seeing, that pretty brunette. I told you they're in love. My guess is, he knows anything, he's talked about it with her."

"Then do it. Get rid of them both. And get me that jump drive back."

51

JACK DROVE HIS rental car back to the Reagan National
Airport lot, turned it in, and caught the first direct flight
back to Atlanta. He had told Rachel he'd meet her tomorrow in Charlotte, and join her as they explained everything to her
dad.

But now he had this meeting scheduled with the police first
thing in the morning. He tried calling Rachel but couldn't reach
her before getting on the plane. He left her this message:

*"Rachel, I'm guessing you're driving to your parents' house now.
I know you don't like to drive and talk on the phone, so you may not
hear this till you get there. I'll explain the details when I see you, but
I've got the proof we need from Jameison's office. I grabbed a jump
drive from his laptop. It's all there. Solid evidence that backs up everything we told the police. A little change in plans. They want me to meet
them first thing tomorrow morning, so I'm flying back to Atlanta, not
Charlotte. Call me when you can. Feel free to tell your dad anything
you want. We got the proof now. Well…bye."*

He'd almost wanted to say *I love you* there at the end. That's
really how he felt, but it was way too soon. He didn't want to do
anything to chase her away.

He laughed as soon as he thought this, considering all the craziness he had already subjected her to in their brief time together.

*

Nigel Avery's eyes locked hard onto the corridor leading to Rachel's apartment. She had to come home sometime, he thought. He hated having to wait around all this time with killing on his mind.

He'd thought it all through on the drive over from the motel, after his call from Jameison. Do the girl first. Even with a direct flight, Jack wouldn't land in Atlanta till 8:30pm, at the earliest. Then he had to drive here. So, he'd take care of Rachel. A simple burglary would do, an act of random violence not connectable to any of the other deaths in this case. About an hour ago, he had put on one of his everyday–man disguises and went shopping for a new weapon in the streets. He decided to drive to the nearest big town, to avoid any chance of someone remembering him.

Now, he waited.

He knew Rachel wasn't out on a date with her beloved Jack. Avery had learned Rachel's only job was working part–time at the school during the day. So, where was she?

*

"There," said Nigel Avery. "Finally."

He'd been sitting there for almost an hour–and–a–half.

Walking along the corridor of the apartment building, he saw a young woman turn down a breezeway toward her apartment. His eyes latched onto a yellow light shining just above and to the right of her doorway. The woman walked right under the light and stopped at the front door. Even though he was still some distance away, he knew what Rachel looked like. He'd taken photos of everyone involved in the case, some extras of her.

He scanned the surroundings, making sure no one would see him get out of the car. The coast was clear. He turned off the overhead lights then opened the car door. He closed it gently, without letting it latch. In and out, he reminded himself. No time for monkeying around. That's how he'd kept clean all these years.

In seconds, he was standing outside her front door. He had seen no one else along the way. He thought about just kicking it in, but why make all that noise so late at night? He picked the lock in under a minute.

As he opened the door, a shapely body, silhouetted by a light from the bedroom, stood in the hallway straight ahead. She stiffened at the sound of the door. She had no chance to turn around. Avery's shot was straight and sure—right through the head. She thumped against a linen closet door and sank to the floor.

He had decided to use a silencer, so the noise was slight. Still, it startled a cat lying on the dining room table. He turned as it ran past him and out the door. A hideous sight. Its face looked all chewed up. Avery hurried into the living room and kicked over a few small pieces of furniture. He yanked free a high-end DVD player lying on a rack full of electronics below a big screen TV, then headed out the door.

As he opened his van, he thought about how this would play out on the next day's news. Imagine someone ending the life of this beautiful young woman for a measly DVD player? He tossed it in the back seat. Tomorrow it would be in a convenience store dumpster, one town over. That was a refreshing thought. Just one more night in this two-bit town, and he was free.

Now it was time for the final task on this cleanup mission. He was about to head over to Jack's apartment, when he got an idea. There was a pretty good chance when Jack got back into town, he'd want to see Rachel. An even better chance that he'd drive over here, once he tried but couldn't get her to answer her phone.

Why chase the mouse? Why not just wait for the mouse to come to him?

52

JACK LANDED IN Atlanta and made it out to his car by 9:30. The wind had picked up. Jack wished he had brought a hat and gloves. He tried calling Rachel's phone again, but still got voicemail. She couldn't still be driving to her parents, so where was she? Maybe her car had broken down on the way. But if that happened, she should still be answering her phone.

He decided to call Rachel's parents. Maybe she was there and in all the excitement forgot to turn the volume back on. Unfortunately, he got their voicemails, too. Now he wouldn't know if she was all right, and he'd have to drive back to Culpepper not knowing.

The beep.

"General Cook, this is Jack Turner. I was hoping to talk with Rachel. I left her a voicemail message, but she's not answering her phone. If she's there, please tell her that I decided to fly back to Atlanta instead of Charlotte and that everything…worked out okay. I just thought I'd call and make sure she got in all right. I'll probably see you tomorrow. I've got an appointment first thing with the police, then I plan to head up your way. Good bye."

Jack turned his car on. Hopefully, Rachel was there and someone, either she or them would call him back soon.

*

Fifteen minutes later, General and Mrs. Cook stepped into the heated vestibule of their 18th century home. They were carrying the spoils of a long evening out spent eating dinner then shopping. After the coats, hats, and scarves were hung up to dry and the packages stacked temporarily on the sofa, and after the General had started a fire in the fireplace and his wife had set a tea kettle on the stove, he decided to check their phone messages.

He listened to them twice, three calls from Rachel and one from Jack. He took notes on the second pass. As he explained them to Anne, it became clear to him that something was definitely wrong. He could detect it in Rachel's voice. It didn't seem serious, more like puzzling. Twice she mentioned something about driving to their house to spend the night. And Jack's message clearly indicated he expected her to be there already, and that he planned to come up here tomorrow…after meeting with the police.

"I should have made her take that house key," Anna said. "She could have let herself in a few hours ago."

"Now don't get all worked up, Anne," the General said. "I'm sure it's nothing." Still, he picked up the phone to call her. "Blasted voicemail," he said. After the beep, "Hey Rachel, got your messages. Sorry we missed them. Your mom says we'll get you that key so it doesn't happen again. Looking at the clock, I'm guessing you're not driving all this way tonight. You know we'd be happy to see you anytime. You and Jack. Just let us know when you expect to arrive tomorrow. Jack left a message, said something about meeting with the police. Please call us back and let us know what's going on. Love you. Dad."

*

Jack finally arrived in Culpepper around 10:15pm and drove straight to his apartment. He drove by slowly, scanning for any signs of someone watching. His landlord's house was dark; that was normal at this hour. He looked down the end of the driveway and noticed his screened–in porch was also dark, no lights on in his apartment, either. Everything looked just the way he'd left it.

He drove down one entire block, then back again, just to be sure. Didn't see anyone sitting inside any parked cars along the road. He double–backed and pulled into his driveway, turned off his headlights to avoid waking his landlords.

He sat in the car a moment, resting his head on the steering wheel, physically and emotionally spent.

As he walked up the creaking steps, his mind was mercifully numb. Only his uncertainty about Rachel's safety kept him from collapsing on his bed once inside. He took off his jacket and draped it over a kitchen chair, then walked into the bathroom to splash some water on his face.

He came back out and decided to try Rachel again. Walking into the living room, he sat on the sofa. That's when he noticed he had a voicemail message. He didn't even hear the phone ring.

"Rachel!" he said. It had to be her.

"Jack? It's Rachel. Just calling to let you know there's been a slight change in plans..."

Jack's heart began to pound.

"...I know you wanted me to go straight to my parents, but I've been calling them for three hours now and there's been no answer. I

don't have a key to their house, and I didn't want to drive all that way if they're not going to be home. I've got a few errands to run, and I'll keep trying to reach Mom and Dad while I'm out. If I don't get them, I may go over to the library, or maybe a coffee shop. Eventually, though, I'll have to go home. Can't wait to hear how your trip went. Hope everything's okay. Can't wait to see you. Bye."

Quickly, Jack redialed the Cooks in Charlotte.

"Hello?" It was General Cook.

Jack swallowed hard. "Hello, General?"

"Jack?"

"Hi, sir. Yes, it's Jack. I'm sorry to be calling so late, but—"

"Jack? Is anything wrong? Is Rachel all right?"

Is Rachel all right? Then, that means... "General, have you heard from Rachel tonight?" Jack's insides were turning.

"We've listened to a few phone messages from her, but we've been out all evening. Jack, what's going on?"

What could he say? Rachel wasn't with them, the library closes at 9pm. Where was she? Had she gone back to her apartment?"

"Jack?"

"I'm sorry, sir. I've got to go."

"Now you hold on just a minute, soldier. You're not going anywhere until you tell me what this is all about."

"General, Rachel may be in danger. This is going to sound crazy, but Rachel and I have uncovered proof that these dreams I've been having—the ones I came up there to see that sleep doctor for—are because...I'm being drugged. Me and three college students. A professor here was treating us like guinea pigs, testing some new experimental drug."

"What?"

"I know, it sounds crazy. The thing is, in the last two weeks two of the students being tested have died, directly because of this drug."

"Died?"

"Yes, sir. I'm bringing all the evidence I gathered to the police tomorrow. After meeting with them, we'll probably drive up there to be with you. I'll explain everything then."

"You said Rachel may be in danger?"

"She might be. I don't know for certain. But really, I've got to go. She's not answering her phone. I'm going to drive over and check on her at her apartment. I'll call you as soon as I locate her." Jack hung up.

As he did, he noticed his cell phone battery icon was in the red. It was going to die any minute.

He hurried out of the house and down the steps. "Oh God, oh God," he kept repeating. "Please let her be there and be okay." He raced his car in reverse out the driveway, and fishtailed onto Rambling Road.

53

JACK PULLED INTO Rachel's parking lot. On the way there, he had tried to suppress any dark thoughts, but it wasn't easy. She wasn't at her parents and she hadn't left any other voicemails after that first one…which was hours ago. He really couldn't picture someone like Thornton coming after her. She was probably fine, but he'd feel so much better if they could connect.

Jack looked but didn't see her car parked in either of the two spaces provided. Two other cars were parked in her spots; maybe that forced her to park somewhere else.

He pulled into the first open guest space, shut off his car, and hurried toward her apartment. As he neared her door, there was Tuffguy, who arched his back and rubbed up against Jack's pants. Rachel had said she never let him out anymore, afraid he'd get beaten up again or run over. Jack thought about picking him up but wasn't sure how well that would go. It did make him wonder if Rachel was home. He couldn't imagine she knew he was out roaming the sidewalks.

That sense of tension turned into dread when Jack reached for the doorbell. Her front door was clearly unlocked, standing open several inches.

"Rachel," he yelled, as he pushed it open further. Standing there in the threshold, his eyes immediately latched onto the motionless body lying face down in the hallway. "Oh, Rachel no." With the light from the dining area, Jack saw a splatter of blood on the hallway wall. He looked down at Rachel. It had to be her. She wore the same sweater she had worn that afternoon. Tears welled up in his eyes.

He took one step toward her body when, suddenly, a bullet pounded into the trim around the front door, inches from his ear. Jack dropped to the floor then looked up at the bullet hole. Was it Thornton? Who else could it be? He had killed Rachel and now he was lying in wait, lurking somewhere outside, trying to kill him.

This was crazy. Had Thornton gone mad?

Jack wanted to go to Rachel. He couldn't just leave her there. Then another bullet smacked into the side of the building just fractions above his head. Jack had to go. He ran in the opposite direction from where the shots rang out. A third bullet slammed into the wall a half–step behind him. He turned the corner and ran through a breezeway, then down the far side of the apartment building, heading for an area covered in shadows.

*

Avery couldn't believe it. He had Jack in his sights. How could he have missed him three times? He didn't have long before the police showed up. He had already taken his silencer off when Jack showed up. People might talk themselves out of calling for one gunshot, but not three.

He quickly put the silencer back on and turned on the car.

He drove around to the other side of the building in search of his quarry. He had maybe five minutes before the cops arrived.

*

Jack hid behind a rusty dumpster at the far end of the complex. He heard a car start up, saw headlights come around the side of the building. The car was creeping toward him, less than fifty yards away. Now he wasn't so sure it was Thornton. It was definitely not Thornton's car. Whoever it was, he was shining a flashlight on the corridors and in between the parked cars. Jack was sure he'd shine it around the dumpster in a matter of seconds.

He lifted the lid and quietly slipped into the dumpster. His gag reflexes activated as he lay down among heaps of rotting trash bags. It must have been days since the garbage had been removed. He lay still, tried not to breathe. He could hear the car; it was closer now, maybe twenty yards away. His mind flashed to the sight of Rachel, lying dead in the hallway, her blood smeared against the wall. It hadn't sunken in yet that she was gone. Anger began to replace his panic, mixed with fear. He wished he had a gun, even a knife would do. He would go after the guy in this car and tear him apart, or else die trying.

Jack saw the light, probably from the flashlight, dancing above the lid of the dumpster. Thin streams of light from the car's head-lights beamed through tiny rust holes. It was all Jack could do to keep from throwing up. It sounded like the car stopped. He listened for a car door opening. If it did, he was sure his time had come. He imagined timing a swift uppercut to the man's face as he opened the dumpster lid. It might buy Jack enough time to run and avoid getting shot.

He waited.

The car continued past, taking the lights with it, leaving Jack in black darkness. After several moments, the darkness was matched by silence. The car was gone. Or, at least, had moved on to another part of the complex.

Slowly, Jack raised his eyes above the rim of the dumpster. The coast was clear. He quickly jumped out, brushing chunks of garbage off his sleeves. He ran toward his car, staying in the shadows. As he got in, he looked around carefully for any sign of the car.

He thought about going back to Rachel's apartment but changed his mind. What good would it do for him to be caught there by the police when they arrived? They might try to blame her death on him. Right now, it appeared no one had seen him. Whoever had killed Rachel was still nearby. Jack didn't know what he looked like, but he knew the car. The killer had to be caught. Jack decided to drive around the area, see if he could spot the car. Maybe take down the license number.

Then he would go to the police.

As he drove away with his headlights off, he could hear the faint sound of police sirens. He thought about Rachel. Tears filled his eyes. He couldn't believe she was gone. They were just getting started, but he had actually begun to imagine she could be...*the one*. He banged his fist on the dashboard.

The police would be arriving any moment. They'd discover her body lying there in the hall. After the CSI's did their thing at the scene, they'd take her away in a body bag. The image brought a wave of nausea. He yanked the steering wheel, forcing the car to the side of the road. He opened the door and threw up. Grabbing a towel he found in the back seat, he wiped himself off then tossed it on the floor.

He drove all around Rachel's complex then through the streets of the surrounding neighborhoods. There was no sign of the car. He wondered who this man was. Was he Thornton's accomplice? Did he work for Thornton or this Dr. Jameison? He still had the hardest time believing the professor would be mixed up in something like this. It was so opposite from the nature of the man he'd known for all those years. There had to be a compelling reason, like the blackmail option. That was the only thing that made any sense.

Jameison was obviously the blackmailer. Ultimately, he was the man behind this entire scheme. Likely, Jack thought, the one who had hired this killer to take both him and Rachel out. If Jack could only find him, there was a good chance he still had the murder weapon in his car.

After driving around the area for another fifteen minutes with no luck, the smell inside the car became overwhelming, leftover smells from his time in the dumpster. Jack decided he needed to get to a bathroom and get cleaned up. But he couldn't go back to his place. If this man knew where Rachel lived, he certainly knew were Jack was staying.

Jack remembered a motel out by the highway. He had thought about staying there before Thornton secured his old apartment.

54

ABOUT TWENTY MINUTES later, Sergeant Joe Boyd stood in the open doorway, surveying the grisly scene. A young coed lay dead in the hallway from a single gunshot wound to the head. No sign of forced entry. No obvious sign of rape. Evidence of a struggle. Could be a simple burglary.

Could be.

"What happened to my nice little town?" Boyd said. "This is getting as bad as Pittsburgh."

He barely had time to take in the scene when Dobbs yelled to him from his patrol car outside. "Sergeant Boyd, it's Hank. He says he needs to talk to you. He says it's urgent."

Boyd walked toward Dobbs, past another officer already dusting the front door for prints. "What you got, Hank?" Boyd asked.

"You're not gonna believe this, Joe. But we got another one."

"Another what?" Boyd said.

"Another corpse."

"What is going on around here?" Boyd shouted. "Four dead students in two weeks."

"This one's not a student," Hank said. "Looks like another suicide. Though I'm not sure about anything now."

"A suicide. Where are you, Hank?"

"You're not going to believe who I'm looking at here."

"Hank..." Boyd was in no mood for guessing games.

"I'm out here at Lake Sampson."

"Lake Sampson," Boyd said. "That even our turf?"

"Afraid so. I've got a dead *professor* here, Joe. His ID says he teaches history at Culpepper. His name's Thornton."

Boyd did not respond. His mind involuntarily started organizing the puzzle pieces.

"Don't you get it—a professor?"

"Yeah, I do. Go on."

"Got a single gunshot wound to the heart—this place is a bloody mess. The gun's here, I got a note here. No sign of forced entry."

"You read the note?"

"Yeah, it says—get this—that he's been hiding a secret gay lifestyle, and implies he was involved with that student who committed suicide a few days ago. You know...the jumper?"

"For crying out loud," Boyd said. "What kind of place is this?"

"Joe, I've lived here most of my life. I've never seen anything like this before—ever."

"All right. What makes you think this professor might *not* be a suicide?"

"It's this note...a fourth-grader could spell better. I can't imagine a history professor writing something like this. And... didn't we learn the kid who jumped had a girlfriend who dumped him? I don't know. This all seems way too fishy."

"Well, bag the note, and we'll check it out later. You alone?"

"Just me and the neighbor who called. He's pretty shaken up."

"All right, seal it off as a crime scene, then get on the horn and wake everybody up. I want every man, every car, up and about. Get two guys patrolling around this apartment complex. Tell 'em to get the names of anyone that looks out of place. Get someone out there to babysit our dead professor till the coroner arrives—and tell whoever you get it'll be a while 'cause I've got the coroner coming here first—and then you meet me at the station in thirty minutes. I'm gonna get to the bottom of all this."

"You think this guy Turner's got something to do with this? That guy we talked to this morning? I got a phone call from him earlier tonight. He was all worked up, saying something about finding new evidence. Solid proof. Didn't he say something about his thing involving a history professor?"

"I think you're right. I hate to say it, but something bigger may be going on here. There's been way too much activity. Something's gotta be agitating it. I want to at least check into his story again. I'll read over those papers he gave me. You send someone by his place and pick him up. Do we know where he lives?"

"I can find out."

"All right, send someone by to pick him up. Tell them not to arrest him, just bring him in for questioning." Boyd thought a moment. "Forget that, Hank. *You* go get Turner yourself. I don't want any screw–ups."

"What about the professor? You wanted me to wait here till the M.E. shows up."

"Turner's more important."

"Alright," Hank said. "How about I see you at the station in forty–five?"

"Right. Forty–five…or sooner. And Hank?"

"Yeah?"

"You keep talking to me if anything changes."

"Right."

Boyd walked back to the apartment to find Dobbs marking off the area with yellow tape. Maybe there was hope.

55

JACK ARRIVED AT the Woodbine Inn in about twenty minutes. An Indian man stood behind the front desk. Jack wondered what he must have thought about Jack coming in like this: late at night, smelling like garbage, his eyes all puffy. The man didn't seem to mind. The handful of cars in the parking lot was probably why. He gave Jack a key to room number ten.

Jack jiggled his motel key several times, and was just about to walk back to the front desk for a new one, when the lock gave way. He threw his briefbag on the far bed and turned to lock the door. No dead bolt, just a little pull chain dangling across the doorway. He drew the curtains together but gave up trying to close the gap after several frustrating tries.

As he walked to the sink, he took off his putrid clothes, letting them fall wherever they fell. He flicked on the light switch in the bathroom. An annoying fan rumbled in the ceiling. As the shower heated up, the fan sounded like it was about to explode, so he flicked off the switch and took a shower in the dark. He stood under the hot water for several minutes, too tired to move. A memory of Rachel's lifeless body jolted him out of his stupor.

He fought back another wave of tears as he scrubbed off the

stench and shampooed his hair. He stood there a long while, then turned the water off, dried off and wandered out of the bathroom. After shuffling toward the nearest bed, he plopped down, his hair still mostly wet. He rolled over onto his face and quickly fell asleep from sheer exhaustion.

*

Forty–five minutes later, Jack awakened to the sound of a car screeching into the motel parking lot. It rumbled right up to one of the parking places near his room. The headlights shined through the crack in his curtains like a laser. He lay still on his bed and listened as the engine shut off, the car door opened and closed. Was it the police?

But there were no sirens, no flashing lights.

Deciding it was just someone coming in late, he rolled over. Soon he heard a nearby motel door open and close. As he lay there, a vague anxiety began to take hold. Soon, the anxiety formed into words: *Where would the guy who killed Rachel be sleeping tonight? This was one of the one of only a handful of motels in Culpepper.*

He sat up, wide awake, then tiptoed across the rug and peered through the cracks between his curtains.

It was *the car*.

The same car Jack had seen from inside the dumpster. Parked right next to his. Did the guy know what kind of car Jack drove? He had to. But Jack had heard him go into the room. Maybe he'd walked right by it. For a moment, Jack thought about calling the police, but that idea was quickly extinguished by a more primal desire to get out of there, as quickly as possible.

Jack got dressed, tossed his smelly clothes in the garbage can. Quietly, he walked across the carpet to the front door, slowly slid the chain out of its groove. He turned the knob and opened the door, praying it wouldn't creak. Closed it over but wouldn't let it latch.

As he stood outside in the corridor, he guessed which room the man was staying in. There was only one other room with a light on. The curtains were closed. Jack walked to his car. He wondered how he could open and close the door without making a sound. He got in as quietly as possible, wincing as the door clicked shut.

As he turned on the ignition he looked up and saw the curtains in the man's room spreading apart. Jack immediately turned on his headlights, hoping to blind the man temporarily so he couldn't see who was driving. He backed out slowly to avoid suspicion and drove toward the main road, back into town.

It didn't work.

Through his rear view mirror he saw a man run out of the room, stop and stare in Jack's direction. As Jack rounded a curve, the man ran back into his room, probably for his keys.

And his gun, Jack thought.

He floored it.

Where should he go? To the police? Maybe it was time. He would at least be safe from this killer, for now anyway. But then another thought. Professor Thornton hadn't killed Rachel. This other guy had. And he probably worked for Jameison. Thornton might have no idea that Rachel was dead. If Jack could find him, tell him about Rachel, maybe he would come clean.

Then Jack remembered, that's what Rachel had suggested from the start, find Thornton. If Jack had followed her plan, she might still be alive. But if he didn't think he could find him during the day, what chance did he have of finding him at night?

Then an image formed in his mind. A Rolodex, sitting on the

corner of Thornton's desk, in his office at the school. Why hadn't he thought of that before? Thornton had probably written something about his cabin on one of those cards. The school was obviously closed, but Jack had keys. Thornton had given him a set for the front door of the Murray Building and his office, in case Jack ever wanted to work there when Thornton was away.

Jack turned left at the next intersection and headed for the university.

*

Avery saw Turner's car lights ahead, turning left at an intersection. He was only a block or two behind. And gaining.

That's what being too tired gets you. He had pulled right into the motel parking lot, right next to Turner's car and didn't see it. He vowed not to miss his chance again.

Just then, his phone rang. He fumbled through the pile of fast food bags on his front seat and answered on the fourth ring.

"Avery?"

"Doc, what a surprise."

"You were going to call me with an update."

"When I was finished with the task. Not quite there yet. Actually, I'm in hot pursuit of the last target. So, can we talk about thirty minutes from now? I'm driving about eighty here on some dark, country roads."

"Just give me a quick update. Where are things at?"

"The professor committed suicide this afternoon. You know about that. The young lady, the girlfriend of that Turner guy, walked in on a burglary. Sadly, she didn't make it." Avery heard Jameison sigh on the other end.

"Have you gotten the jump drive yet?"

"That's what I'm after right now, and to take out the guy who took it."

"You gotta get that jump drive, Avery."

"Don't lecture me, Doc. I know what I'm doing." Avery looked down the road. Turner was turning at another intersection, left this time. Avery guessed by the direction Jack was heading for the University campus. "Look Doc, I've really gotta go." He hung up before Jameison could reply.

56

JACK PULLED UP to the Murray Building and, for the first time, got a front row parking spot. Not hard at 1:00am. He got out and looked back toward the main entrance. No sign of the killer's car. No sign of anyone. The temperature was just above frigid, but most of the snow had melted off that afternoon, gathering in little clumps around the trees and light poles. He walked toward the front doors.

*

Avery had pulled his car off the road a half–block back from the main entrance. The streets around the campus were deserted. At the moment, he was eyeing Jack through a clump of hemlock trees. He recognized the building Jack walked toward as the same building where Thornton's office was.

*

Jack walked up the steps and pulled out his keys. Took him a few tries to figure out which one unlocked the front door. He pulled it open, stepped inside, and turned to lock it behind him.

*

Avery was lying on a small hill, still hidden in the trees, looking through his night–vision binoculars. If Turner locked that door, it would make getting inside extremely difficult. And noisy. Avery wished he'd brought along a rifle instead of his Beretta. An infrared scope would come in handy right about now. He put his binoculars down and steadied the pistol under his other arm. Jack's body was plainly visible through the glass.

*

The glass door shattered. It felt like someone had hit Jack in the shoulder with a hammer. He fell to the ground. He looked up to see the cracked glass spreading out like a spider web, a bullet hole in the center. It took him a moment to realize he'd been shot.

The killer's here. Jack reached for his wound and felt warm fluid oozing through his fingers. He had never felt so much pain. He had to get up. Now. He rolled over on his uninjured side and lifted himself off the floor.

*

Avery swore as he lunged through the trees, sprinting for the door. He couldn't let Jack get away. He knew his aim was perfect— straight for the heart. The bullet must have veered slightly when it hit the thick glass. He should have compensated.

*

Joe Boyd sat at his desk, reading over the copies that guy Turner had given them earlier in the day. Beside him, a notepad. He was trying to get his hands around the situation. Thought the best way to do that might be to pretend the outlandish story Turner had told them might actually be true. Through that lens, the dots were starting to connect.

He was startled by the phone ringing. It was Hank. He picked it up. "You on your way here?"

"I was," Hank said, "but I just heard over the radio a report about a gunshot at Culpepper. Someone said they heard a loud noise like a gunshot, then breaking glass."

"You've got to be kidding me. Did the caller say which building?"

"The Murray Building," Hank said. "The thing is, Joe. I was looking into this thing a little this afternoon. That's the same building the professor works at. You know, the suicide in the cabin out by the lake."

"This has all got to be connected," Boyd said. "I can get there in ten. Meet me there, quick as you can."

*

Jack ran down the dark hallway, holding his arm close. He tried several office doors, but all were locked. Should he still try to make Thornton's office? *Could* he make it up three flights of steps? The elevator was on the far side of the building. The shooter would be on him in moments.

He made it to the edge of the stairway and heard the glass door open, then the sound of cracked glass underfoot. He looked in time to see the man raise his pistol in Jack's direction. Jack lunged for the steps as a shot rang out. A bullet soared past where he had stood a second ago. He scrambled up the stairs ignoring the pain in his wounded arm. He could hear the man's footsteps down the hall.

When he got to the second floor, Jack saw a janitorial closet across the hall. He couldn't outrun this guy down another long hallway. He made a run for the closet, relieved to find it open.

Once inside, he heard footsteps rapidly climbing the stairway.

He didn't move or breathe. Heavy steps stopped on the second floor. Jack could almost feel the man's presence, barely a few feet away. His shoulder began to throb. He applied hand pressure to the wound, then thought about the blood. Surely, a blood trail led across the hallway to this closet. He imagined the killer noticing the blood, smiling, then firing several shots through the door.

To Jack's relief, a few moments later he heard footsteps run up the stairs toward the third floor. It wouldn't be long before the shooter came back down again. Next time, he might notice the blood. Jack took a chance and flipped on the light switch. He grabbed a white towel then quickly shut the light off again. Letting his jacket drop to the floor, he wrapped the towel tightly around his shoulder, trying to slow down the flow of blood.

Taking his shoes off to deaden his footsteps, he slowly opened the door. The hall was empty. He ran toward the opposite end, trying to make the elevator. He remembered the History Department's faculty lounge was on the fifth floor. He had a key for that room also. And there was a phone there. The shooter probably expected Jack to head to Thornton's room. He hoped this guy didn't know about the lounge.

As he turned the corner along a short section of hallway, he heard footsteps running back down the stairs. The shooter must have realized his mistake. Jack began to feel dizzy and lightheaded. He turned left again around the next corner, now facing the long hallway on the other side of the building. The elevator was only thirty or forty steps away.

Did he have time? The footsteps grew louder.

"Give it up, Jack," a man's voice yelled softly. "Stop running and maybe we can talk."

Jack ignored him and kept running, but he was running out of steam. He mashed the elevator button. It lit up. He mashed it again and again. "C'mon, c'mon!" he muttered. The doors finally opened. He dropped down and dove in. A bullet pinged just over his head. As the doors closed, he heard the man swear.

Jack was breathing so hard he thought he might pass out. He lifted himself off the elevator floor and pushed button number five, trying to calm down as the elevator began to rise. He couldn't remember: did this elevator tell people in the hall what floor the elevator was on?

Finally, the doors pulled back. The faculty lounge was down the hall on the right side, not more than fifty feet from where he stood. He stepped out into the hall, listening for any sounds.

"Oh, Ja–ack," came a sinister, sing–songy voice.

Jack looked up. At the far end of the hall, in the direction of the lounge, the silhouette of a man standing dead–center in the hall, his gun raised. This is it, thought Jack. He closed his eyes, and tried to turn his thoughts toward God.

A shot rang out. Jack winced, waiting for the blow.

But nothing happened. He heard a noise, a thump. He looked up to see the man's body lying at the other end of the hall.

What the...?

57

FROM AROUND THE corner, Joe Boyd tried to focus in the darkness on the body he had just shot. He approached the man cautiously, gun aimed directly at his head. He was lying on his back, his legs bent in an odd fashion. Boyd stood over him. The man's eyes opened slowly. A trickle of blood made its way down the side of his mouth.

It took a moment, but the man finally focused on Boyd's face. "You must be Sgt. Joe Boyd. I get that right?" He coughed.

Boyd nodded, evaluating the wound. It was mortal.

"Pleased to meet you. The name's Nigel Avery. At least the name I've been using lately." He coughed again. "Should have worn that vest. Thing is, it chafes under my arms." He was smiling.

"Wouldn't have mattered," Boyd said. "If you had a vest on, I'd have just shot you in the head. Can't have a man shooting up my town, now can I?"

"I suppose not." It was clearly hard for him to breathe.

"Mr. Turner," Boyd yelled down the hall. "Is that you?"

"Yes," came the reply. "I'm shot."

"Paramedics are on the way. You're safe now. I see a bench about halfway down the hall. Can you make it there?"

"I think so. It's my shoulder."

"My partner will be here in a minute," Boyd said. "One of us will be there to help you."

"Paramedics coming?" Avery said.

"Yeah, but we both know you won't be here by the time they arrive."

Avery smiled weakly. "Your bedside manner sucks."

Boyd couldn't help but smile at that.

"So where you think I'm headed?" Avery said. He seemed to think a moment, then said: "Wherever it is, I figure it can't be good."

Boyd couldn't tell if he was being serious. "I don't know if it'll help your chances any, but maybe you should use this time wisely. You shot that girl over at that apartment tonight, right?"

"You want me to do your job for you, Sergeant?"

"I'm supposed to be in bed right now, Mister..."

"Avery. Least you could do is remember my name."

"Did you do it? Are you my shooter?"

Avery nodded. "You find out about the professor yet?"

Boyd nodded. "That you, too?"

Avery said, "Let's just say, you might want to look a little further into that suicide."

Boyd heard footsteps coming up the stairway, heard Hank call out his name. "Up here, Hank. I'm okay. Got one man down, and another one shot down the hall. That one's Jack Turner. The paramedics here yet?"

"Just pulled up. They're not sure where to go, or if the scene's secure."

"Send them up. There's an elevator down the hall."

"Right." Hank came up the rest of the way, took a look at the body near Boyd's feet, then down the hall. "Mr. Turner?"

"I'm right here."

Hank went to him.

Boyd looked back at Avery. His eyes were now closed. Boyd bent down to check his pulse. When he did, Avery's eyes opened. "So what's all this about anyway? Why are you doing all this? Who are you working for?"

"Don't think I got time for all that," Avery said. "Ask that guy Jack. I think he's figured it all out. That's why we're here in this hallway so late at night. That's why you had to get out of bed." He smiled. "Guess this time, the good guys win."

Those were his last words. Avery's eyes became empty, staring up at nothing. Boyd closed them over, checked his pulse anyway.

He stood then joined Hank, who was helping Jack Turner to his feet.

58

"IS HE DEAD?" Jack asked Sgt. Boyd, as he and the other officer named Hank helped him to the gurney, where the paramedics took over.

"He is now," Boyd said. After they strapped Jack in, he extended his hand. "Hey, I'm sorry we didn't listen to you today. Your story just sounded too weird."

Jack shook Boyd's hand, but grimaced as another round of pain shot through his arm.

"Think we're ready to hear your story now," Boyd said. "Soon as the dust settles."

"I'll tell you everything I know. In the meantime, you might want to look at this." He held out the jump drive. Boyd took it from him. "Everything's on that, proof of this whole scheme. Click on the folder with Professor Thornton's name."

"He's dead too."

"Thornton...is dead?"

Boyd nodded. The paramedics were ready to load Jack into the elevator. "Hank, why don't you stay here, start securing the crime scene? I'll go down with Mr. Turner."

"Sure, Joe."

The elevator doors closed.

"That guy up there, the one who shot you…he 'fessed up to it. Tried to make it look like the professor committed suicide. I haven't heard all his reasons why yet, but Hank wasn't buying it."

Jack sighed. "Did he confess to killing Rachel, too?"

"Rachel?"

"The girl who was killed at the apartment complex. Rachel Cook. She was the one with me today. She and I were…well, we were starting to date." Jack sighed. The look on Boyd's face confused him. He seemed to be almost smiling.

The elevator opened to the first floor. Boyd stepped out into the hall, followed by the paramedics, pushing and pulling Jack's gurney. Boyd continued down the hall toward the main entrance. Jack heard their feet and then the gurney wheels rolling over the glass.

When they got to the doors, Boyd stopped and looked at Jack. "There's somebody out here who wants to see you." They made it through the doorway into the cold night air. The parking lot was lit up with flashing lights, bouncing off the buildings and trees. The paramedics followed Boyd, who seemed to be walking toward the open backdoors of an ambulance. When they got there, he kept walking, around the ambulance on the right side.

Jack saw a police squad car. Boyd opened the back door. A young woman emerged wearing a light coat.

"Jack?" she shouted as she ran toward him.

Jack could hardly believe it. Tears filled his eyes. Then he began to laugh at the same time. "Rachel?"

"Jack, you're all right! They said you got shot." She threw her arms around him. He hugged her tightly. Then they kissed, over and over.

"Rachel, I thought you were dead. I saw you lying there in your apartment hallway."

"Oh, Jack. It was Mary," Rachel said, standing up, releasing a different kind of tears. "My roommate. She came back late this afternoon to get all her things. I can't believe she's dead."

"But, I saw the sweater, the same one you were wearing when I left you."

"It was Mary's. I was just borrowing it. I gave it back. She must have decided to wear it home."

"And your parents said they hadn't heard from you. Where did you go?"

"When I couldn't get hold of them, I decided to hang out at the library. I knew you didn't want me to stay at my apartment. I would have warned Mary, but she told me she was leaving before six. I don't know why she was still there so much later. After the library closed, I went over to Starbucks, but I forgot and left my phone volume off."

Jack held her face in his hands. "I'm really sorry about Mary, Rachel. I know you two were good friends. But I thought...I thought I lost you. I can't believe you're all right." He hugged her again with his good arm.

"One of the paramedics spoke up. "We really need to get him to the hospital."

"I know. I'll get my parents to take me."

"Your parents are coming?"

"They're almost here. They called about ten minutes ago." She leaned over and they kissed once more. The paramedics loaded Jack into the back of the ambulance.

*

Boyd watched this scene unfold. He was glad somebody had something nice going for them through all this.

Hank came up behind him. "So, what do you think, Joe? Crazy, isn't it?"

Boyd looked at the ambulance driving away, then at all the emergency vehicles in the parking lot, then at the entrance to the Murray Building. He shook his head and said, "I'll tell you what I think. I think I should have stayed in Pittsburgh."

59

Two Months Later

JACK AND RACHEL got out of Jack's BMW and walked toward the Culpepper police station. Sgt. Boyd had agreed to meet with them for an informal, confidential briefing on the case. Jack knew it would be a fairly complicated, multilayered investigation, especially when he learned the FBI had gotten involved.

Jack was still living in Culpepper and would be for at least several more months. In the aftermath of Professor Thornton's sudden death, and the resulting scandal that followed, the History Department at Culpepper was scrambling to put the fires out. Jack offered to finish out his lecture series in Thornton's classes, as agreed, and even to finish teaching the rest of Thornton's classes for the semester. The school instantly accepted.

Jack's agent didn't like the idea. She was afraid Jack would fall behind on his writing deadlines. Jack didn't care. He said yes for one reason only: to get to spend more time with Rachel. They walked hand–in–hand through the police station's front doors. Jack's arm and shoulder were still very tender from the gunshot wound, but they were healing nicely.

Officer Hank Jensen met them in the lobby. "Hey guys, Sgt. Boyd's on the phone but he should be off shortly. I'm supposed to take you into an interview room where you guys can chat." He started walking down a hallway, and they followed. After a few more turns to the right, he pointed toward an open doorway on the left. "Can I get you a cup of coffee or bottled water?"

"Water for me," Jack said. He'd already had a perfectly brewed cup this morning. Why ruin the memory now?

"Me too," Rachel said.

"Be right back." Hank left the room.

Jack reached for Rachel's hand on the table. "How's the unpacking going?" Rachel had moved to another apartment. After Mary's death, she just couldn't stay there anymore.

"I've only got a few more boxes to go, then I'll be done. How about you? Are you nervous?"

"About this? Not really. Are you?"

"A little," she said, "I don't know why."

Sgt. Boyd had already told Jack that he wouldn't be facing any charges. Even for stealing Jameison's jump drive. Boyd was going to explain why today.

Jack stroked her hand with his thumb. "I've been kind of looking forward to this little talk. I still have so many questions about what happened."

Sgt. Boyd walked into the room carrying a large mug. Hank Jensen was right behind him with the waters. He set them down and left the room, closing the door on his way out.

Boyd greeted both of them, shook their hands and sat down. "How's your shoulder healing up?"

"Doing pretty good," Jack said. "Wakes me up sometimes when I roll over on it."

"I guess after what you've been through, if that's the only problem you're having in your sleep, you're coming out ahead."

Jack smiled.

"Well, I've got a lot to get to today, and I'm sure you two are plenty busy. So let's get right to it. Thought I'd start off mentioning none of this is being recorded. Everything that's said here is totally off the record. Is that okay with you?"

"Fine," Jack said. Rachel nodded.

"Let me tell you why right up front. I mentioned, Jack, when I called that you wouldn't be facing any charges for stealing Dr. Jameison's jump drive from his office. The reason is...Jameison is dead. When he saw all the evidence stacked up against him, he knew we had an open–and–shut case. So he put a gun to his head. That pretty much made all our problems go away. With him dead, Nigel Avery dead, and the professor dead, there's nobody left to put in jail."

Jack took a swig of his water bottle. "You mentioned, *with all the evidence stacked up against him.* Was there anything else besides what was on the jump drive? I was even concerned it might be inadmissible, because of the way I...acquired it."

Boyd leaned back in his chair. "There was plenty of other stuff. For starters, we found a DVD Thornton had made that spelled out everything. Looks like he made it the morning before he died. Then at the cabin, we found a digital recorder in Thornton's bed. Looks like he turned it on when Avery broke in and attacked him. Captured the whole thing. It gets even better. We found a surveillance van Avery had been using while he was in town. He recorded everything, including his detailed conversations with Jameison. Oh, by the way, you've got some electronic bugs in that apartment of yours, and on that landline. Not that anyone's listening anymore, but thought you should know."

"That's kind of creepy," Rachel said.

"You can hire somebody to get rid of them," Boyd said.

"You mind if I ask what's gonna happen to the jump drive I got from Jameison? Specifically, the content on the drive?"

"I don't mind. Turned it over to the FBI. I told them what you told me about your crazy dreams, about what you said the drug Jameison invented was capable of. They seemed very interested. I'm sure they found plenty of samples and other documents on this drug when they raided Jameison's office. I wouldn't be at all surprised if they contacted you for a firsthand account. You're one of the few people still alive who've actually used it."

Rachel leaned forward on the table. "But what about the newspapers and what they said about who was responsible for killing my friend Mary and Professor Thornton, for that matter? And what about Ralph Riesner and Jared Markham? This drug is really responsible for their deaths, too. The papers blamed some drifter named Arnold Shepherd. Who is that?"

Boyd sighed and leaned forward in his chair. "Now we're getting to the main reason why I wanted this meeting off the record. The guy who shot you, Jack. The man responsible for these killings here in town, told me his name was Nigel Avery. But he said something that made me think it wasn't his real name. We found ID's for several more aliases in his van. Once the FBI got involved, we talked it over. The agent in charge said they were pretty sure this guy was a former special ops guy, former CIA. But seeing that he was dead, and so were all the other guys we might have indicted, we decided not to press it. We had plenty of incriminating evidence to prove what happened, but no one to arrest."

"That doesn't seem fair to the victims' families," Rachel said.

"It's not," Boyd said. "But in a way, justice was served. All the men responsible are dead. The official reports will show them as responsible, so all the families can hire civil attorneys to sue their estates. I'm sure there's plenty of money in Dr. Jameison's coffers. Maybe some in Professor Thornton's, too. I wouldn't be surprised if the University didn't take a hit over this."

"Well, at least that's something," Jack said.

It seemed that Sgt. Boyd was all done with this briefing. "You guys have any more questions?"

"Nope," Jack said. Rachel shook her head no.

"Are you okay with everything I said? Have any problems with it?"

"Not at all," Jack said. "I'm relieved. I was dreading the thought of having to spend months dealing with all the legal issues, maybe having to testify at Jameison's trial."

"If Jack's okay, I'm okay," Rachel said.

"Great," Boyd said. "I'm so looking forward to getting my little town back to where it belongs."

60

L ATER THAT NIGHT, Jack arrived back at his garage apartment on Rambling Road at about 10:30. He and Rachel had spent a wonderful evening together, starting with an exquisite dinner at River Bend restaurant, followed by a romantic movie at a local theater. Both had to be up early tomorrow for classes, so they ended the evening early.

As Jack sat on the sofa, he reflected on the things he'd learned at his meeting with Boyd. He spent the most time thinking about Professor Thornton. The betrayal still stung a bit, though for the most part, Jack felt sorry for the man. What his life had become, how it ended. He didn't want to dwell on the situation too long. There was no fruit in regret. Nothing to be gained by living in the past.

Well, he thought, almost nothing.

He leaned forward on the couch and looked at three things he had laid out on the coffee table. A quote from an old Humphrey Bogart movie went through his head, from *The Maltese Falcon.*

The stuff dreams are made of.

There was a bottle of wine, a wine glass, a TV remote and a DVD documentary about a daring mission that took place in the

Pacific theater during World War II. The mission was flown by a squadron of P–38 Lightnings. Most WW2 buffs who knew about fighter planes, favored the P–51 Mustang. It was a great plane, but Jack had always liked the P–38 best.

It was now a very rare warbird, only a handful of them left in the world. Jack had seen one years ago at an airshow, only once. He wondered what it must be like to fly it. Of course, he knew he'd never get that chance.

Until now.

He looked at the bottle of wine on the coffee table. It was one of two Professor Thornton had given to him. Both had been laced with that colorless, odorless, tasteless drug Dr. Jameison had created.

The drug really was harmless, after all. Ralph Riesner had died because he took it then watched a horrific slasher film before bed, causing him to endure perhaps the most dreadful nightmare any soul had ever experienced. That, and his heart defect were really the things that killed him.

Jared Markum had committed suicide because he had been studying about the Holocaust in–depth. His drug–induced dreams had placed him in the role of a Nazi SS officer participating in the atrocities committed against the Jews. Apparently, he couldn't get the guilt he felt, or those images out of his mind. Besides that, his girlfriend really had dumped him.

Again, the drug itself hadn't actually killed him.

Now that Jack knew he wasn't going mad, that the dreams could be controlled, he had begun to long for the thrill of his dream experiences again.

He sat there on the edge of his sofa, feeling a bit like the code-name Jameison had given him: *Bre'r Rabbit.* In that *Uncle Remus* story, after *Bre'r Rabbit* had been captured, he begged *Bre'r Fox* and *Bre'r Bear* not to throw him into the briar patch. Of course, they did, thinking it was the thing he feared most.

Actually, it was just the opposite.

Bre'r Rabbit wanted to be thrown in the briar patch. Part of the moral of the story was: A place others dreaded became the place *Bre'r Rabbit* most longed to be.

Jack poured himself a glass of white Zinfandel and sipped it nice and slow. Then he popped in the DVD, the one with the secret World War II mission where a squadron of P–38 fighters had been dispatched to intercept and shoot down a Japanese admiral's plane. The same Japanese admiral who had orchestrated the attack on Pearl Harbor.

*

An hour later, Jack finished the DVD and his glass of wine. He yawned deeply, the third time in the last hour.

It was time.

Jack turned the TV off, turned the lights out and plopped down on his bed. He'd always wanted to fly a P–38.

As he drifted off to sleep, he couldn't restrain his smile.

ACKNOWLEDGMENTS

There are a few people I absolutely must thank for helping to get *When Night Comes* into print. Starting with my wife, Cindi. Not just for her encouragement and support. Over the years, her editing skills have grown to where the editors at my publishing house requested I not send in a manuscript until she's had a chance to go through it. On this novel, I promoted her to senior editor. She provided excellent help on edits with the storyline and characters.

I want to also thank my great team of Beta readers, all who caught many things Cindi and I missed, even after several passes. Thank you Terry Giordano, Patricia Keough–Wilson, Tonya Brown and Sarah Bulls.

I also must absolutely thank my friend and fellow author John M. Wills. John spent the better part of his life protecting and serving fellow Americans, first as a police officer in Chicago then with the FBI. John helps me get things right on police matters in my novels, not just in *When Night Comes* but several others. Besides his books, John also writes book reviews for the New York Journal of Books, and he writes monthly articles on Officer.com. Check out his books at any online bookstore.

WANT TO READ MORE?

Want to read more of Dan Walsh's novels?

Since 2009, Dan has written over a dozen other novels, mostly for the inspirational and Christian fiction market. All of them are written in a similar style, with character–driven storylines, page–turning suspense and a strong romantic thread. But most of these novels are a little different from *When Night Comes*. Most have a stronger spiritual theme or message woven into the story.

But if you mostly like reading suspense novels, Dan recommends these two as the most similar to *When Night Comes*:

THE DISCOVERY

www.danwalshbooks.com/books/the–discovery/

WHAT FOLLOWS AFTER

www.danwalshbooks.com/books/what–follows–after/

To get a sneak peek at Dan's other novels or see what others are saying about them, go to this link, then click the book cover you're curious about:

http://www.danwalshbooks.com/books/

WANT TO HELP THE AUTHOR?

If you enjoyed reading this book, the best thing you can do to help Dan is very simple—*tell others about it*. Word–of–mouth is the most powerful marketing tool there is. Better than expensive TV commercials or full–page ads in magazines.

Dan would greatly appreciate you rating his book and leaving a brief review at any of the popular online stores, wherever books are sold. Even a sentence or two will help.

ABOUT THE AUTHOR

Dan Walsh was born in Philadelphia in 1957. His family moved down to Daytona Beach, Florida in 1965, when his dad began to work with GE on the Apollo space program. That's where Dan grew up.

He married, Cindi, the love of his life in 1976. They have two grown children and three grandchildren. Dan served as a pastor for 25 years, then began writing fiction full–time in 2010. His bestselling novels have won many awards, including 3 ACFW Carol Awards (Book–of–the–Year) and 2 Selah Awards. Three of Dan's novels were finalists for RT Reviews Inspirational Book of the Year.

If you'd like to get an email alert whenever Dan has a new book coming out, or a special deal on one of Dan's books, you can check out his website below and sign up for his newsletter. From his homepage, you can also contact Dan or follow him on Facebook or Twitter.

http://danwalshbooks.com

41800910R00213

Made in the USA
San Bernardino, CA
21 November 2016